Let the Wind Eavesdrop

A Novel By

Sydney Gibson

Edited by A.E. Vikar and K.T. Carroll

Disclaimer: This is a work of fiction. Names, characters, businesses, places, events and incidents are either the product of the author's imagination or used in a fictitious manner. Any resemblance to actual persons, living or dead, or actual events is purely coincidental. Any content with cannot be used or distributed without the permission of the author.

Cover Art by Benjamin Thorne

Copyright 2016 Sydney Gibson

This novel is dedicated to all us who believe in true love and the magic behind it.

A special thank you to KT and Ben for helping out with this crazy last minute idea.

And a huge thank you to my supportive fans! You keep me writing even when I want to quit!

The poem you read in this novel is Blue Song by Tenneesse Williams. One of my favorites in this world, and I wanted to honor his impact on how I view love. Look up his works and you'll fall in love.

Chapter 1

Some say if a love is strong enough, it can overcome the physical obstructions placed in its way, it can transcend space and time together. That love, a true love, is the most powerful force a human has to offer the world and themselves. I never thought that to be true, nor did I want to believe it. Until I wanted to meet her so much, I broke all the barriers set before me. My love for her was the most powerful thing I had ever met or allowed in myself. It all started with a creaking floor board in my grandmother's house.

Standing in front of the old house, it still looked as good as the last time I had been here, close to twenty years ago. I loved this little white cottage tucked up on the hills in Nantucket, the ocean wind had worn down the paint lightly with the mix of ocean salt it would carry up and out of the water, cascading down on to the cottage.

The white wooden siding mixed with the faded blue shutters always gave me a sense of home whenever I stood on the front path that led up to my grandmother's cottage. I hefted the bags in my hand and took steps towards the front door. It had been a long flight down from the city I called home to my childhood summer home.

I smiled as I stopped in front of the worn dark blue door with the same welcome sign with sailboats and shells that I had given my grandmother for her birthday when I was seven. I set my bags down and dug into the manila envelope that held the keys and all the other paperwork I needed to prove I was now the owner of this small cottage. I dumped the keys out and slid the key into the lock. Lifting up on the doorknob as I unlocked the door, pushing it open I expected a dusty, dank interior. Instead, I was welcomed with the warmth of old memories mixed with the early morning sun pushing through the windows that faced the gentle cape.

I dropped my bags by the front door and walked towards the back deck, twirling the keys on my fingers as my boots made soft creaking noises as I walked across the old wooden floor. I could not hold back the small smile that crept up as with every step, more of the good memories of my time here filled my head and my heart.

I pushed open the old door that led me out onto the old deck that faced the amazing ocean view, the old Adirondack chairs where exactly as they had been all of my life. I stood and let the gentle breeze the morning offered, sift through my hair as I took deep breaths. Trying to clear out the rest of the city smells and memories I had eagerly left behind. After what felt like a few hours of staring out into the water, I pushed off the doorframe and walked back inside.

I picked up the thick manila envelope and dumped out the rest of the contents, there was the deed to the cottage and the land around it my grandmother owned. Including a copy of her will and the last letter she left for me. I smiled as I read my name at the top of the letter I had read a million times in the last few months since my grandmother passed away. I had been named after her and I was certain because of that one fact, it was why she and I became pretty much inseparable until I moved to Toronto to find myself five years ago.

I ran my fingers over the top of the letter, smiling as I read the gentle handwriting of the woman, "Dear Francesca, my favorite granddaughter..." I laughed out loud, I was her only granddaughter, but she always made an effort to tell me I would always be her favorite. I set the letter down as I scanned over her last words to me and felt my heartache at the fact I had been so distant in the last five years and allowed my self-created sadness pull me further away from the one woman who made me who I was today.

It took the last final heartbreak of my fiancé cheating on me to pack up my life one night and fly back to the states, running to the one place I felt the most love and the most at ease with myself.

I folded my arms, hearing the gentle creak of my leather jacket as I walked around the house, checking out the state it was in, my grandmother's lawyer had told me that in the last few years, she had rented out a room to a grad student or two trying to escape the mental strain of school. She had always been present until the last year when she moved into the hospice, she rented the house out to one student that had been named in her will for receiving the large collection of books my grandmother always had around her. I walked around the living room, smiling at how very little changed in the years I had been gone. I walked upstairs; checking on the spare room she had rented out, it was clean and obvious that those who stayed here cared for the room as much as my grandmother. I moved to the master bedroom and sighed as the room was the perfect spot in the entire house. Large peaked ceilings were highlighted by a large floor to ceiling window that gave even a more spectacular view of the ocean and the cliffs that I knew I could easily lose myself in.

All of the furniture was present and untouched, I looked at the massive canopied bed that I had spent many a night lying with my grandmother as she read to me from one of her many books. The only thing that was missing was the books on the bookshelves that lined the walls of her room. It was apparent the student had taken the books as soon as they could. I sighed, wishing I had been a little more of sound mind to respond as soon as I heard of my grandmother's passing. I could have at least saved the one book I loved the most. I continued through the upstairs, finding everything to be in working order. I walked back downstairs and picked up my bags, lugging them back up to the spare room and to the master bedroom.

As I dumped one of my bags of random things, I felt the floor board underneath me creak and shift. I kicked at it with my boot, noting that it was extremely loose and I would have to fix it. I smiled at the idea of getting my hands dirty with fixing the house up and brightening it even more.

I spent the rest of the morning unpacking and sorting my things out, I was staying at the cottage indefinitely, perhaps permanently. I no longer had anything or anyone to go anywhere for. I changed out of my tight black jeans, hung up my leather jacket and tossed my boots into the closet. Opting for comfortable pajama pants, I walked back down to the kitchen to make coffee. I was excited that I had everything I needed to make a simple cup of coffee all the way up to a full meal. The lawyer had ensured that the cottage would be stocked with food when I called and told him I would be living there.

I held the cup of coffee in my hands, loving the heat it sent through my hands and my body. I went to go sit on the deck when I heard my phone ring upstairs, I let out a sigh. I had forgotten to call my best friend the moment I arrived at the front door, she was now panicking since it was four hours past my arrival time. I set the cup down and ran upstairs, moving to the spare room where I had set my purse and bags down. I dug around and grabbed my phone as it vibrated and rang in the pockets.

I smiled as I answered. "You are worse than my mother."

"I will kick your ass worse than your mother ever did if you don't check in at the time we agreed. I was worried your plane crashed, or you were taken away by a swarm of sea crabs." Amy huffed on the other line as I pictured her pacing up and down the length of her tiny apartment we once shared.

I sat on the edge of the bed, catching a glimpse of myself in the mirror hanging over the dresser. I looked tired, life had made me tired in the last few months. I ran a hand over my hair and cringed at the dark circles that made my hazel eyes look darker. "I got lost in unpacking and checking out the house."

"Is it as magical as you described it Frankie?"

I smiled. "Even more, I missed this place. I think it's exactly what I need to start my life over." I leaned on my knees. "You are still coming down next month, right?"

"Heck yes! I will not be able to go for long without my best friend! Plus! I want to see the ocean and lighthouses and eat crabs." Amy began talking excitedly as she rambled about food like it was the air she breathed.

I stood up, smiling and laughing at the constant energy my best friend had. I walked towards the door to head back to my coffee, when I tripped on a floorboard and stumbled. "Ow! Shit."

I leaned against the wall, rubbing my stubbed toe and looking for the culprit. It was a pushed up floorboard that was almost under the bed. I mumbled to Amy as she continued telling me about her last few nights at work and how many times she was groped. I got down on my hands and knees, and pulled at the floorboard, wanting to rip it out for the shock of anger it sent through my body. The floorboard pulled up easily and as I held the board up, I could tell someone had pried it up on purpose. I frowned, suddenly wondering if it was one of the students, trying to hide whatever weed they were hiding from my grandmother. I looked down into the gap and caught a glimpse of something white.

I reached my hand in and felt it was an envelope, thick with at least a few pages inside. I pulled it out and read in the most scribbled but oddly beautiful handwriting, "To the heart I lost." I squinted at the envelope, the paper was faded, yellowed and looked to be at least a few years old. I held it, flipping it around, deciding if I should open it and take a chance that it wasn't a suicide note or some sort of weird manifesto.

"Huh? Yea, Amy, I'm listening. I just smashed my foot on an old floorboard." I sighed as Amy returned to rambling. I grabbed the board and set it back in place. I then stood up and held onto the letter as I walked back to the kitchen. Setting the letter down next to the coffee, I stared at it. It was drawing me in, the more I stared at the swirls and edges of the handwriting. I opened my mouth to interrupt Amy, when I heard a knock at my front door, I turned to look at the door. "Hey Amy, can I call you back? There is someone at the front door. I promise I'll call you before I go to bed, yes, and I will text you when I get up, and yes I will send pictures of the townsfolk and crabs I find in town." I smiled at her random, yet normal for her requests. I grinned rolling my eyes. "I love you too, Amy."

I let out a sigh of relief as I set my phone down and headed to answer the second knock that was echoing through the house. Looking through the small window, I saw it was just the mail man. I opened the door grinning. "Hi Tom."

The mail man was the same old mail man that I remember as a kid. Tom had to be close to a hundred years old, since he was already old when I was little. Tom had white hair and his uniform was always pristine, he grinned when he saw me. "Little Francesca? Is that you?"

I nodded as I held onto the door. "It is, not so little anymore, though." I half smiled at him. "Still on the old route, I see."

Tom held his smile and nodded. "Almost thirty years and haven't missed a day." He pulled out a small box, holding it out to me. "I'm so very sorry about your grandmother. She was quite a lady. I was surprised to see a package for this address, I was certain the last woman who was here had moved out months and months ago." I took the package and signed for it. Looking at the package made my heart twinge when I recognized my grandmother's handwriting.

I held the package close to my heart as Tom finished up, he winked at me. "Good to have you home and in this house. I'll see you tomorrow Francesca." He turned to walk away and stopped, looking back. "If you need anything, let me know. I still live in the old yellow house down the street" He smiled and tipped his hat to me before disappearing behind the trees that lined the small street.

I closed the door, still holding the package close to my chest. I set it down on the counter, I wasn't ready to open it. I still was having a hard time with losing the one woman who I sought so much strength in. I just ran my fingers over the elegant handwriting that was always my favorite part of my grandmother, and the letters she would write me all the way till the end. I picked up my coffee cup, my eyes falling back onto the yellowed envelope. Lifting it up to hold it against the light, I noticed there were pages full of words.

I bit my lip and walked out onto the deck, the ocean air filling me up. I sat in one of the wooden chairs and hesitated for a moment before talking myself into opening the letter. I owned the house, so technically I owned whatever I found in it, right? That was a good enough excuse. I set my cup down on the arm of the chair and ran a finger under the flap. It opened easily and I gently pulled out the thin sheets of paper.

Unfolding them, I swallowed at the amount of words that filled every page. The handwriting was not my grandmothers, and I could tell it wasn't a man's handwriting either. There was something so delicate and elegant about the penmanship, that led me to believe it was a woman.

I glossed over the first sentence and by the second paragraph, I returned to the beginning and started over, reading slower this time.

"In constant search of solitude, and I find it. I find it doesn't suit me as much as I hoped. I love the ocean here, the lovely older woman who has entrusted me with her home as she fails ill. Perhaps, it's her illness that has me looking at myself and the life I have chosen. Alone, broken hearted and consumed by a mission I cannot recall why I started, maybe it was for love. But in the end, it was love that broke me and set my feet running the furthermost away from any sense of hope and love."

The letter continued on, it was obvious the writer was intelligent as words flowed seamlessly. I felt my heart breaking for this person as they wrote their heart, and heartache out onto the pages before me. I had to bite my lip as I read the last page.

"So I pour my heart out on empty pages, hoping along the way I can find my way back to something that resembles happiness. But again, I do intend to tuck this letter into the floorboards where no one will ever see it, nor will I. Maybe that is what I need. To find hope in knowing no one will know the pain I put myself through as love continues to escape me day after day.

To whomever may come across this, if you read this, please take all of my ramblings as my gentle advice to find a love that you will fight for and hold onto it, never lose the things that make you human and happy. Life and love is far too precious to ignore.

-C"

I set the last page down, my eyes were glassy from the sense of heartbreak in the words. It did put in perspective what I was going through. It was as if the writer and I had experienced the same loss. I wanted to hug whoever it was on these pages and let them know they weren't alone.

My fiancé had cheated on me and I caught him. The worst of it all was he cheated on me with someone I called a friend, someone I trusted to pour my heart out to about my relationship issues; she used that to gain ground with my fiancé. I picked up and ran from the entire heart ache and loss of trust I experienced.

I sighed and looked at the date scribbled in the corner of the first page. It was dated almost two years ago. I folded the letter and tucked it back up into the envelope. I held it tightly as I watched the waves on the distant horizon.

Something struck me, I shot up from my chair and ran back into the house. I ran to the desk next to the front door and pulled out the notepad and other stationary bits that my grandmother always kept there. I sat down at the kitchen island and scribbled down everything that was in my heart, just like the one whose letter sat close to me. I wrote and wrote, as if I was writing back to them, letting them know they weren't alone, sharing my story of how I had loved and lost and did the same thing. Before I knew it, I had filled five pages and my entire being felt light. I shoved the pages into the envelope, sealing it and setting it down in front of me. I smiled as I wrote on the front. *"To the heart I will find again."*

I picked up the letter, walked upstairs, and pulled up the floorboard to shove my letter in the spot. I smiled as I set the board back and walked into the bathroom to take a long bath. Before I slid into the hot water, I moved the yellowed letter that inspired my own start towards healing a broken heart, next to my bed. I tapped it once before I headed back to the bathroom. Maybe after I was long gone, after I sorted my life, the letter would find another lost soul and inspire them.

Chapter 2

I took advantage of the fact that I didn't have to get up for anything. The morning light poured through the uncovered windows, casting rays of light and shadows in patterns that made me smile. I snuggled deeper into the plush pillows and blankets of the giant bed. I was content to stay here for the rest of the day or my life, watching the ocean from my bed. I had slept easier than I had in months, after pouring my heart out on paper, I felt lighter. Lighter, happier, and ready to start my life again. I laid in bed for a little longer after waking up, trying to motivate myself to get moving. I wanted to stay in bed all day, but the bare walls around me begged me to get up and start bringing them back to life.

I swung out of the bed and walked around the room, loving the feel of the wooden floors on my feet. I pulled out fresh clothes from my suitcases, tossing them on the bed. Today, I would explore the town and see what had changed in the years I had been gone. I would also have to stop at the hardware store for supplies to start fixing things up. I smiled and hummed to myself as I moved around the room. I half skipped to the spare room to find my baggy blue jeans, when I tripped on the floorboard again. Stubbing my big toe again.

I cursed as I sat on the bed, rubbing at my abused big toe, and stared hard at the floorboard. It was loose and I was beyond certain I had secured it properly last night. I dropped to my knees and yanked at it, pulling it up easily and staring at it. I wanted to break it out of the anger it brought in me, and the now growing bruise on my toe. "You little shit." I set the board and looked down in the hole to see if my letter was still there.

As I reached my hand in, wrapping my fingers around my letter, I pulled it out. I was going to set it by my bed until I could properly fix the board, making damn sure it would not pop back up. I walked back into my room, more so limped, and tossed my letter on the side table, groaning as I heard a few pages of the older letter flutter to the floor. Maybe I should go back to bed for a few more hours.

I turned to pick up the errant pages that skittered close to my sore foot. I went to gently folded them back up and set them under my letter, when I paused. My letter looked different, it was yellowed and dirty. I moved closer and picked it up, flipping it over to the front. I was confused as I read. *"One's heart is not to be made fun of."* in the same elegant handwriting as the first letter. I sat forward on the edge of the bed, staring at the letter. I went through the motions of last night in my head, going over how anyone could have gotten into the house. I had locked all the doors, twice, before I went to bed. I had heard no one in the house or near the house all night, just the waves crashing in the distance.

I tapped the letter on my knee and took a breath. "Shit." I opened the letter, revealing two pages filled with the elegant handwriting. I scanned over them, taking notice that the date was missing from the upper corner. I furrowed my brow more as I started at the beginning of the letter.

"I am not sure if this is some sort of prank, try to get the quiet, moody grad student to emit any sort of emotion, but the words on these pages lead me to think otherwise. Although, signing it Francesca has thrown me for quite a loop. Mrs. Owen is a woman who deserves more than to be the scape goat for a silly prank or an attempt to anonymously share emotions. I am also curious as how one found the hiding spot, I was

certain I had secured this floorboard to the point it would take a crowbar to pry it up.

Aside from that, whoever you are, your words have been heard, and it some strange way, have brought me comfort. Whether that was the intention of your prank or not, it has. I understand where you are coming from.

I'm not sure how you got into the house, and how you were able to find my letter, and if you are a broken-hearted burglar, but if you are in need of someone to listen, I'm here, Francesca.

But first I challenge you, tell me how you found my letter and how did you get into this house? I have the only keys and I keep this house locked up tighter than my own lab. I also have a shotgun under my bed, and I am not afraid to use it."

I laughed at the last part. "Something about that last sentence has me thinking you have no idea how to use a shotgun." I held onto the pages, there was something strange going on. I stood up and set the new pages on to the table, staring out the window as I tried to think of possibilities. The cottage had been empty for a few months, so I would not be surprised if I had a squatter with a sense of humor to deal with.

I checked over my bags and other things, noting that nothing seemed out of place. I folded my arms and added better locks to my hardware shopping list. I showered and dressed in my baggy jeans, a loose sweater and tied my hair up. I looked far different from my usual city wear of black on black with a splash of black, but this was me starting over, and I wanted to be comfortable.

Downstairs in the kitchen I dabble with making a bowl of cereal and pulled over the package Tom dropped off the day before. I sighed hard in between bites of my whole grain granola. The package was covered in my grandmother's writing and her careful wrapping.

This was the last thing I would ever get from her, and in a weird way I didn't want to open it. I finally caved after finishing the bowl and gently tore open the edges, trying to save as much as I could. The box was a plain one, one of her many shoe box type boxes she would keep her knick-knacks in. It was blue, her favorite color, and old. I lifted the lid and grinned as I saw a book nestled comfortably in a bed of tissue. On top was an envelope, my name delicately drawn out.

I opened the letter as I set the book on the counter. It was my second favorite book of hers, an old copy of *"King Arthur and the Knights of the Round Table."* One that was battered in a gentle way, from all the readings I forced out of her as a kid, and occasionally as a teenager.

I peeled open the letter to read the short note from my Grandmother.

"*My dearest Francesca,*

I had this planned. It could take years for you to come home or it might not. I had to pay the estate lawyer extra to make sure the moment you took up the keys to this lovely cottage, you would get this package. I knew this book was one of your favorites and perfect to start your own collection, the rest of my books have found a lovely home with a lovely woman. Don't worry about them, they will be loved as much as I loved them. I do hope you can meet the dear woman, she is quite remarkable in her own right, and I think you two would get along quite well.

This cottage is yours, forever and more, as long as you choose it. It's a magical place, in more ways than one. I never could tell you the magic it held after you left, but now, knowing you, you have taken up residence to heal a broken heart or soul.

Francesca, you will find the love you have always dreamt of and asked me about as I read you fairy tales. In this cottage, you will find it and them. I promise you, the walls of my home have the secrets, and the floors hold all the magic you will need. As long as you open your heart and your soul to the possibility of a love greater than you.

I will always love you, my favorite and only grandchild. You brought an old woman more joy and life than you can ever imagine. I will always cherish the memories I have with you.

Love you my dearest girl,

Grandma Francesca

P.S. I will give you a small hint to finding the magic I speak of, your favorite book. Search it out and everything will be revealed."

I wiped away the tears as I read over and over my grandmother's words. She was always the one person in my life that understood me and accepted me no matter what I did, or who I became.

My heart weighed heavy with the regret I felt for being separated from her, out of my own selfish choice. I clutched the letter to my chest as I let slow sobs out as I watched the waves, and took deep breaths, allowing each gentle sway of the water take away the sadness. My selfish chase for the sake of true love had cost me time with the unconditional love of my grandmother.

I tucked the wrapping and the letter carefully into the box, holding on to the book as I walked back up to the master room. After setting the box, and the book, on the shelf next to each other, I smiled at them. They were now symbols of the true start to my new collection and my new life.

Staring at the sledgehammer and the regular roofing hammer, I was lost at what exactly did I need to fix up the broken bits and pieces of the cottage. I had an old red plastic basket in my hand, filled with glue, nails, caulk, and a box of white lights that I had intentions of looping around my bed. I had ambitions it would add a little more fairytale to my canopy bed at night.

I had spent the last hour in the hardware store trying to navigate and refresh my handyman skills. I smiled at the cashier, who I knew was staring at me trying to place exactly where he had last seen my face. After finally choosing a hefty roofing hammer, one I knew could be heavy enough for fixing the floorboard, and possibly heavy enough to take out that suspected squatter in the middle of the night, I headed towards the counter to pay and tell the cashier who I was.

I walked over to the counter, setting the heavy basket down, and smiled at the salt and pepper haired man. "Did you need anything else, ma'am? Need any information on roofing or weather stripping? I have some pamphlets off to the side, next to the gumball machine."

I shook my head and smiled. "No thanks, Sid. I think I can manage fixing up the shutters and floorboards."

The older man paused in grabbing the bits and pieces from the basket, and looked at me harder, trying to once again, place my face. I finally broke, ending the guess who game. "Little Frankie? Remember me? Mrs. Owen's granddaughter? You used to give me free gumballs after I would try and tell you it shorted me a quarter."

Sid grinned and blushed a little. "Frankie. Yes, of course I remember you. You, um, have grown up." I could see his eyes try to not roam over the curves I carried. "Last time I saw you, you were at old Natty's dress shop. Your grandmother and you were trying on dresses for the end of summer crab dance." He took a deep breath, his smile faded slightly. "Sorry about your grandmother, she was a hell of a woman."

I nodded, keeping my tight smile. "Thank you and yes, she was." I fidgeted with my purse. "I'm living in the cottage now, so you'll see a lot more of me." I motioned at the random tools. "I want to clean up and fix up the house, just like it was when I was little."

Sid smiled and now had a pep in his movements. "Well, Frankie, I will be happy to point you in the right direction." He looked down at the basket. "It looks like you have a good start in the tool department. The grad student who lived in the cottage after Francesca went into her, um. Anyways, that grad student did a lot of the repairs on the roof and the back windows, herself. So, you'll be good when the storms come."

I looked at Sid as he mentioned the grad student. "The grad student? Can you tell me a little about them?"

Sid nodded as he threw some items in a wooden box for me to carry home. "Good kid, for the life of me I can't remember her first name. I guess it's all the wood glue I've inhaled over the years." I couldn't help but chuckle along with Sid at his silly joke. "Pretty girl, real pretty. She moved into the cottage right before Francesca grew really sick. One of your grandmother's favorite tenants, always see the two walking through town. That girl would help your grandmother with groceries and what not, but was always very quiet. Ran into the two at the farmers' market and weaseled out that the girl was a medical research student, a legitimate doctor studying something I could barely understand. All I could gather was genetics, chromosomes, fertility, and I only knew some of the words from watching Law and Order over the years."

Sid winked at me as he tapped at his cash register. "The girl stayed on after to take care of the house and moved out more than a handful of months ago." He looked down his nose at the total of my goods. "Let's call it an even forty dollars. Sound good little Frankie? Err... I mean Frankie?"

I nodded and pulled out the money, handing it over to Sid. "Did this girl tell you anything more? Or leave a forwarding address?" I was suddenly intrigued by this grad student that both Sid and my grandmother took a liking too.

Sid shook his head as he opened the register. "Nope. She was real quiet and real intelligent, too. I think she felt she would intimidate us small town folk with her big words, but once in a while I could make her smile with one of my hardware jokes." Sid leaned on the counter, sighing heavy with a smile. "She was quite a looker though. Tall, brunette, pretty in all the right ways."

I smiled and laughed, picking up the box. "Sid, how would your wife take to you talking like that?"

Sid winked at me. "I tell her the same thing every night. That she will always be pretty in all the right ways. Happy wife, happy life." He walked around the counter and held the door open for me. "Like I said, anything you need, come find me. I will help you fix that house up."

"Thanks Sid, I appreciate it." I walked out into the small street and was met with the gentle ocean breeze I knew I would come to adore. Sid nodded and as I walked down the street to my car, I heard Sid bellow out behind me. "It's good to have you home Little Frankie. That cottage and this town missed you."

I paused for a moment and looked over my shoulder at the older man I used to swindle for gumballs as much as possible. "Me too, Sid. Me too."

I made a few more stops at the farmers' market and the tiny bookstore on the edge of town. As I drove slowly back to the cottage, enjoying the afternoon sun, I was thinking about the grad student and who she was. I knew I would have to poke around a little more in the townsfolk and what they knew. I was pretty certain she was the heir to my grandmother's books and would have the book I wanted.

Back at the cottage I set to work on plugging up the small window air leaks, straightening molding around the rooms and lastly, I set to the floorboard that was my big toes arch-enemy. I set the nails and glue to the side, and stared at the hole where I had placed my letter. I chewed at my lip for a second, before an idea struck, and ran back to my room and grabbed the stationary I had left out. I quickly scribbled a note as I crouched over the top of the dresser.

"Prank? Maybe, but I fear you are squatting in my house. A shotgun? Well, I have a sledgehammer and the giant arms to swing it faster than you can dig out the so-called shotgun under your bed.

The words were mine, in case you care. My heart and my soul. If you are the original author of the first letter, then I thank you. If this is some cruel prank, you better piss off and get out of my house before I get really mad. I have stubbed my toe twice as a result of your stupid joke, a third time will not be welcomed with smiles.

Oh, and if you somehow manage to pry up this floorboard after I double nail it and glue it down, I will grant you one wish.

Hugs and kisses.

Francesca."

I smiled wickedly as I quickly sealed the letter and dropped it back into the small void. I then set to work double nailing and sealing the floor board with glue. When I was done and the glue was set, I was positive the floorboard would withstand a wrecking ball. I kicked it with the tip of my boot in victory and moved back down to the kitchen for a celebratory glass of wine. I sat out on the back deck with my wine, and let my thoughts drift to the mysterious grad student and how long it would take me to track her down and get the book I so dearly coveted.

Chapter 3

The next morning, I attacked the day with renewed vigor. Cleaning the cottage from top to bottom, repairing the little things that caught my eye and making notes of what I needed before heading into town. The day matched my mood, sunny, bright and eager.

I had my list in my hand and was in town by lunchtime. I hit up the hardware store again, spending a few more minutes with Sid as he helped me select better tools and supplies I needed. He filled me in on the happenings in the town, such as, upcoming festivals and who was doing what. I could not wipe the smile off my face, as I listened to the older man.

As I set all of the things I needed down on top of the old counter, or the things Sid suggested I needed to fix the cottage, he began to tally the total. Pushing keys on the cash register, he looked at me above his glasses. "So little Frankie, how does a fifty spot work for you today?"

I smiled as I dug around in my purse, handing over the money. Sid was giving me a huge discount, and it made me love him a little more. "I'm not going to shake the little Frankie name, am I Sid?"

Sid blushed slightly and smiled as he opened the register. "Sorry, old habit. There were two Frankie's in this town for a long time." He closed the register and grabbed an old peach box from under the counter to start packing up my things. "How are you settling in so far?"

I helped him, tossing the bags of nails in. "Better than I expected. I love that cottage, it's such a peaceful place. I'd forgotten what it was like to sleep with nothing but the sounds of the ocean to keep me company." I set a tape measure on top of the pile. "Hey Sid. Do you know anyone who might be able to tell me about the brunette grad student? You know the one that's pretty in all the right ways?" I winked at Sid as he cleared his throat.

Sid shoved his hands deep down into the pockets of his apron, tapping his carpenters pencil on the counter. "Hmm. You could try old Tom, the mail man. You remember old Tom the mail man? He knows everyone up and down this whole little town. Let's see, Natty is another one. I know your grandmother used to go to her once a week at least to pick up yarn for her Afghans. The last few months before your grandmother moved, that pretty girl never left her side. Making sure she got where she needed to with ease." Sid picked up a jar of gumballs and pushed them towards me. "For old times' sake." He smiled as I took one. "I wish I could remember that girl's name for you little Frankie, but it's been awhile since I saw her last and like I said, she never really said much. Just waited for your grandmother to do her business."

I thanked Sid and grabbed my box of things. Outside of the old hardware store, I took in a deep breath of the afternoon air, loving the sunshine and the smell of the ocean in the breeze filling around me.

I glanced around the old town as I pushed on my sunglasses, seeing Natty's Dress and Things shop was still where it had been since it opened in 1963. It also looked the same as I am sure it did on opening day. I almost had a notion to walk over and reunite with Natty to ask about the pretty in all the right ways brunette, but when I moved closer, I saw the closed sign and laughed to myself. Natty was still closing up shop on Wednesdays so she could go out to the beach and dig for clams.

I chuckled, it felt like I was in a time warp as everyone I met from my childhood, never changed one bit over the last twenty years.

I walked to my car and pushed the supplies into the back seat, thinking about having to look in the barn and see if the old blue truck was still there. I had a sudden overwhelming need to put my city life completely behind me while I was at the cottage.

I pulled into the drive path to catch Tom as he walked up to the house to drop off mail. I hopped out of the car, leaving it running so I could ask him a few questions.

I almost startled the old man when I yelled his name from the bottom of the drive path. He clutched the mail to his chest as I stopped in front of him. "Jeez! Don't scare an old man like that Francesca or your mail won't make it to the door!" He took a breath and handed me a thin stack of letters. "Where's the fire?" He smiled a little, at my flushed, embarrassed cheeks.

I blushed harder and shrugged. "Sorry about that Tom, I wanted to catch you and ask you a few questions about the cottage. Sid pointed me in your direction."

Tom laughed. "Sid? Oh boy. What does Sid have to say about anything? All he knows is nails and how to sniff the wood glue and not get caught."

I shook my head and laughed with the old man. "That's true, Tom. But Sid did tell me that you might be able to fill me in on the last renter who stayed in the cottage before my grandmother passed." I suddenly felt sheepish in my intense need to find out who this brunette was and why my grandmother was so taken with her. And to find my books.

Tom pushed his blue postal hat up, wiping at his brow. "Hmm. There was that young man, an English major. He was always trying to publish the next great novel. I had to hand him the rejected manuscripts back almost once a week. Then there was the German girl, engineer student. She helped your grandmother fix the roof trusses, big girl. Strong girl." Tom raised his eyebrows at me. "I do mean big. Then there was the brunette medical student. Pretty girl and your grandmother's favorite."

Tom looked at me, with a soft smile. "She was the last one to live here. She packed up the house when your grandmother was moved to the hospice. Took her mail to her every day. Real good kid."

I bit my lip at the memory of when I received the phone call telling me she was being moved into hospice care. I was too caught up in my own life disaster to give it, or her, a second thought. It had become one of my biggest regrets, not going to spend more time with her during that time. I gripped the letters in my hand. "Do you happen to remember her name?"

Tom cocked his head to the side. "Oh shoot, I should. I saw her every day for two years. Chatted with her and everything. Smart girl, like Einstein smart." He furrowed his brow. "I'll have to ask my wife, I never forget names and faces but for some reason I'm drawing a blank." He smiled and winked at me. "Maybe you scared it out of me Francesca."

He turned and started to walk away. "I must finish my rounds! I will see you same time, same place tomorrow." Tom patted me on the shoulder as he shifted his mail bag higher up onto his shoulder.

I sighed hard and looked at the mail in my hand, it was random junk mail and a letter from the city. I sighed harder when I saw it was his handwriting. I moved to properly park my car, when I heard Tom come back around the bushes. "Carey! Her name was Carey!" He grinned and tapped at his temple. "Still as sharp as the day I was born."

I waved back at Tom, laughing as he disappeared back around the bushes, and let out a breath, "Carey. It's a start." I walked to the car with a smile and a plan forming in my head of how I was going to track this brunette Carey down.

After emptying the car, I got set to work on the little things I wanted to get done before dinner. I had planned on going to the grocery store to pick up a few things to try and make the crab cake recipe I found in the old recipe box, still jammed in the one cabinet. In the meantime, I fixed shaky cabinet doors, resealed a few of the kitchen windows and the giant window in the bedroom. I smiled at my handiwork and that there was no longer a draft pushing through the gaps.

I wiped off my hands and walked past the spare bedroom when something in my heart and mind told me to stop and check the floorboard. It literally felt like someone was pulling on my heart as I walked by the door, so much so, I had to place my hand over my heart to feel if there were strings attached.

I was pushed into the room and gasped lightly when I saw the floorboard that I had nailed, glued and almost welded down, pried up and loose. I knelt to the floor slowly, hesitating for a moment before picking at the edge. Finding the board moving easily, I pushed it to the side.

I sucked in a deep breath as I sat on my heels, slowly reaching my hand inside the hole. Closing my eyes when my fingers grazed the edge of an envelope, and pulled my hand back quickly as my heart raced. Looking around the room, I tried to find anything that would clue me into that someone had gotten in while I was gone.

I hopped up and ran around the cottage, checking doors and windows. After finding everything intact, I raced back up to the spare room, and dropped to my knees near the hole in the floor. My heart was racing, my hands shaking as I dipped back in to grab that mysterious envelope. Once again feeling the edges of the envelope, I grasped it between my thumb and first two fingers, and pulled it slowly free.

The envelope was yellowed, like the others, and sealed, veritably untouched. I flipped it over and the same messy but elegant handwriting was scrawled across the front, reading. "*My one wish.*"

My finger moved on its own, tearing open the letter. There was only one page, but it was filled from top to bottom. I didn't skim the words as I had before with the last letter, this time I read slowly.

"*You must be the infamous little Frankie. Mrs. Owen has told me stories upon stories about her favorite granddaughter, but she also told me that you have been living in Toronto for the last year and a half, which makes me semi question the validity of your words in your last correspondence.*

If you are the brunette in the pictures on the wall in the sunroom, I dare to say you would have a hard time swinging a sledgehammer at my head."

I paused reading and holding the letter against my thigh. I had moved to Toronto three years ago, and then my grandmother became sick eight months later. Glancing at the letter, something was nagging me in the back of my head. I let it go, and returned to reading the letter.

"I took your letter to Mrs. Owen. She just smiled and said I should keep writing you. That you would be a good pen pal to have, that you would also surprise me. Then she told me that I should tell you to look in the barn behind the truck? Whatever that may mean.

However, your grandmother has never been wrong about anyone she has met, including me. She offered me a home when I was lost and did not have one. She gave me a place to find warmth and hope in a heart that was long given up on. So, I am going to write back to you and hope that this isn't some elaborate prank or joke on my behalf.

Your words, in your first letter, gave me the feeling that I was not alone in how I feel about the world around me and how I fit into it all.

My one wish, since you owe me one for prying up the floorboard you thought to be impenetrable, is this, that you find the peace in your heart and find someone who can appreciate you for you. I can tell in your first letter that you are just more than a beautiful broken hearted girl. Whoever broke your heart didn't deserve you.

I hope you write back, the house is lonely now and I have rather gotten used to seeing this floorboard poking up as if to say hello. Hmm, maybe that is two wishes.

Oh, and by the way, my name is Carey. It's nice to meet you Francesca, Little Frankie.

Till next time,

- C."

Carey. The pretty brunette grad student. Another piece to the puzzle I was searching for just fell into my hands.

I folded the letter back up, tucking it away in the envelope, and stood up to walk back to my bedroom, setting the letter on top of the other two.

Carey's words echoed in my mind. I could tell in her letters that she was intelligent as Sid said, but there was something more to her words, something that made my heart skip and fill up with a strange, long forgotten sensation. I walked to the large window, folding my arms across my chest as I stared out into the waves. My eyes caught onto the lighthouse that sat out on the cove. I stared at it, thinking about the strange comment about when I moved to Toronto. There was no date on this letter like there was on the first. A small mystery was brewing in the floorboards of my cottage and it filled my mind, chasing away the linger thoughts of why I had left Toronto in the first place.

I chewed on my lip, thinking for a little while, before I eventually went back to the kitchen and grabbed the grocery list, knocking over the small amount of mail Tom had given me earlier onto the floor. His letter stared at me like a red flag, a stop sign, and everything else you could identify with suddenly stopping in place.

I picked it up, with my jaw clenched, and tossed it in the small basket that held the extra keys to the cottage. There I spotted the barn key. The words Carey passed on from my grandmother slid to the front of my mind. I snatched the bulky keys up and ran out to the barn.

The grin on my face when I saw the beaten up blue truck felt like it was going to split my face. The old 1947 Ford pickup truck seemed to grin back at me. The old blue paint was peeling, and there were rust spots dotting the entire length of the truck, but I didn't care. I ran fingers down the side as I walked slowly around the truck, relishing the feel of the pebbly metal. The old truck was a sight for sore eyes and made my heart swell at the memories it brought back to me. This had been my grandmother's sole form of transportation from when I was four years old until she stopped driving.

Making my way to the rear of the truck, still grinning like a fool and eager to find out if the old girl would still run, I saw it. An old trunk tucked a few feet behind the rear hatch. Again the strange feeling that my heart was being pulled into the direction of the trunk, I was moved to it as if my legs and feet were being controlled by someone else.

The old steamer trunk was one I had vaguely remembered hiding in the back of the closet in the front room. I never went into it as a kid, knowing it was private and special to my grandmother. I never touched it and soon forgot about it. I bent in front of the lid, smiling at how perfect the condition was. It was easily as old, if not older than the Ford.

The lid lifted easily when I pulled it open. Spotting quickly a single envelope on top of the jewelry tray with my name written in my grandmother's handwriting. I smiled and picked up the letter, slipping it into my pocket, before lifting the tray to find all of the photographs that filled the hallways, and the albums that filled the spots on bookshelves that were not taken up by the massive collection she kept.

Tears fell as I glanced at photos of my grandmother and I when I was little, when I was an awkward teenager, to the last time I saw her. A few weeks before I moved to the city.

I picked up the picture in its plain wooden frame, sniffling. How could I have ignored this woman, the one woman I cherished more than anything else? All for a love that I thought was all I needed. I held onto the frame with both of my hands, running my fingers over the picture. I missed my grandmother painfully in this moment as she continued to give more than I deserved.

After a moment I went to set the frame back with the others when I caught the edge of a picture out of a frame. I tugged at it, thinking it was another of the collection, but, instead of me and my grandmother, the picture was my grandmother sitting on the patio with a brunette.

The brunette in the picture was young and absolutely beautiful. One look at her had my heart beating quickly. I unconsciously bit my bottom lip at how stunning this woman was. She had long brown hair that was trying to fight the ocean wind, doing nothing to cover up the deep golden brown eyes of the woman and the gentle, genuine smile she held. There was something about her eyes that kept me staring intently at the photograph. It took me a minute until I broke away from her beauty to read the letters on the brunette's shirt, MIT. This brunette in my hands had to be Carey, the Einstein smart, pretty in all the right ways brunette girl.

I flipped the photograph over, hoping there was a date or a note on it, but there was nothing. I chewed on the inside of my lip, tapping the photograph on my palm. Standing up I closed the trunk and held onto the photograph. Finding that I kept looking at it and the beautiful woman sitting across from my grandmother.

There was something about her that had me drawn in, it was similar to the feeling I got every time I walked past the floorboard, or curled my fingers around the yellowed envelopes she left me. I was now on a mission, not just for groceries, but more pieces to the puzzle.

Before leaving the barn I checked the old Ford, yelling in victory when it started up on the first try and purred like it had just rolled off the factory floor. I pulled the truck out of the barn, pulling my black sports car in its spot. I then covered up the last part of the city I had visible with an old canvas tarp.

As I was about to pull out of the drive path, I stopped, another idea popping into my head. Running back into the house and to my bedroom I scrambled for the stationary I had jammed in the bedside table.

My hand moved fast as I wrote.

"My grandmother was the first one to call me little Frankie. It seems I will never shake that nickname loose. Even now, years after I left this town, I'm still recognized as little Frankie.

I am curious as to what my grandmother has told you about me. Most of it could be good, but most of it could be embarrassing. Since you went over your wishes, I will ask one from you. What has my grandmother told you about me?

Tell her that I found the trunk behind the Ford. Tell her thank you, I have long forgotten about all those pictures and what they meant to me.

You must be someone pretty special yourself. My grandmother has a way of finding the special people and giving them a home and a place to be themselves. That's what she always did for me growing up.

I must say Carey that whoever broke your heart or whatever broke your heart to make you feel so lost. They don't deserve you being heartbroken or sad about it. You do that and whatever it is, has won. You seem to be smarter than the average bear, don't let the weaker ones have power over you. Follow your heart and be true to it. I understand heartbreak and have lost myself in it over the last little while, but being here in this cottage and finding my grandmother again. It's the light at the end of the tunnel.

She is right, about being pen pals. This cottage can be lonely when it's empty. Almost too perfectly lonely.

I have also gotten used to the strange letters in the floor and I think I am beginning to look forward to them. So, yes, if this isn't a weird creepy prank. Please write back.

Oh, can you tell me when my grandmother told you I moved to Toronto and why? And last question, what is the date today?

- Frankie aka Little Frankie

P.S. Did you go to MIT and what for?

P.P.S. Can you tell my grandmother that I love her dearly, always will and that I'm sorry?"

I sighed as I scribbled out the last line. I had always hoped I could tell my grandmother one last time that I loved her. I slipped the letter into an envelope, sealing it, taping it closed, and scribbling on the front of it, "*One Wish, Two Wish.*"

Kneeling on the floor in the spare bedroom, I lifted the loose board, and set the envelope into the hole. Pushing it deep into the sub-floor to make sure it was in there as good as it could be before I put the board back. I then lightly nailed the board in place, kicking it for good luck with the toe of my boot. I stared at it, squinting and wondering how it was possible that these letters were making its way into a sealed house.

The thought lingered in my head along the drive back into town, my eyes constantly drifting to the sight of the beautiful brunette named Carey, in the photograph I had stuck in the dashboard next to the speedometer.

Chapter 4

The first stop I made when I was back in town, was Natty's shop. I grabbed the photograph of Carey and tucked it into my back pocket before hopping out of the old truck. The sun was warm and as I shut the truck door, I realized I couldn't remember that many sunny warm days in the city. I would only take notice of the dark gloomy ones, but now, being here every day seemed warm and bright. I idly wondered if it was a sign.

Walking into Natty's old shop was another time warp event for me. Literally nothing changed, even Natty standing behind the counter sorting through her boxes of yarn. Natty still looked as eccentric as she did when I was a kid. Her wild hair was now silver. It was a wild kind of hair that didn't make her look crazy, just made her look like she was always caught in a windstorm.

Natty always favored old baggy jeans and the thick sweaters that came with living on the eastern coast near the ocean. Her jewelry is what I remember most, big rings with turquoise stones, still on her fingers almost twenty years later.

The bell above the door tinkled as I walked in, Natty never once looked up as she hollered towards me. "Questions? Ask them. Looking is free and welcomed."

I smiled at her thick accent that made her sound like she belonged in the Kennedy family. Natty was born and raised on the coast, and I was certain she never left it. I uttered a quiet thank you and took the opportunity to look around the old shop. This was where my grandmother and I had picked out my dress for the end of summer dance, my prom dress, and the last time I saw my grandmother, picking out a cocktail dress for the event in the city where I had met my fiancé. The shop was still filled with dresses, sweaters, and all sorts of random knick-knacks that made Natty's a one stop shop for anything your summer cottage would need.

I picked up a large sweater that was soft, and perfect, for the cold nights I knew were to come as summer began to drift away into fall. I walked over to the counter and set it down, Natty peered over her glasses. "Oh good choice, those are handmade in Pennsylvania by the Amish." She looked up at me and had to push her glasses up as she squinted. "Little Frankie?"

"Hi Natty."

Natty smirked. "Well I'll be. Old Tom had mentioned the cat drug you back to town." She pulled off her glasses, as she reached for my left hand. Holding it up as she leered at the ring finger. "I thought you were engaged to that handsome man boy from the big city. The reason why you disappeared like a bad summer rash around here." She turned my hand slightly before letting go. I tucked it under the sweater feeling embarrassed.

"I was."

Natty smiled. "Was. That's why you're back in town. Broken hearts need the ocean air most." Natty picked up the sweater. "Tom tells me you've taken over the cottage. About time someone brought life into that old house."

As she folded the sweater I gripped onto the edge of the driftwood counter. "How long has the cottage been empty?"

Natty tossed her head back and forth. "Ehm. Almost a year now, the girl moved out about a year ago."

"Carey?"

Natty nodded as she expertly folded the sweater. "Shame to see her go, she was a good kid. Smart girl."

I took a steady breath. "What was she like? Carey?"

"Pretty girl, very pretty girl. Treated your grandmother like she was her own, even took care of her right up until she moved into hospice." Natty wrapped the sweater in tissue, tucked it into an old burlap bag and set it on the counter. "She seemed a little lonely, a little heartbroken. Same look in her eyes you carry now, Little Frankie."

I swallowed and looked off to the side. "Do you know where she moved to? Carey?"

Natty sat on the stool behind the counter. "I think she moved to Seattle, months and months ago. Last day I saw her, she was picking up some sweaters and blankets. She thanked me for my kindness and was endearing. Told me she had gotten some job as a research doctor in a fancy hospital."

Natty waved her hand around dismissively. "Don't ask for the name of the hospital, you know I don't give two clams about details that have nothing to do with me." Natty smiled as I laughed lightly. "The girl took care of your grandmother, and she had a huge part in figuring out what was ailing her. Created a treatment that had the last few days of Francesca's life pain free and happy."

I bit the inside of my mouth to hold the tears back. "I should have come home sooner."

"Yes, you should have. Your grandmother loved you dearly but, would snap at any one of us that spoke ill of your disappearance and not being here for her." Natty frowned and raised her eyebrows. "But you're home now. Your grandmother was one of my best friends and I have always looked at you as a niece I never really had. I'm happy you are home to brighten that cottage back up."

Natty patted my hand, "I still dig clams up on Wednesdays if you want to join me. Best clam chowder you will ever have." She winked at me.

I smiled at the older woman, "Thanks Natty. Is there anything else you can tell me about Carey?"

"Nope, you know all I know." Natty paused. "Wait, she did mention something about your grandmother being something special. I already knew that, but the girl was adamant on telling me there was more to just her kind heart. She tried to get me to tell her where Francesca's family was and how to get a hold of them."

She frowned lightly. "No one knew where you were in the city, little Frankie. I'm sorry."

I felt my chest tighten as I nodded. "That's my fault. I was wrapped up in a man boy, lost my way." I whispered that last part, and picked up the burlap bag, "Thanks again Natty." I turned to walk away out the door when Natty called after me. "There is one weird thing, hit me like hurricane. Carey, right after your grandmother went in to hospice, started asking about you. What you were like and when the last time you were at the cottage, mentioned something about letters?" Natty shrugged and furrowed her brow. "The girl was under a lot of stress though, your grandmother and her finals."

I paused in mid-step, and turned as my throat suddenly became dry. "How long ago was that?" My heart pounding as the words came out.

"Like I said, right after your grandmother became really ill. Almost two years ago. You had been gone awhile by then, kid."

I tried to smile to hide the strange feeling that washed over me, two years ago. It correlated with the date on the first letter I found, but how could it be? Two years and yet I was getting letters in the floor within days, like it was nothing. What was going on? This strange puzzle, mystery of this apparently amazing brunette was getting deeper and stranger.

 I promised Natty I would stop by for clam chowder next week and walked out into the street. I tossed the sweater into the truck and climbed in, pulling out the photograph, I held it in my hands, staring at Carey. Who was this woman? Why was I so drawn to her? Why did the simple looks of her picture make my heart beat in a way that I never felt before and how was she writing me letters from the past?

I was quiet and lost in thought as I went to the grocery store for supplies before heading back to the cottage. I was extremely sad about the things Natty told me about my grandmother and me being gone more than anything else.

After I put the groceries away, I went right to the trunk full of photographs, and busied myself through lunch and into late afternoon. Sorting through the photos and hanging them all back up in the hallway and in my bedroom. All the photographs were a part of my life where I was happiest and I threw it all away in a moment for a blue eyed man boy who promised me the world.

When I was finished, the entire cottage was filled with photographs of my childhood. I found another photograph of Carey and my grandmother. It was obvious that Natty took it, since both women were knee deep in mud holding up clams in every photograph she was in. I laughed and couldn't help but run my finger over Carey's face. She was absolutely stunning, I couldn't ignore that. Something in her eyes told me so much about her soul. I could see her heart in the gentleness of her eyes, I could also see a slight sadness to them. There was something deep inside of me that made me want to know this woman, meet her and hug her. Hug her sadness away and hug her for being there for my grandmother when I wasn't.

I let out a sigh and walked up to my bedroom, setting the photograph on the almost empty bookshelf holding the single book my grandmother had sent to me. I walked to the side table and picked up the few letters from Carey and set them next to the book. His was mixed in with hers. I groaned, I should read it in case he was determined to come after me.

I walked back to the kitchen to pour a glass of wine or anything strong to help me read his letter. I passed the spare bedroom and glanced in, my eyes locking on the floorboard pushed up. I smiled lightly and walked over to it, and didn't hesitate to pull it open and wrap my hand around the letter I knew would be there. I held it up in the dwindling afternoon light. "*As you wish.*"

I set her letter off to the side, next to the large bottle of wine I had stashed in my bag. A last minute pilfering of the man boy's expansive wine collection. It only seemed fair after all he put me through.

I tore open his letter and blew out a puff of irritated air, it was typed not handwritten. Typical of him.

"*Dear Frankie,*

I hope that you know what you have done. I have already moved your things into storage and passed the key onto that little annoying Russian friend of yours. She felt it necessary to call me a selfish pig asshole, interesting coming from a street urchin. Amy will be bringing you the key and you have three months to clean out the storage unit, I have graciously paid three months' rent for you.

I know I apologized for my actions, but your reaction and unwillingness to listen and accept some facts, proves to me you have a lot of growing up to do. I have moved on and so should you.

I do appreciate that you mailed the engagement ring back to me, saves me some time having my lawyer draft up the request.

I wish you the best and hope you realize that I did love you, Frankie.

All my best,

Christopher."

I crumpled the letter up and ripped it apart, stomping outside to throw the pieces into the wind, yelling at the ocean as tears streamed down my face. The ocean only responded by crashing the waves harder against the show. Drowning out my screams of anger, sadness and utter hurt.

I stood outside well after the sun dipped down into hiding, leaving me in darkness. Just the rotating light from the lighthouse at the edge of the cove as my only company. I went inside when the cold was too much. I set my wine glass into the sink and picked up the bottle and Carey's letter. I needed to drown myself in a large, hot bath and bottle of wine. Christopher was an asshole, a pompous, self-involved asshole man boy. I was agitated as I filled the bath with the hottest water I could pump out of the old pipes. Taking large sips from the bottle, I shook my head and laughed at how stupid I was about Christopher and falling for him like he was the one.

I cringed happily as I dipped myself into the almost lava hot water, enjoying the sting as it burned away the anger left from the impersonal and pompous letter from him. The bubbles came up to my neck, I let the wine bottle float around in my hand as it graced the top of the water. I closed my eyes as the heat and alcohol did their job. I began to relax. I rolled my head to the side and saw her letter sitting there. I traded the wine bottle for the yellowed envelope as I pushed up to keep the paper from getting wet.

I smiled instantly at the sight of her sloppy handwriting.

"*Little Frankie,*

First off. Today is August 23rd, 2012. A Thursday. I normally am diligent about the dates on anything I put to paper, but I think my last few letters to you have been rushed.

Your grandmother has told me nothing but good things about you. She truly adores you and as she tells me more stories about you, I can see why. A feisty, courageous, smart as a whip, big hearted girl. All her words. She told me the story about when you were nine years old and you stood between her and the man who tried to take her purse. She said it was that summer you convinced her to go to the movies in the city? Mrs. Owen told me to have you tell me the rest of the story.

I dare say that I'm far from special, I just think she has taken pity on me and allowed me to stay with her. To answer one of your postscripts, I did indeed go to MIT. Fertility research with a minor in curative medicine properties, basically a Marie Curie wannabe. I'm almost done with my graduate degree and am looking forward to a short break. Can I ask why do you ask about MIT?

My heart was broken, it is one of those things that come in life and how we all navigate it. Love is one of those things we all deserve, but not all of us can navigate its road's successfully. Maybe one day, I will ramble on about it to you, my pen pal, after I have had a night of heavy drinking. Till then, all I will say is thank you. These two glasses of wine I have had while writing you, is truly not enough liquid courage to spill my heart to a floorboard and the beautiful woman under it, But, thank you for the words of encouragement, Frankie, and making a Yogi bear reference.

I have to keep this letter short, I promised to take your grandmother out to see Natty later today. I should shower and put the wine bottle back in the cupboard.

Oh, Toronto. Your grandmother told me you just moved to the city a few months before I came to live here, that you met a handsome man that swept you off your feet. Natty calls him man boy in her usual sarcastic tone. Mrs. Owen said, to tell me all about the man boy so I can relay it to her. I think she likes these letters as much as I do. She is as curious as I am about the one who whisked you away from this lovely little ocean side town.

She also wanted to say you're welcome for the trunk and that it will take you back to your heart and what it will need to find it again. Just keep looking. I did sneak a few looks at some of the recent pictures she had of you, how could anyone break the heart of a woman as beautiful as you. It amazes me, the world is a very confused place.

These letters have been a small comfort, I find the more I ask about you, the more Mrs. Owen lights up and the more I light up, too.

Till you write again,

Carey.

P.S. Mrs. Owen says she loves you more than the ocean and the sea. There is nothing you have to be sorry for; she is still with you. You just have to look in the pages (I am quoting her words exactly, as she requested.).

P.P.S. I should apologize for my comment about how beautiful you are, I have drank a little too much wine. But, you are very beautiful, Frankie. You probably need to hear that more, maybe you can ask the man boy to tell you every day. You deserve that."

I could not help but smile at how many times she called me beautiful, even if it was apparent the wine was doing most of the talking. It didn't matter, it helped take the edge off of Christopher's letter. I sighed and set the letter down, dragging my lobster red body out of the hot water and dressed for bed. I then walked to my bedroom, bringing the rest of the wine with me as I crawled into bed with my stationary.

I sat for a minute, recalling when I was nine and had done my best to scare off a mugger trying to take my grandmother's purse. I laughed at how brave I thought I could be when it was my grandmother who talked the mugger down and gave him enough money to satisfy his need for a clean bed and a hot meal. I started scribbling the story down for Carey when it hit me. I snatched her letter back up and looked at the date she had written. It was two years ago exactly. I set the letter in my lap, how was that possible? Maybe it was a mistake, but how could it be? She was talking to my grandmother while she was still alive. Then, there was what Natty told me, Carey had been inquiring about me and mentioned something about letters. I rubbed my eyes, trying to rub out the buzz I had from drinking half a bottle of expensive wine in a hot bath.

I stood up and grabbed the photo of my grandmother with Carey. The date printed by the old developer at the drugstore read July 12th, 2012. I sighed and rubbed my eyes again, my mind was having a hard time absorbing these small facts. I crawled back into bed and started a new piece of paper, the only way I would get more of this puzzle put together is if I asked.

"Carey, I need a nickname for you since you seem too attached to the little Frankie name like the rest of this town.

You told me that today is August 23rd, 2012. But, my calendar says, August 23rd, 2014. Which one of us has had far too much wine?"

I paused, my eyes were growing heavy as the wine was now mixing with the emotional exhaustion I had from the day. I didn't want to not leave a letter for her, so I scribbled quickly.

"I think I have had too much wine as well. I can barely stay awake. I promise, first thing in the morning I will write until my hand falls off. The mugger story, the man boy who is the biggest pompous dickhead in the world, and how I could ever think I was in love with him...ugh.

All of it, I will tell you.

Till tomorrow,

Little Frankie.

P.S. Thank you for calling me beautiful, it was something man boy never told me enough, you are right.

P.P.S. You are also beautiful, stunning if I dare say it. I found two pictures of you tucked in the trunk, that's how I knew about MIT. You have the most gentle honey gold brown eyes I have ever seen. I wish I could take away some of the sadness I see in them, Carey. You are equally as beautiful, if not more.

P.P.P.S. I owe you for taking care of my grandmother. Natty told me you were with her every step of the way and did so much for her."

I stopped writing as tears began to hit the paper, smearing the ink I had just freshly put down. I wiped away the tears, leaving black smudges. I was now drunk and sobbing, I tucked the letter in an envelope and stumbled to the spare room. Writing on the front of the letter. "*I promise you tomorrow.*"

Out of nowhere I kissed the letter before I dropped it in the hole, covering it up with a gentle slap of my hand. I pushed up and stumbled back into bed, passing out in sobs while the wine pulled me into a deep, drunken sleep. A sleep that was laden with images of a brunette woman who seemed to be in the past while I was in the future.

Chapter 5

The loud vibrations of my cell phone running around the wooden floor, brought me out of my deep sleep. I groaned as I leaned over the side, trapping the phone in my fingers. Pulling it up to my one open eye, I answered it as I fell back into the fluffy pillows.

"Amy."

"Hey pretty lady! About time you answered this phone. I've been calling on the hour, every hour. It's almost three. You starting to take after me already?"

I pulled the phone away to glance at the time, it was 2:55 in the afternoon. I had almost successfully slept the day away. I groaned again, that wine was definitely stronger than I thought. "I drank too much last night, I guess."

I heard Amy whistle and make one of her off handed comments before she got to the point of her call. "So I'm standing at the truck rental place. How big of a moving van you think you are going to need? I swindled that douchebag into paying for a van. I'm going to head over to the storage unit as soon as I'm done here. Anything you want in particular? Anything you want to throw out, burn, turn into recyclables?"

I rolled over to lie on my side, looking out the picture window at the sunny afternoon sun as it hit the tips of the waves, throwing sunlight in different angles into my room, I let my mind sway with the ocean. I didn't want to think about Christopher, or the storage unit, but I had let the letter sit for a few days and knowing the eagerness of my best friend to see me, I knew she would be on top of bringing my last remaining pieces of city life to me as soon as possible.

"Anything marked with a C and a smiley face, burn. The rest bring to me, we can sort through it together. You should only need a normal van, I have maybe thirty boxes of stuff left in that unit."

"Aye Aye. I will be up in three or four days. I have to work a few more shifts at the hotel before I can take vacation time." Amy let out a dramatic sigh.

I smiled at the thought of finally seeing Amy, it had been almost a month since I saw her last and opted for the solitary life by the water. "That'll be perfect, I should have the cottage all fixed up to your high standards of living."

I could feel Amy's award winning smile through the phone. "You know what I like, anyways, I gotta bolt. I have to haggle with this rental guy with all of my best talents." She blew me a kiss and hung up just as I heard her begin to haggle like an aggressive stock broker on the floors of the stock exchange.

I tossed the phone on the side table and rubbed at my eyes, I could feel the last edges of the wine escaping, at least I didn't wake up with a hangover. I took a deep breath and sorted through what I had to do for the day. Then it hit me, I hadn't written Carey like I promised. She would have already gotten the first half drunken ramblings I left her by now. I slid out of bed and grabbed my stationary and began to write.

"*Carey,*

I'm still trying to figure out a nickname for you, but I'm coming up blank. Maybe you can tell me something about you that would clue me in on some fun nicknames for you.

I'm sorry for my drunken ramblings, half drunken ramblings. I only drank a half bottle of wine, but I did not forget my small promise to you. I owe you two stories.

I will start with the boring, horrible one, the origins of man boy and how I became swept up in a whirlwind romance I thought would end perfect like in the movies. Man boy, Christopher, is...was my fiancé. I know. I was on the quick trip to marriage and a life of wealth and anything I could ever want. Everything but a man who loved me enough to stay honest and loyal to the woman he proposed too.

I guess I should tell you how I met him.

I met Christopher almost three years ago at a press meeting for a local politician. I was writing a story on the politician, yes, hard to believe from my letters that I am a journalist. I'm actually not too bad at it. I do investigative reporting for the largest newspapers in Toronto. Just on hiatus for a little while. Anyways, I ran into Christopher at the press meeting, literally. Clocked into him as I was running around the corner to chase down one of the assistants to the politician. I used to say it was love at first sight, but now I think it was lust or admiration clouding my vision. Christopher is a lawyer, one of the top business lawyers in the city and he was there supporting and fundraising, and I got lost in his deep blue eyes, white smile, and the way he charmed the pants off anyone in the room. Yet, he managed that night to make me feel like the only girl in the world.

Fast forward, we started dating and I thought I had found my knight. Christopher took me to fancy restaurants, to the theater, we traveled and I was beginning to live a life that took me far from the one I had here in this cottage. I lost myself in a man who could negotiate and talk his way out of and into anything. After six months of dating, he proposed to me. I thought it was genuine until two months ago when I found him knee deep in his personal assistant atop of the desk I helped pick out for his office.

You can imagine the rest. He had been sleeping around on me for the last four months. Wanted to still marry me because I was better suited for a high profile life than his assistant girlfriend.

The only regret I have is that he took me away from my family, from my grandmother and I couldn't see my way out of the shine of a fancy life he gave me. That's why I'm back at the cottage, trying to find the life I had that was far better than the one he could have ever given me. Tell my grandmother that the man boy was exactly like that weatherman she always hated on channel 9, the one who did the weekend forecast. She will know what I mean.

Looking back, he never told me I was beautiful. Actually you are the first person to tell me I'm beautiful in a long time. I wish I could meet you, Carey. For that reason alone, and thank you in person.

Now, story two. The how I tried to save my grandmother from the crime of the century. What she told you pretty much sums it up. I had swindled her into taking me to the movies in the city, since this little town only gets whatever the old man who owns it wants to see. I was so excited to be out in the city and show my grandmother what it was like. She never traveled outside of this little town, always preferred the ocean to the masses of people crammed together. As we stopped at a drug store to buy candy to sneak in, a dirty looking man popped out of the alley, asking for her purse. I sprang into action, standing my tiny little kid body in front of my grandmother. Telling the man in my strongest little kid voice to back off. I was furiously protective of my grandmother when I was little, and all the way up until man boy brainwashed me. Maybe that's what true honest love is, you will do anything you can to protect the ones you love, regardless of your own safety. I'm not sure if I will find that kind of love outside of family again.

The dirty man went to push me out of the way when my grandmother reached out and gently grabbed his hand. He froze and I could see all of the anger, the drug hazed intentions of robbing an old lady and the sadness disappear in her simple grasp. My grandmother talked him down and gave him a handful of money, which he actually hesitated to take until she persuaded him to take it. He actually thanked her and apologized to me before he ran down the street.

I looked at my grandmother in awe, like she was truly superman. She smiled before I could ask her what had happened she told me. "Sometimes a gentle hand is stronger than a firm voice. But thank you my little Frankie, for being my protector."

It was something that always stuck with me forever, still does. I can see that day clearer than any other. Can you ask my grandmother why she wanted me to tell you that story?

Anyways, those are my two stories. I wish I had more to say about man boy, but he was my greatest mistake and maybe my greatest failure.

So, now it's your turn. What does the beautiful mysterious brunette from MIT have to tell me? I think maybe two stories will make this fair? Anything, anything about you that will bring me closer to unraveling the mystery of you, I want to know more about you, Carey. My heart seems to want to know more about you.

Please write back as soon as you can, I find talking to you to be healing to my heart.

Little Frankie.

P.S. Play the song Broken Arrow by Rod Stewart for my grandmother...she will tell you why.

P.P.S. I asked about MIT because I wanted to make sure the stunning woman in the photograph with my grandmother was you. Which must also mean you are a stunning and fiercely intelligent woman?"

I smiled as I wrote the last bit, I knew I was mildly flirting with the brunette stranger, but it felt right. It felt right calling her beautiful and pouring out secrets and stories I had never shared with anyone. I sealed the envelope, scribbling "*Bottle of Rain*" across the front. I hopped off the bed and went to run to the spare room when something caught my eye, literally stopping me mid step.

On the bookshelf next to the King Arthur book and the photograph of Carey and my grandmother, sat another old book. Just a few inches away as if it was set there unknowingly of the other items. I walked to the shelf, confused and saw that it was my grandmother's copy of Aesop's Fables. I stared at the book confused, I had not been able to find any of her books in the house. I tapped the letter against my hand, almost afraid to touch the book thinking it was figment of my wine hazed imagination.

I took a breath and decided to drop the letter and come back later, maybe I was seeing things.

I grinned as I found the floorboard pushed up as usual. I reached in and grabbed her letter, setting my thick one in its place. I clutched the letter against my chest and couldn't wait to read it.

After pushing the floorboard back in its place I leaned against the bed in the spare room, running my fingers over the black inked words. *"I give you today."* Just those simple four words had a profound effect on my heart as it beat a little faster.

I unfolded the letter and smiled, the letter was short as I had expected, but it didn't matter, it still made me grin like an idiot. Was it possible I was smitten with this woman's handwriting?

"Frankie,

I should probably try and call you that instead of little Frankie. Your grandmother remarked you were not a big fan of it. Which in a way makes me want to call you it more, to bring out that feisty side of you she often tells me about?

No need to apologize on the length of your letter, I'm just happy to hear from you. I also have to keep this brief. I am about to head out of town for a few days for some school work related conference. Basically I'm interviewing with a few research companies and medical schools. I hate to leave your grandmother and this quiet town for the surging noise of the city and the people who carry along with it, but I need a job. I'm getting tired of buying the cheap ramen noodles and would like to upgrade to the finer things in life, like microwave dinners.

There won't be a letter from me for a few days, but I promise the moment I'm back home at the cottage, you will receive one. I will tell you all about my trip and anything I can think of, unless you ask me something in your next letter.

Now to the curious thing, the dates. It appears I'm living two years in the past and you are two years in the future, it seems highly impossible even for my scientific mind. I asked your grandmother about it and she gave me a cryptic answer, a smile and a wink. I would dare to venture so far in the possibility of time and space transcendence, but, you are not Marty and I'm not Doctor Emmett Brown. (Insert laughs here for my cheesy pop culture reference.)

Anyways, I have decided to test a theory. I had begun cleaning up your grandmother's belongings for. Packing up her books and other cherished items for safekeeping. She told me of one book she used to read to you when you were little. I have set that book on the shelf in her room, on its side. I have no intentions of touching it or moving it, even as I leave. So if for some reason you are in the future, you will find the book in her room. If you do, write back to me which book it is and what I have written in the front cover.

I must be off, I want to get this letter to you before my flight leaves. I promise, with all of my heart that I will write you as soon as I am back. Please don't forget about me.

Carey

P.S. you do enjoy the postscripts

P.P.S. The man boy is a damned fool if he never told you how beautiful you are, every day. Because you are a woman who deserves at least that much.

P.P.P.S. Calling me stunning might give me an ego little Frankie, but it fills my heart with compliments from a beautiful woman. So thank you. "

I could not wipe off the stupid, silly grin that I knew was plastered to my face. I was developing a crush on this woman, or these letters. I really didn't care to spilt hairs over it. I was happy, she made me happy in the little comments and the way she half wrote in cursive but changed halfway through a word. I let out a sigh and stood up, to walk back to my room, to write her another letter, so she could have two when she returned.

I started thinking about where she was going, if she was still there now. Mainly all of my thoughts leading to how I could find her, thoughts that seemed to halt as I glanced at the bookshelf.

The book laid on its side, slightly away from the other things. I stared at the worn blue book with faded gold lettering, a thick layer of dust covering it and the shelf it laid upon. Telling me that it was something that had gone untouched longer than just a day. My heart seemed to stop as I walked to it, setting Carey's letter down next to the others. I reached out with a shaky hand, picking up the old book that I had flipped through a million times with my grandmother.

Aesop's Fables.

A book full of magic and hope, that's why I loved it so much as a child. I took a deep breath as the snippets of what Carey's experiment instructions were. I ran my fingers over the cover, fingertips leaving clear trails in the thick dust. My finger paused at the edge of the pages, I could feel the dust, and I could feel that this book had been on this shelf for a few years. I hesitated for a moment before I flipped open the front cover. I could feel my heart start pounding from a dead stop to a full blown, just ran a marathon, pace.

In the front cover, in her handwriting, "*Better bend than break. The oak and the reed is my favorite fable in this book. You should read it Little Frankie, never let anyone break you. -L*"

I was breathing heavy. The book was not on the shelf when I passed out the night before, I remembered because I had stared at her picture a million times before the wine pushed my eyelids closed. The only book I had was the one my grandmother sent me. I looked at the shelf, the book had left a clean imprint in the dust I had ignored cleaning up until I had more than just three items to store on it. But this book, the one in my hands, reappeared out of nowhere and had defied the ideas of time and the laws of science.

I knew all of my grandmothers other books were gone, nowhere to be found in the house. I had searched thoroughly through the cottage. I assumed them to all be in the hands of the brunette woman who could make my heart stop in simple scrawls and loops of her handwriting. The woman I had never met until I stubbed my toe on a floorboard, a woman no one knew where she was now. Yet, she had given me this one book out of thin air.

I whispered to no one. "How did she do this?" My heart was now pounding so hard, I could hear it thump in my ears.

Was it possible we were breaking all of the laws of science? All I knew was that whatever it was, it had to be magic involved. Magic that was making my heart beat honestly for the first time in years. I sat on the edge of the bed, the book gripped between my hands to keep them shaking any more than they already were.

I needed to find out more about Carey, and where she was. Because as I slowly knew I was falling for the woman, I needed to know how to find her. More importantly, I needed to know if she was real.

Chapter 6

I sat on my bed staring out the window, the book still in my hands. Every time I tried to figure out how Carey was able to get the book to the shelf, I would drift off and stare at the waves. This was definitely something that went well beyond my journalistic education. I opened the front cover one more time, my fingers running over the simple words Carey had written. My heart picking up pace as my finger ran over every little ink mark she had left.

I took a deep breath and stood up, moving to the bookshelf, I set the book next to the one my grandmother had sent me. They fit next to each other perfectly, the book was definitely from her collection. She had always tried to buy books of similar age and coloring.

I glanced at the picture of Carey and my grandmother before turning back to the bedside table and pulling out the stationary again. Carey had said it would be a couple of days before she would be writing back, but I wanted to make sure she knew I had gotten the book. I sat and wrote slower than normal, my heart and my mind still digesting the book's appearance.

"I always thought myself to be the reed and not the oak, but I feel like I have broken like the old oak, putting faith in the strength of others to carry me.

This is also one of my favorite fables next to the lion and the mouse.

How did you know?"

It was a simple question but I wanted to know. Know how she knew that the book was one of my favorites and that I would find it like I did. I sighed as I sealed the letter and walked slowly back to the spare bedroom. I pulled the floorboard to the side and sighed harder as I felt my first letter still there, I set the second one underneath the first. I wanted Carey to read that one before we began the discussion if we were breaking the laws of time and space or if this was really an elaborate prank. I was hoping that it wasn't a prank because of the profound effect this woman's simple letters had on me. She was slowly bringing my heart back to me when it was lost in the city. After putting the board back, I dressed in an old pair of pants and a thick sweater, deciding to spend the last few hours of the day cleaning up the barn to keep my mind off of things.

I burnt the daylight faster than I thought. I had managed to clear out the small work table and area my grandmother had used to make all of her own picture frames. I smiled and thought about picking up where she left off, or at least finding some sort of creative outlet to use the work table. In time, I would have to discuss going back to work, after the short leave of absence I had taken was over. Amy would be bringing the rest of my city life, my laptop, and other things I suddenly did not feel so necessary to have at an arm's reach. I dusted off my hands and grinned as the late evening sunset was pushing amber light through the cracks of the old barn, highlighting the cozy feel it gave off. I closed the large doors and headed back inside the house. I found it fascinating that my days went by quickly, but also slower than when I was in the city.

I set the small wooden box I had found hidden under a canvas tarp in the work table drawer, on the kitchen counter. It had all the tell-tale signs of my grandmother's handiwork, the artistic and the not too true carpenter way it was put together. Lastly, it was dotted with the infamous swirls of Celtic knots she had always adored. My grandmother would spend a lot of her time drawing out Celtic knots, painting them and trying to instill them in anything she could. She had also taught me how to draw some of the less complicated versions, but I long forgot how when I opted for more exciting things like college life, and swarmy lawyers with bright smiles.

I made a hot cup of coffee, running my fingers over the old box and its smooth knot work. I could not remember seeing the box when I was little, or anywhere in the house in the few times I visited as an adult.

Lifting the lid of the box, I smiled at the dark blue material inside, cradling the smaller boxes inside. I pulled the four smaller boxes out and set them on the counter, each one was similar in shape but varied in size. There was also a small note at the bottom of the larger box, I lifted it up and immediately recognized the handwriting as my grandmother's.

I flipped open the single page.

"I know you will find this, Frankie. That's why I had it hidden in the barn. I knew when the time was right you would find it.

In time, you will know what to do with these and you will find the one they will eventually belong to, as they will belong to your heart.

Love you always, my dear."

I swallowed the tears back as I set the paper down and turned to open each one of the boxes. In the first box I picked up was her wedding ring, the other box held a smaller ring that looked like an engagement ring, and the last two held another ring that looked like a man's wedding ring and lastly, there was a necklace.

The necklace I had always remembered her wearing. It was a worn down Claddagh with an emerald cradled between the hands. I held it in my hands and squeezed, I could almost feel my grandmother in the gentle grooves of the necklace and the charm. She had never taken it off and remarked once, or twice when Natty made fun of her, that she would be buried in it.

I packed up the rings and set them back into the box, slipping the necklace around my neck. Pressing my fingers against it as it settled right under my collarbone. I felt like my grandmother was suddenly with me even more than ever before. I took the box back up to my bedroom, setting the old wooden box on the shelf next to the books. It felt as if that was where it needed to go.

Holding the cup in my hands I walked out into the backyard, down the small steps and down into the cool, damp sand of the beach. The wind was cool and full of the ocean as it blew around me gently. My heart was heavy, heavier now I as I realized how much I did miss my grandmother being gone. My grandmother knew it, and yet she had made efforts to make sure I was still loved when I certainly didn't feel like I could be, or should be.

Finding a rock, I sat down. Propping my feet up on the edge as I huddled over my knees, watching the seagulls and the waves battle each other in the ebb and flow of nature. My thoughts moving to my grandmother and Carey, mainly Carey. I suddenly had the urge to have her sitting next to me on this rock, to be anywhere near me so I could hear her voice, feel her presence next to me. I wondered what her smile was like and what I could do to bring it out of her, and for a split second I wondered what it would be like to hug her and have her read from the books on the shelf.

I smiled and laughed out loud. "You are definitely smitten. Smitten with a woman who might not even be real." I sighed hard, trying to shake out my last thoughts about the brunette, but I couldn't shake how it would feel to have her close to me, so close she was in my arms.

I sat there until the sun disappeared into the ocean, looking as if it was drowning itself slowly, but happy to do so. The sand was much cooler under my feet now as night had set in and the tide had moved in, washing my steps away as soon as I laid them down. Glancing up at the cottage, I saw two headlights pull into the driveway. I squinted and paused, I wasn't expecting anyone for a few more days.

Hustling back up to the house, I let out a sigh of relief when I caught sight of the large moving van parked crookedly and heard Amy chattering away on her cellphone. I walked around the side of the cottage and stood, with arms folded, staring at my best friend as she sat on the wooden split rail fence, her legs swinging easily.

I waited a minute before breaking her conversation. "When are you ever early? Two days early?"

Amy swung her head in my direction, grinning as she almost dropped the phone from hopping off the fence and running towards me. She almost tackled me in a tiny aggressive hug.

"Frankie! I called you! The front door was locked and I couldn't find the key under the mat."

I mumbled against the tiny girl. "That's because it's tucked up under the mailbox by the door." I wrapped my arms around Amy, squeezing her. "I am so glad you are here."

Amy leaned back in my arms. "The ocean side town too boring for your taste? Need a little Amy in your life?" She winked as she hopped out of my arms. "Come on. Let's unload the truck. We have to take it back in the morning. I got it for free if I promised to drop it off at the rental place the next town over."

I laughed as I walked after Amy, her random hyper chattering about how she called in sick for the next two days before her vacation and was sure she would be fired, but didn't care. She grumbled about the drive down and how she haggled the rental guy into giving her the van for free, and lastly cursing Christopher to hell and back for how he "done did me wrong." I just listened and smiled, enjoying every minute.

It only took us an hour to unload the van. I really only had a handful of small boxes filled with my extra clothes I had left behind, my electronics, my knick-knacks and my own book collection. I dug around in the box of electronics, pulling out my work laptop and my tablet. Setting them up in the kitchen to charge, I smiled as Amy came downstairs.

"Wow, Frankie. This little cottage is pretty amazing. I thought it would be a tiny sea shanty the way you used to describe it." She flopped herself into the chair by the small table in the kitchen I had yet to use. I watched as her eyes drifted to the massive ocean view and became lost in the simple beauty it offered. "This places feels magical, it's so perfect."

"I hope the spare room will be enough for you, I cleaned it up yesterday, but I didn't expect you here till the end of the week. The sheets are fresh, and in the morning we can get newer blankets if you are too cold."

Amy kept staring out the large sliding door. "You think you will come back to the city?" She slowly turned her eyes to meet mine. I could tell she was serious and asking me more than just the simple question, it was her way of asking me if I was alright. I had left without much of a quick phone call to her. I cried too hard after the huge blow out with Christopher, that all I wanted was to be away from him and the city, and everything else.

I shrugged as I reached for two wine glasses. "I don't know, Amy. I think there is a lot I missed by being in the city, and every day I'm here I really don't think about leaving. It's perfect for what I need right now, but who knows if at the end of my leave if I will be ready to come back." I poured the rest of the wine I had borrowed from Christopher into the glasses. Handing one to Amy I held it up, "To new beginnings in the shanty by the sea."

Amy smiled and clinked her glass before taking a huge sip. "This is tasty stuff. Oh! Reminds me, I got you a little something." She ran to her giant bag and pulled out two bottles of wine. Walking back to me she held them up. "Compliments of the man boy's super private stock. I slipped them out when he was getting me the storage unit key." She winked. "It's the least he could do."

I laughed out loud as I grabbed the two bottles. "Yes it is."

Amy and I finished off the bottle I had taken and made it halfway through a second before we decided to call it a night. I helped carry her bags upstairs, getting her settled in the spare room. I hugged her. "I'll see you in the morning, and we can drive around the town and see what kind of trouble we can get into."

Amy smiled, "It's a deal." She threw her bag on the bed and dug around, pulling out her pink skull covered pajamas. I shook my head and turned to walk out when my eyes caught the floorboard, still in place.

I looked over my shoulder as thoughts of Carey flooded my mind, bringing me even more warmth than the wine had. "Amy, this floorboard is loose. It has a mind of its own and pops up here and there. If it does, just wake me up and I will push it back down. I haven't found the perfect glue yet." I grinned as I turned and looked at Amy.

She tilted her head and stared at me. "That smile, I haven't seen it in a long time." She pointed at me. "Did you meet some handsome sailor, or crab fisherman that has brought that stupid grin back?"

I could feel myself blushing. "No. No sailor or a crab fisherman." I turned to walk out the room as I heard Amy holler after me. "A lumberjack? A net weaver? Oh come on Frankie! You are going to have to tell me at some point."

I laughed. "Goodnight Amy." I quickly closed the door to my bedroom and moved to the bookshelf, picking up the picture for a hundredth time.

Staring at Carey, I whispered into the night. "Definitely not a sailor or a fisherman, just a beautiful student."

I fell asleep as quickly as I had the night before, the wine doing its job of making sleep come quickly and happily.

That night I dreamt about one night Christopher and I were out on the town. He was taking me to a new restaurant opening that he knew the owners and wanted to schmooze the crowd that would be there. The dream moved quickly through the dinner and the boring conversation of politics and business. While the boys began to smoke cigars, I excused myself, wanting a breath of air and a break from the tedious conversation about politics.

I walked out the front door, breathing in the deep, crisp, clean air of the night. I smiled as I looked up in the night sky; the stars seemed to be sparkling bright as I looked up into the sky. I pulled my wrap closer around my shoulders, my dress was not made for cool nights, but to bring cool envious stares instead. I continued to take deep breaths, pulling my wrap even closer, I heard a soft, smooth voice off to my right. It took me a minute to realize that the voice was calling my voice, and another minute to realize it was a woman calling me. I turned and my eyes fell upon a stunning brunette, tall, lean, and elegant in her simple outfit of jeans and a white V-neck shirt covered by a loose grey jacket billowing slightly in the wind. I smiled as she walked towards me slowly, she uttered my name again. "Frankie?"

I cocked my head trying to recognize who it was, but it was taking me longer as I stared at the brunette. Her hair was up in a ponytail, revealing the beautiful angles of her jaw and the long neck. I felt my heart skip slightly at the sight of this woman, she was gorgeous, but I couldn't recall ever meeting her.

I went to open my mouth to ask who she was when I felt a hand on my arm, pulling my attention from her.

I turned to look to my left and grinned as I saw Christopher's grin. "There you are Frankie. I thought you had escaped. It's time for dessert, and then we can go to the cocktail lounge you and Amy were talking about."

I smiled and turned to him, my world wrapped up in his blue eyes. "I stepped out to get some air, you know how much I hate cigars." I kissed him gently on the cheek.

He pulled me and nodded towards the restaurant, I eagerly followed but something pulled me to look back at the brunette. She was just a foot away from me, her eyes staring at me as if she was looking at a ghost. I smiled politely, and as I turned back to Christopher I heard her say. "It is you, Little Frankie."

My head shot back around, focusing on what she had just said. I furrowed my brow and asked. "What did you just say?"

The brunette smiled and hung her head down, turning slightly to look back at me, she said. "I finally met you, and it's at the wrong time, Little Frankie." She hurried back down the street, disappearing into the small crowds of people who littered the city streets on any given night. I was pulled, again by Christopher, back into the bustle of the new restaurant that was packed, the sound of a champagne cork being let go woke me up from the dream.

My heart was pounding and I was breathing heavily. I rubbed my eyes, the dream was a mix of reality and fiction. I had gone to a restaurant opening with Christopher, but it was years ago and right after we had started dating. Everything in the dream had happened, me getting bored with the company and heading outside for air, even the part where Christopher found me was what actually happened, but I never remembered the encounter with the brunette who knew my childhood nickname. I stretched as I felt groggy from the wine.

It was still dark out, very late at night now. I rolled out of the bed and stood up. I was sweating mildly from the dream and felt like I had just run a marathon as I stood next to the window, cracking it slightly to cool myself down. The ocean wind pushed through happily, fluttering a few pages of the letters and pushing the picture on the shelf to the floor. I walked over to the picture and as my fingers picked it up, and felt a warm sensation against my chest. Forcing me to put a hand on it, I felt the necklace under my palm. It was warm and it felt as if it was pulsating.

I flipped the picture over and as soon as I looked at Carey smiling, it hit me. Hit me like a freight train, so hard I had to lean against the bookshelf.

The brunette calling my name was Carey. The tall, elegant, stunning woman with her hair up, looking at me as if she was looking at a ghost, she was Carey.

I let out a strangled breath, "Oh my god...Carey. It was you." I slid down to the floor, holding the picture. I was changing my past with every letter I sent her, she was searching me out and the past me has no idea who she was. I clutched the picture to my chest, closing my eyes praying that she would come home soon and write me. There was no doubt in my heart now that I had to find her that I was meant to find her.

Chapter 7

I couldn't sleep for the rest of the night. My mind was running a million different directions, not one of them getting me any closer to how this was happening and how I could get to her. I never let go of the picture even after I pushed myself up from the floor and crawled back into bed. I held it close to my chest, right under the necklace that never seemed to cease its gentle pulsing against my skin. I figured it was just my heart still racing from my dream.

I went back through my memories of that night. I remembered it clearly because it was one of the few times Christopher had treated me like I was the only woman in the world. He had done that in the beginning of our relationship until he knew he had me wrapped around his little finger, and so consumed in the life he had to offer me. Squeezing my eyes shut and pushing my face down into the pillow. I could clearly remember what I ate for dinner that night, the taste of the fancy cocktails at the lounge we went to after, the way his cologne smelled on the lapels of his thin woolen coat, and even the crazy cab driver who tried to runs us over.

Those were the memories I could hold in my hand, as they felt so real and my mind had gone over them a million times. Then, came the brunette, Carey. She felt new. She felt like a fresh edit to one of my newspaper articles, smashed perfectly into a piece I had written over and over until a fresh breath of air and ideas filled my head. Carey was new, a new memory that slid itself into an old one.

I knew it was real, she was real, and that moment she approached me was real. It was not my sleeping brain that conjured it. I was certain my sleeping brain would conjure other ideas about Carey, and they would be less than innocent. My feelings and thought about her were changing every moment and growing stronger.

After agonizing inside my head for a few hours, I got up with the sun. Realizing the only way I would know the truth, or something that I could call the truth, was to wait for Carey to set a letter into the floor. I walked downstairs, pausing at the spare bedroom, peeking in, hoping to see the raised edge of the wooden floorboard. Instead, all I saw was my best friend tangled up in her bed sheets like a pink tornado and snoring as she mumbled in her sleep. I stared at the floorboard, hoping that it would pop up any second and ease my strange anxiety.

It didn't.

Amy rolled over and in a half asleep voice. "Don't even think about waking me up for another twelve hours." I half smiled and closed the door.

I stood in the hallway between the kitchen and the front living room. I stared at all the photographs I had hung back up, noticing my grandmother wearing the necklace in all the photographs. I couldn't remember when she got it, just that it was on her neck in every single picture. From when I was a tiny newborn until the last summer I was here. My hand found the pendant again, holding it tightly as if it was her.

I glanced over into the kitchen as the window whistled through a crack in the glass door that led out to the back deck. It pulled my attention to the bright, tiny green lights on my laptop and tablet. Letting me know they were ready as soon as I was. I grumbled and decided to try to cure my insomnia with work emails that I knew were piling up. As I took a step to the counter, another quick whistle of wind pushed past me and rippled against the frames on the wall. I turned to look as one frame made a louder clank than the rest. I reached out to still its movement and prevent it from deciding it wanted to fall off the wall.

I smiled lightly when I saw it was the picture of Carey and my grandmother sitting on the back deck. I took an extra moment to straighten it when something in the photograph caught my eye. Pulling the photograph off the wall and walked to the bright underside light by the sink. Turning it on, I held the frame up so I could see it clearly. Around Carey's neck was a necklace, and as I squinted at it, I saw that it was the same necklace my grandmother was wearing.

I swallowed hard as I set the photograph down. I did not recall seeing it the first thousand times I looked, or more so stared at Carey in this picture. Then again, I was only really looking at the golden brown eyes of the smiling brunette and very little at the rest of the photograph.

I flipped the photograph over, still no date on the back. I studied the photograph and was able to figure out that it was a late summer evening by the sweater my grandmother was wearing. It was her fall favorite, one she brought out at the first sign of the leaves changing. Fall was at least a month away, maybe a month and a half away.

I set the photograph down on the kitchen counter as I walked to the table, sitting down, my head was full. Full of mysteries that were showing its face every day. I stared at nothing in particular as I tried to remember if I had seen the necklace in the photograph. After a few minutes of boring a hole into the darkness of the kitchen, I smiled and took a breath. Maybe it was my mind working overdrive, trying to pick up any of the small clues it could that would bring me one step closer to her.

Opening my laptop, I fell into distraction of work and personal emails. Sorting through the almost fifteen hundred work emails that awaited me. Many were nonsense, just finalization emails of the last article I had submitted before my life and world changed. I groaned slightly as I opened the final print of my article, one about the political aspirations of Christopher and a few other politicians he supported. It was an article to help him highlight the good they were doing just in time for the upcoming elections. I clicked out of it as fast as I had clicked in.

I went through the rest quickly, answering a few and replying to my editor when I thought I would be back. I told him that I would be taking the full four months of leave and near the end I would make my final decision, but I would be willing to do some small articles in the next month. After clearing out my work email, I moved to my personal account. That one was just as full as my work account, emails from friends and intended wedding guests asking the ever popular question at the end of an engagement, what happened? Why was the wedding suddenly off?

Ignoring all of them, I leaned back in the chair, the only people who had to know why and what happened were Christopher and my best friend, who was sleeping in the room above me. The rest, well the rest could find out from him. I had no intention of explaining the actions of cheater and a liar to anyone, my heart was still far too broken to explain it carefully and without spite. I took a slow breath, remembering clearly the image of him and Ashley on the desk. Ashley was going to be one of my bridesmaids, a close friend that I had met through Christopher and we hit it off immediately. She even helped pick out the engagement announcements and she was going to go with me to New York City for my dress fitting. I suddenly groaned and rubbed at my face. I should have known better, or been a little more suspicious of Christopher and her and the close relationship they had. How could I have been so dumb?

I groaned again and returned to the computer, closing out of the emails, I was about to shut the computer down and go crawl deep under the covers and sleep. Then, an idea hit me, I still had access to the local police department people search program. My heart began to race as my fingers flew across the keyboard, logging in and typing her name into the search fields.

When I hit enter, forty different results appeared. I had to sift through them until I found two who fit her approximate age based on what she told me about her time in grad school. The first one was a short stocky brunette who lives in Minnesota and has two parking tickets, the second was an eighty five year old who was spending her golden years down in Boca Rotan, Florida. There was a third, and when I clicked on her, I grinned and blushed. There was my Carey.

Carey Murphy, thirty-one years old. Her birthday passed a few days ago, I smiled and debated sending her a late birthday card through the floorboard. I kept on, she had no criminal history, few parking tickets that were paid promptly. I chewed on my lip as I sifted through her last known addresses. MIT was one, there was her home address in Seattle. I smiled. "Born and raised in Seattle. Can't stay away from the oceans can you?"

I scrolled down to another address that was right outside of MIT and the last known address for her was my grandmother's cottage. I went through more pages and I found nothing. There was no further record in any of the databases I had access to. I went to a few other sites that I often used to dig up information on people I was writing about, but came up empty. It was as if she disappeared the moment she left the cottage. The morning sunlight creeping across the floor pulled me from the computer. I had searched for hours and I could feel it in my back as the old wooden chair was not meant for sitting in one spot for too long.

Shutting down the laptop, I set the timer on the coffee pot. It was six in the morning and I knew I could at least squeeze in a quick nap before Amy would be up searching for food, then jumping on me to go get more food after she ate everything I had left in the cupboard and fridge. Walking past the island, I paused, staring at the photograph of Carey, I sighed. Scooping it up and hanging it back on the wall before I went upstairs. I would sleep on it, sleep on the newest mystery, and clue the wind had brought my way.

Entering my bedroom, I could feel the warmth the morning sunlight had brought to the room. It poured through the large window, cascading a golden glow over my bed and hitting the angles of the walls in just the right way. For a moment, I felt like I was in a different place, a castle tower almost. I hugged myself as I walked across the warm wood floor and hopped into the perfectly warm bed. Pulling the large covers up close, I rolled onto my side so I could look out. It had become a habit, rolling over and staring at the view.

It was the only time I felt my mind and heart empty out together and replace the thoughts of him, my broken heart and everything else, with just the gentle back and forth of the water.

My eyes closed on their own, slipping into a gentle sleep I kept my hand around the necklace, wondering if Carey did the same thing at night.

Amy did as I expected, and woke up three hours later. She ate the rest of the cereal I had and then, jumped on the bed until I woke up. As soon as she saw my eyes were open, she dropped to her knees and crawled to sit next to me against the headboard. "Time to wake up! There are eggs, bacon, waffles and maybe mimosas in our near future!"

She leaned against me as I sat up, frowning at her. "You are better than any alarm clock. You know that?"

Amy winked at me before she leaned her head back, looking around the room. "This is quite the little bedroom. One that looks like it was made for a princess." Amy smiled as she rolled her head to look back at me, "So what are we going to do today? Burn some of his things? Plow the fields?"

I chuckled lightly. "We are going to do whatever you would like, my dear." I rolled out of the bed and stretched, reaching to put away the stationary I had left out on the table. I asked over my shoulder. "How did you sleep? Any problems?"

I could hear her stretch, and sigh. "Nope! Slept like a baby! It was amazing. I can't remember the last time I slept without hearing sirens, cabs honking and the drunk woman downstairs yelling at the Chinese delivery guy." She bounced out of the bed and stood next to me. "This place is amazing, I think if you stay I might think about staying here, But! First, we have to check out the diners, see if they are worthy of hanging around."

I smiled and grabbed Amy into a half hug. "Best you will ever have." I squeezed her a little tighter. "Thank you for coming."

Amy squeezed me back. "There's nowhere I wouldn't go for my best friend." She reached up and kissed me on the cheek. "I'm going to go get ready. I'm beyond starving. Oh! We have to get more cereal and food in general. Your cupboards are now bare." She giggled and bounced past me, half pointing at the bookshelf as she went, hollering. "Maybe we can find some things to fill up that sad-looking bookshelf!"

I kept smiling as my eyes settled on the bookshelf, whispering, "I think someone already has a plan for that."

The day started with us eating at the old restaurant my grandmother would go every Saturday morning, filling Amy up with all the best breakfast the small town had to offer. We then went to Natty's where the two eccentric women hit it off and bonded over crazy jewelry. By the time we left the old woman's shop, Natty and Amy had made plans for a big afternoon of making clam chowder the next day. Amy and I then drove around in the old blue truck exploring the entire town and the oceans edges. I spent most of the day telling Amy about the spots I used to play in as a little girl, telling her stories about my grandmother and what she was like. Amy had never met my grandmother, we had met when I moved to the city and the few times I came back to the cottage, it was only for a day or two.

When the day finally dipped into the late evening, we rolled the old blue truck up into the driveway. Amy hopped out first and started grabbing the bags of groceries that were piled up in the truck bed. "Can we order pizza or ribs?"

I shot her a look as I pulled up brown bags full of food. "We just went grocery shopping, there is enough food in here for months and you want to order out?"

Amy shrugged and walked towards the cottage, mumbling something along the likes of you can take the girl out of the city, but not the city out of the girl. I giggled as I followed her into the cottage. She quickly abandoned helping with the rest of the groceries in the name of changing out of her shopping shoes. I let out a huff and went back to the truck to haul the rest back into the house.

On the third and last trip, my arms full of the last four bags of food, I heard Amy yelp and start hopping around the room. Thumping against the wooden floor, the sound echoing through the entire cottage.

"Amy? You okay up there?" I walked to the staircase, jogging up the stairs to her room. I found her rolling on the bed, holding her toe. "Amy?"

"Oww! The floorboard jumped out at me! I smashed my toes on it when I went to go grab my other shoes to finish helping you." She pouted at me and held up her red, sore toes. I smiled and shook my head. "I'll get some ice for you."

I took two steps out of the room when I spun around and walked back into the room, dropping to the floorboard in question. It was pushed up, telling me like it always had that Carey was back. I pulled the floorboard to the side and stuck my hand in, ignoring the moans from my best friend as I felt a thick envelope underneath my fingers. I felt my heart race when I saw her handwriting on the front. I quickly tucked it in my jeans pocket and set the floorboard back. I wanted to rip it open right then and there and read it all, but the groans and moans of Amy pulled me back into reality. I ran downstairs, filled a red checkerboard towel full of ice and ran back up. I sat down on the bed, Amy immediately throwing her legs over my lap so I could treat her apparently life threatening injury. I held the ice against her toes as my mind only focused on the envelope in my back pocket. Amy sat up and leaned against me, "I thought you said you fixed the floor?"

"I said, I tried, but, it has a mind of its own." I shrugged and looked at her. "I think it adds character to the place."

Amy frowned. "Breaking your house guest's toes is adding character?"

I laughed patting her knee. "It does. I will push it down again, re-secure it." I raised my eyebrows at her. "How about you go down to the kitchen, get the good wine out and call in a take-out order from Bobby's BB-Q? He will deliver and has the best sandwiches in town." I winked at her. "The number is tacked to the fridge."

Amy immediately perked up, hopping out of the room and down the stairs. "I knew I could persuade you!" She hopped down the stairs, issuing a series of ows as she worked her way down. I let out a breath as I stood up and hustled to my room. I dumped the ice into the bathroom sink before I sat down in the chair I had placed near the giant window. I held the letter in my cold hands, shaking a little. I laughed lightly, I wasn't sure if it was from being cold or from the simple sight of her handwriting. It had only been maybe a day or two at the most, but it felt like the first time I saw this handwriting.

"*Time is a mystery.*"

The black ink stared back at me as I stared at the front. I took a deep breath, my heart racing as I pulled it open. There were a few pages, making my heart race even more.

"*Frankie,*

As promised I'm writing to you without even unpacking. I must admit I found myself coming to the floor board as soon as I walked in. You brought a smile to a tired traveler when I saw your letters waiting for me.

The trip went well. I have a few job offers I have to sort through. I think when I go to visit your grandmother tomorrow, I will ask for her advice and opinion on where I should head to. It appears she has the best insight on just about everything. Other than being interviewed a thousand times at the conference, I rather enjoyed the short trip to Toronto. I was able to go sight-seeing in parts of the city I had neglected over the years and my many trips there. I did have one strange moment, and it involved you. It has me thinking about this floorboard and our last back to the future themed conversation."

I paused, reading and held the letter in my lap, my heart was pounding as I could clearly remember my dream from the other night. Carey standing in front of me as I was whisked away, smitten by the man on my arm. I swallowed hard and continued reading.

"*I'm not even sure it was you, I have only seen pictures of you in the cottage. But, I. Hmm...How do I tell you this? I think I met you the other night? But you didn't know it was me.*

I was out on the east end of the city, enjoying a late dinner alone after the last round of interviews when I felt a pull to walk down to the corner. It was a strong, deep pull in my heart. And for a moment I could hear your grandmother's voice in the back of my head, clear as if she was standing next to me, reminding me to always follow my heart whenever it pulled me in a direction. The pull was strong, stronger than anything I had ever felt. So, I walked. I walked for a block and came across a restaurant opening. Black shiny cars everywhere, people standing in line all a mix of black suits and black cocktail dresses.

Then, there was you. You walked out of the restaurant and it was if the world slowed down. You were wearing a midnight black dress with a sheer black wrap that was patterned with crystals. It was beautiful, you were beautiful as you stood there. Your head looking up into the night sky, closing your eyes slowly as you took in the cool air around you. I was drawn to you, and before I could stop myself, your name rolled over my lips as my legs moved on their own. When I was a foot away from you, you turned to me. A confused look on your face and it was as if I was a stranger. The sparkle in your hazel eyes as you looked at me, for a moment it took all of my words away. In that moment I lost my chance to say something more than just your name. You asked me what I said, and I couldn't answer quickly. Bad habit of mine, shyness when it's least needed.

When he came out and grabbed your attention, I realized that I was a stranger to you. That you, in that moment as we had never met. I found you at the wrong time, met you at the wrong time. I could see in your eyes how in love you are/were when he came for you and made me envious of him.

After that moment, I started putting pieces together. That, and your second letter about the book I left you. I can't rely on my science because it betrays all the hard evidence I hold in my hands now. I exist in the past, and you live in the future. The you I met is happy, engaged and living a life most would be happy to live. I won't lie and say that it didn't make me jealous for a split second to be so close to you and then, have it interrupted, there is something about you Frankie. Something that I have not felt in a long time and seeing you, standing there as if you were a dream. It made me feel alive, my heart felt alive for the first time in a long time.

Maybe I can do something and make sure you have that happiness with him, warn you, and warn him. Maybe there is something I can say to you so you can prevent him from straying from the most beautiful woman I have ever seen, and let him know he should hold on to you. You should be the only girl in the world. You should be the only girl anyone who has you ever looks at. I know I would...

But! I'm going to test this time/space continuum theory I have about you and I, before I do anything. I will leave you a letter when I wake up tomorrow giving you the clues.

I must say goodnight, as my words are blurring together and my handwriting is worsening. I wanted you to know, that you made me smile as I read about you trying to protect your grandmother. I have found that she also has a calming effect on me whenever she is around. I can imagine that it affects anyone she comes across. She talks about you a lot, how you were always her protector and that she wishes we could meet. Something about how we both need to find where our hearts belong.

I will write to you tomorrow after I visit your grandmother and play the song you asked me to for her. I promise this Frankie. I wish I could tell you or show you how much light you have brought into a darkened heart in just a few letters.

-Carey

P.S. I went to MIT to work on fertility in genetics and the remapping of the human genome so I could isolate how the chromosomes shape in the first stages of pregnancy. Hoping I could do a little good with some kids and their mother's. That, and I was drawn there because of love. She went to Harvard and I went to MIT. That's where I lost my way. There's a little more to that story than that, a broken heart of a hopeless fool in love.

P.P.S. I have no real exciting life stories, just facts. My life's song is "Your Song" by Elton John. I have always wanted to sing it to the one I wanted to marry. Always have since I was a little girl. I know a strange and unusual proposal, I know. But, a nerdy doctor like me has romantic fantasies. I love the ocean, I'm always drawn to it and have resigned that I must live by the ocean, perhaps I was a mermaid in a past life? Lastly, for now, I love books. They are my passion and I think that is why your grandmother and I bonded. Her collection is unlike any I have ever seen, and I'm honored she has entrusted me to care for it.

P.P.S. One last thing, pick one. Seattle, New York City, Sydney, San Diego. I need help in choosing a job offer and these are the best options."

I looked at the last few words, sad that there were no more for me to read. I went to set the pages down, when I saw a little arrow on the corner, telling me to flip the page over. On the back there was a few lines.

"*The lion and the mouse. I can see that, Little Frankie. Especially, after the story of your grandmother and the mugger. Never let anyone break you or tell you that you are nothing, other than strong and brave. I can see it in your eyes, I did that night.*"

I wiped at my eyes, wiping away the tears before they broke. Carey had met me that night and the past me, the one who was engaged and happy, ignored her. I folded the letter up and held it. The only thing I could do was write her back and tell her to let Christopher make his mistake, let him do it so he could set me free. Then, tell me where I could find her, because it was becoming clear that we were meant to meet through the floorboard. That I was falling in love with the gentle, quite brunette who was slowly melting my heart with every scrawled word she wrote.

Carey was not hiding her emotions, or feelings in the letter, but I could tell in her attempt to say she would search Christopher out, or even the past me, and make sure I was happy. She was resigning to the fact that I was engaged, and that I appeared to be in love with him. Maybe that was why she was a little more honest about her feelings, it was if she was letting go of me.

I had to write her back, to tell her to sit and let the future become my past.

I held onto the letter, re-reading the part where she described meeting me. I wished I could go back to that moment, leave Christopher and go to her. I sighed and wiped at my eyes as I heard Amy trudge up the stairs. Her hands full with a bag of pretzels, "Frankie, the food will be here in a half hour." She paused and furrowed her brow. "Are you crying? Did you get another shit-o-gram from the greasy douche?"

I shook my head and laughed lightly. "No and I don't expect to hear from him ever again." I took a steady breath and looked Amy in the eyes. "I think I'm falling in love with someone who I have never met, or never will meet."

Amy rolled her eyes/ "What does that mean? Have you been watching "The Notebook" over and over like you do when you're depressed? I told you to knock that shit off and watch "Pretty Woman" instead. You can never go wrong with prostitutes and love."

I nodded to the picture on the shelf. "The brunette in that picture, with my grandmother. She lived here almost two years ago, I have never met her in my life. Just know that she was the last of the renters who lived here before my grandmother passed away." I watched as Amy walked over to the almost bare shelf, leaning closer to the picture.

"She's kind of hot." She looked over her shoulder at me. "And no I'm not talking about grams." Amy turned back to the photograph, picking it up as I kept on.

"The floorboard that you tripped over. I did the same thing the first night I was here. I found a letter tucked into the subfloor. I read it and it compelled me to do the same. I wrote out all of my feelings and my heartbreak. I dropped it into the floor, closing it up like it was a time capsule. The funny thing is, the person who wrote the first letter wrote back, and we have been writing back and forth."

Amy turned to look at me, her face all screwed up. "How much have you been drinking exactly? You are the only one living here. Are you writing letters to yourself Frankie?"

I laughed and nodded towards the pile of letters next to the books. "There. Those are her letters. Her name is Carey, and she is a grad student. Now a doctor, I think. There are just a few letters, but somehow the floorboard is like the DeLorean. It takes me to her in the past and brings her to me in the future."

Amy picked up the letters, setting the bag of pretzels down on a shelf. The look on her face told me she was still judging me. Before she could remark how crazy I was I smiled. "I haven't figured it out yet and neither has Carey. We are still working on it and it's harder that she's the only who can talk to my grandmother about the house."

I held out the newest one for her to take. "This one was waiting for me when you went downstairs to order the food."

"Wait. Grams is still alive? I thought..." Amy trailed off, the letters in her hands as she sifted through them.

I nodded slowly, curling up in the chair more. "She is, but in Carey's time, she's still alive. Grams also has been leaving me clues around the house and in the mail. It's like she already knows I'm here and is pushing me to find peace and..." I drifted off. "To find Carey."

Amy said nothing, I looked over at her. She was engrossed in the letters. I left her until she was done. When she was done, she folded the letters up and sat on the edge of the bed. Her eyes going to the window and staring at the ocean. "Do you remember seeing her that night with Christopher? I remember you being a little quiet at the cocktail lounge until I got you a few shots. Did you talk to her that night?"

I whispered. "I didn't, until I had a weird dream the other night. When I clearly saw her, it was if my mind was inserting a lost or new memory. I remembered that night clearly, because it was the first night he told me he loved me, but I never remembered seeing Carey until that dream." I sighed and leaned my head against the back of the chair.

I felt her hand on my knee squeezing gently. "She's falling in love with you, Frankie. You can see it in every word she writes."

I whispered. "I think I am too." I looked at Amy in the eyes. "But, how do I find her?"

Chapter 8

Silence was the uncomfortable answer from Amy. She had no answer when I asked how would I find her? How would we find her? When Amy looked at me with her blank questioning face, I explained as simply as I could how the time difference worked. It seemed the constant back to the future reference was the only one that made sense. I was altering the past from the future and in turn, Carey was changing the future.

Amy chewed on her lip. When I was done, she flipped through the letters a few more times until she looked at me. "I think the only way we can figure this out is if we change the future."

I kept my gaze on the massive window, the ocean was now a bright but, deep blue. Late afternoon was shifting with the sun, embracing the early evening. I pulled my knees up closer to my chest. "What is it Amy?"

My best friend stood up from the bed, her hands moving just as fast as her words, "I think we change the future. I think you write this girl a letter, give her a day or date in the future." She pointed at me hard. "In your future. Tell her to come back to the cottage or a café, or wherever suits your fancy. Or!" Amy clapped her hands. "You go find her. Somehow you can alter her future. She asked you for advice on which city to choose, choose one for her then, go search her out! Frankie! You have all the power." Amy leaned closer to me. "You have all the power to bring her to you."

I rolled my head to look at the excited girl. The strange ideas slowly sinking in. Before I could say anything, Amy dropped to her knees in front of me. "More importantly, you write her back and you tell her to leave Christopher alone. Leave that shit bag to follow the path he was destined to with you. Let your heart break. Then, tell her that she is the one you will wait for." A slow smile crept across her face. "I can see that you are slowly falling in love with this woman. She's the fisherman lumberjack that is bringing your long forgotten smile back. The one that always lit up the room upon your entry."

I smiled lightly at the last few words. I went to say something when the stationary and a pen was jammed into my lap. "Write her. Now." Amy stood up as the doorbell rang. She turned to the stairs and hustled over to the door. Food always took a precedence in her life when it beckoned. Before running down the stairs, she winked at me. "Remember. You have all of the power."

I let her words sink in deeper. I took a deep breath, pulled the stationary closer, setting the pen to paper as I began to write.

"*Carey,*

I have so much to say. But, I want to start with this. Please don't go and find him, don't warn him of what is to come. It needs to happen, because without him breaking my heart I would have never found my way home. I would not have found you. If you do find me, tell me to go home sooner. To go see my grandmother in the last few moments I missed. I envy you because you have the moments I long for with her.

But, please. Please let my heart be broken by him. This is the path I know I need to take. For whatever reason this floorboard time machine is working for us, it has been given to us for a reason. I'm still trying to figure it all out. Please, Carey. Leave your future to be my past.

To answer your question, yes that was me. You were not hallucinating or dreaming. I was wearing a midnight black dress, I was happy, but, I was also ignorant of the truth behind the happiness that I thought he was giving me.

That night. The night you saw me outside the restaurant, I also dreamt about it last night. I remembered that night for so many other reasons than a beautiful brunette coming out of the cool city night. Filling my heart with warmth and bringing a shiver to my skin that wasn't from the cold. It was if you were placed there in my dream. It felt so real, that moment. It felt like a new memory brought to life. Oh, Carey. What I wouldn't give to have that moment back, to have the strength I have now to look past the charms of a bright smile. You took my breath away that night, made me gasp at the sheer sight of you. You make me want to be alive, just in the simple messy scrawls of your doctor handwriting. It gives me hope and a chance. You took my breath away with your words in the last letter, actually you made me blush in an empty room. Yes, you are that good with words."

I paused, setting the pen down as Amy yelled at me to come and get it. My mind was stuck on replaying that first view of Carey, walking towards me with a calm sense of determination in the golden brown eyes that captured much of my thoughts.

I picked the pen up, continuing to scrawl out words.

"I'm still figuring out how this floorboard works. I have an idea, as well on how to test it, but I will let you go first since you are more of a scientist than I will ever be.

I hope my grandmother gave you good advice; she was always dead on with what direction one should take. She always told me to follow my heart...maybe I should have paid more attention. As for what I think with what city you should pick. I like New York City the most. It reminds me of a completely different world when you are in the heart of it and it's close to the ocean. The perfect place for a mermaid.

I wanted to write more, and I will later. My best friend is currently downstairs yelling at me to come to dinner. So, I will leave you with my coveted postscripts. But, I wanted you to know what it means to me to hear that I have brought a little light into your heart, because I feel the same. Although, I only know you through pen marks on paper, it feels like I have known you my entire life and I want nothing more than to meet you. Hear your voice again and tell you things as you stand in front of me, instead of waiting for a rickety old floorboard to speak for us.

Please tell me everything about your visit with my grandmother. I cannot express how much I miss her.

Till you write again,

Frankie

P.S. The one who had your heart, she may not have understood what luck she had in having you. I have never come across anyone like you and don't think I ever will. I want to be nosy and ask what the whole story was. But, I think I just did.

P.P.S I have so many pictures in my head of you jumping around in a mermaid costume singing old Elton John. Now, I know you are the owner of her books, which means I must find you as soon as possible. My childhood and my happiest memories are all tied to her many colorful books we read together. I would sit on her lap in her big chair, facing the ocean. She would read as I stared out into the waves, letting my imagination carry me into places I wished I could go. However, real or unreal they were.

P.P.S. Random facts about me, one of my favorite books was Chronicles of Narnia. We spent an entire summer reading that together. I love the ocean as well. I feel sick if I'm not around it for too long. I never wanted to be a mermaid though, a pirate yes.

P.P.P.S I have a question about the necklace you wore in the one picture, when did you get it? It looks familiar to me. Being an investigative reporter, I'm a determined snoop."

I folded the pages up, tucking them into an envelope as best as I could. In a gentle hand I wrote on the front, "*Mysteries of the heart need to be solved.*" I then made my way to the floorboard, sighing sadly that it was still tucked in its place. Amy's toes would be safe for now. I smiled to myself as I lifted the board.

Before I went to set the letter in the darkness of my strange mailbox, I pressed a kiss to the back flap of the envelope. It came from nowhere and I wasn't even sure why I did it, but I did. I quickly tucked the envelope into the space, setting the board back into place, I stood up. Folding my arms close to my body I walked out of the room drawn out by the sounds of my best friend bellowing that if I didn't hurry up she would not be responsible for the lack of food.

By the time dinner was close to being done, I wished there had been a lot less food. I quit after a few ribs, marveling at Amy and her ability to eat at least three pounds of ribs. Amy kept the conversation light, noticing that I was still lost in my head. We laughed over memories of our first meeting and all of the crazy times we shared.

I had met Amy on a job trying to investigate a health code conspiracy in the bars of the city. I went into the bar Amy was working at and she picked up that I was snooping around. She tried to block me from the deep secrets of the back room until I told her what I was doing. She gave me all the names I needed and wanted. Together, we were able to break the case and brought down a handful of crooked health inspectors. Changing the entire bar and restaurant row on the main street in the city, for the better. Since then, Amy was attached to me like she was my twin sister.

I gathered up the empty containers, moving to the kitchen as Amy poked around for dessert. It was now later than either of us expected. I yawned, pulling the overflowing trash out of the garbage can. "Amy, I think I'm going to call it a night after clean up. This ocean air is so soothing and so relaxing." I let out a sigh that turned into a yawn.

"Can I talk you into a good ole fashioned girls' movie night? You know, like the ones we used to have before you got lost in the blue eyes of a d-bag?"

I smiled lightly at Amy, nodding my head. "We can unpack my TV and set it up in the bedroom. I think my box of movies are on top." I grabbed my sweater, pushing open the back door letting the cool evening wind greet me. I pulled the garbage behind me.

I looked up into the night sky, the dots of light linking together to form the constellations I had learned about as a child and slowly forgotten as an adult, all blinking as if to say hello and welcome back.

I tossed the stretched white garbage bag into the old metal can, setting the lid on top, I leaned against it. My head drifting up to look in the sky. I squinted trying to jog my memory to remember which one was the big dipper and which one was the little dipper. I smiled as the constellations began to come together and shine brighter as I recognized who was who. For a moment, I wondered if Carey was doing the same thing. Looking up in the sky like I was, piecing together stars wherever she was. I wondered if she could see the night sky clearly like I could out here, the lack of city light pollution giving me the purest view of night I had in a long time.

Lastly, I wondered if she was looking up in the sky thinking of me like I was her.

"Frankie. You've got mail." Amy rushed out the back door, holding up an envelope in her hand; waving it around like a winning lottery ticket. She winked at me. "I learned my lesson last time, look before entering. The floorboard was popped up the moment I opened the door." Amy poked my shoulder. "I'll leave you two alone."

Before she ran back into the house, she called out after me. "Remember, you have all the power Frankie!"

I smiled, shaking my head. I looked at the letter, thinner than normal but her handwriting still made my heart beat a little faster when I saw it. I walked from the garbage can and chose to sit on the edge of the walkway that took one down to the ocean. Its walls were made of stone and provided a solid seat for anyone who wanted a short reprieve from their journey. I sat, letting my legs swing freely. The moon was high, giving me enough light to read. Turning the envelope, I smiled when I read, *"Experiment of time."* Underneath the bold words was a smaller sentence, "*I wrote this before I got your last letter, I will read it immediately. But I need you to read this one before tomorrow.*"

I peeled open the letter, even more eager to read what Carey had written.

"*Frankie,*

Please follow me on this strange idea that I came up with. A theory of sorts. One to test how you and I are connected in the relative idea of time and space. I poured over my old science books and even asked a physicist or two I had classes with. None of them could really explain to me how our connection was possible.

I became frustrated and during the visit with your grandmother today, she smiled and winked at me. Only saying that magic cannot be explained by those who choose science over it. She was one the one who gave me the idea I'm about to present to you.

Tomorrow. At approximately two o'clock in the afternoon. I want you to stand in the middle of your grandmother's bedroom, or your bedroom now. Face the wall with the bookshelf. The sun should be at a perfect angle and reflect off the ocean. I want you to stand there and when everything is done, please write me back and tell me everything that happened or if anything at all happened.

If my theory is correct, I think I know how this connection we have works.

Just promise me, Frankie. Two o'clock.

One more thing, while visiting your grandmother today she wanted me to tell you that you have more power than you think you do. I'm not sure what she means, she wouldn't explain it to me. Only telling me a similar thing.

Till tomorrow, Frankie. Sleep well and dream of what could be. I will be thinking of you and waiting for tomorrow.

Carey."

Folding the letter back up, slipping it in the envelope I went back into the house. My heart pounding at what my grandmother said. She was behind this, behind the magic that was bringing Carey and me together. I didn't know how it was working or how she knew. But, I knew she was the one strong link between Carey and I. Gently pushing us together in her own special way. I shivered, not from the chill the night ocean air that had soaked into my bones, but from the excitement of what tomorrow would bring; what Carey would bring.

Amy and I fell asleep watching "The Princess Bride". We had stayed up late watching movies and eating popcorn like we had in the first few months of our friendship and up until Christopher changed so much. I rolled away from the snoring Amy, hogging the one side of the bed and all the blankets. Leaving me to shiver with the corner of a sheet. I opened my eyes, reaching for my phone to see what time it was. The light in the room made it feel like it was early morning. My phone told me otherwise, it was five to two in the afternoon. I jolted up in the bed, panicking. We had slept the entire day away and I almost slept through Carey's test.

"Shit!" I went to hop off the bed only to find my legs were still tangled up in the sheets. I struggled to escape the white cotton shackles, when the light in the room moved to light the bookshelf and the wall around it. The gentle movement seemed more than natural, it pulled my attention away from the sheet and to the wall. I paused everything, my attention and eyes locking in on the wall as the daylight grew a little brighter.

Before my very eyes dark, faded swirls appeared on the wall. They were small at first, and I couldn't make them out. Then, I recognized my name at the top near the crown molding. I freed myself from the bed and walked closer, standing in the middle of the room I stopped as more faded scrawls appeared on the wall. I took one step closer and recognized the scrawls of her handwriting. I gasped, as I watched the words form sentences, then paragraphs as it appeared faster. I swallowed and began reading from the top.

"*Frankie,*

Hopefully you followed my instructions. I hate defacing the walls of your bedroom, but, again this was your grandmother's idea. If this works, you should see the words appear to you as I write them. Tell me what you see, how the words look when I write them with this giant marker I found in the barn. Then, tell me what I write. You have told me about all your favorite books and I had yet to share anything I love. What follows is something I have never shared with anyone, a poem. The one poem that I read over and over, one that keeps me balanced in my heart when I find rough seas ahead. I have always wanted to read it to the one that could capture my heart. You're the first one to do so, Frankie. In many ways, that caught me by surprise."

I could feel the tears as they made their way down my cheeks. I was reading as fast as I could. I even moved closer, my hand reaching out to touch the old black marker on the wall. When my fingers pressed against the words, it felt as if Carey was there with me. Suddenly, the writing stopped for a moment. I stepped back, thinking I had interrupted something. I whispered. "No, please don't stop Carey. Please, I beg of you."

Amy mumbled at me. "Frankie, you really have to stop talking to yourself. Especially when it wakes me up." She groaned as she rolled over, "I need tums, pepto, or a good kick in the stomach."

I didn't hear her, I was too busy staring at the wall, trying to will Carey to keep going. Keep writing. I didn't hear Amy get out of the bed and stand next to me. "Was this here yesterday? I don't remember the graffiti."

I went to hush her when the scrawling started again. Her handwriting moving slower as the words appeared clearer, as if she was taking care in every stroke she made. I heard Amy make a noise and mumble. "What the hell?"

I grabbed Amy's elbow, silencing her. "It's Carey."

Amy uttered out a confused curse word. We both stood enraptured as the words flowed across the wall, instantly aging the moment they were written. I read with Carey as she finished each word. The poem forming itself in a matter of moments. Each word I read made my heart beat faster, and harder for the woman writing them.

"I am tired.
I am tired of speech and of action.

*If you should meet me upon the
street do not question me for
I can tell you only my name
and the name of the town I was
born in–but that is enough.
It does not matter whether tomorrow
arrives anymore. If there is
only this night and after it is
morning it will not matter now.
I am tired. I am tired of speech
and of action. In the heart of me
you will find a tiny handful of
dust. Take it and blow it out
upon the wind. Let the wind have
it and it will find its way home."*

When the last word was finished, I reached out again and pressed my fingers against the wall. The poem was one I had read back in my literature days in college. I knew it well and loved it for the desperate romantic feeling it gave me. I looked back at Amy, who was sitting on the floor, staring at the wall, wide eyed.

Her eyes drifted to mine. "That, that was some crazy shit. You saw what I saw, right? Words appearing on the wall like magic."

I nodded, turning back to the wall. Hoping there was more. "I did. It's her." I ran my fingers over her messy but elegant way of writing, "Carey."

I read the wall over and over, waiting for her to keep writing. After a few minutes, I stepped back to sit next to Amy when I noticed a new book on the shelf. My heart skipped with my hand as I reached out to pick up the dusty old book. It was a collection of short stories, poems and essays by Tennessee Williams. I opened the front cover of the book. Carey had written in the blank page facing the title page.

"This book I have carried since high school. I want you to have it Frankie.

I have also chosen New York City. I hope one day I will see you there.

C"

I flipped through the book, pages dog-eared at her favorite spots, favorite poems and passages. Lastly, I found the dog-eared page holding the poem she had just written for me. I let out a sigh and pressed the open book against my chest, my eyes going to the wall. It was all something I could explain and yet, I really didn't want to. Instead, it drove my heart faster with my mind. I moved past the semi catatonic Amy, still staring at the wall, and went to collect my stationary. I wrote as fast as my heart beat, telling Carey everything that happened. What she wrote and how it all appeared on my wall like old worn out graffiti.

I sealed the envelope and ran to the spare bedroom, mildly saddened there was nothing from her. I dropped my letter in the empty space. Noting that my last letter was missing. I tucked the floorboard back and ran back to my room. Amy was still staring at the wall, chewing on her lip trying to process what we both had seen.

Finally, she turned to me. "We need to find this girl, and find her yesterday."

I grinned. "New York City. That's where we find her." For some reason, in my heart I knew that is where she would be. Carey would be in New York City now, in my present. I would begin looking for her there and start laying down the path for her and I to meet, in our letters.

The only thing that pulled Amy and I from our staring and discussion of what we both witnessed, was her obnoxious ring tone coming from the other room. I sat on the bed while she ran to catch the caller before it went to voicemail.

I sat down with my eyes following every curve and angle of the brunette's words. I imagined her standing in front of me, her hands moving with slow determination to get the poem onto the wall without smearing any of it. I wondered if she was left handed or right. I imagined her strong slender fingers clutching to the large marker, her golden brown eyes squinting ever so slightly in the bright light of the early afternoon. I imagined her turning to me as I sat on the bed, a warm smile covering her face as her eyes met mine. Then, slowly holding her hand out for me to take, pull me up to stand next to her as she read the poem aloud to me. Her smooth voice carrying the words from the wall to my ears, moving closer as she bent closer to me. Her lips brushing across mine, our breaths mingling together.

"FRANKIE! Emergency!" Amy's voice shattered the daydream I was happily losing myself in. I turned to look at her, unhappy she broke my lovely trance right before a kiss. "Amy, you don't need to yell."

Amy held out her phone, one hand on her hip. "I have to go back to the city. The pipes burst in the building and flooded my apartment. That was my landlord, I have to go back and meet with the insurance adjuster and get a quote on damages." She threw her hands up, "It looks like my closet got the worst of it, all of my shoes. MY SHOES!" Amy turned and walked out of the room, still talking as she opened drawers. "I have to be there as soon as possible. Will you be down for driving me? We can make it a fun road trip? Mix tapes and road snacks?"

I walked to the room, leaning against the doorframe. "Yes, I will take you to the city. I can stop and talk to my boss while you sift through a soggy wardrobe." I watched Amy throw clothes into a duffle bag. "But, this has to be a quick trip. I don't want to be away from the cottage for too long."

Amy paused mid-fling of sweaters. "You mean you don't want to be away from the girl in the floor too long." She winked at me, "I don't blame you. If I had a hot ghost write on my walls, write a love poem for me, I wouldn't want to leave the house either."

I laughed, shaking my head. "She isn't a ghost. She is real. I think, but either way I don't want to be gone too long. Every letter we share gets me one step closer to finding her. I don't want to waste time." I took a slow breath, "Carey is remarkable and I want to tell her that face to face."

A t-shirt flopped against my face. "Then go get dressed, gas up old blue and we can hit the road in an hour." Amy winked at me. "We can be back by this time tomorrow if we hustle our cute little asses."

I smiled, trying to cover up the blush that I knew covered my face. I threw the shirt back at Amy, "I will meet you at the barn in fifteen."

It only took us five hours to get to the city, old blue had more in her than I thought. She actually drove better and faster on the highway than my expensive little black sports car. As Amy and I came upon the city skyline, I felt my stomach drop a little. There were so many memories tied to the city, good ones and bad ones. I had only been gone for almost two weeks, but as I navigated the city traffic it felt like I had been gone an entire lifetime.

Amy bounced in her seat, excited to be around her natural habitat of steel, smog, and convenient twenty four hour shopping. I had to shush her a few times, trying to maneuver the giant old Ford truck through city streets. I did smile a few times when we received the honks and waves of admirers of the vintage truck. It was an anomaly to see such a beast in a city that harbored sleek modern everything.

When I finally pulled up in front of Amy's apartment it was almost dinner time. "Amy, I'm going to drop you off here since there is no way in hell I can park old blue anywhere. Then I think I'm going to head over to my office and park her there. I'll take a cab back and help you out. Afterward let's go to dinner and enjoy the city a little bit." I smirked at her, "As much as I hate the city, I kind of missed it and Danny's over on sixth."

Amy kissed me on the cheek quickly. "You missed the cute bartenders at Danny's. I miss the giant corned beef sandwiches." She pushed open the truck door, "But it's a date! I will hurry this up. I think I'm going to claim everything in the apartment. Maybe I can get new furniture or at least a giant check to take a trip to Fiji." Amy hopped out of the truck, blowing me another kiss. "Hurry back lovah!"

I laughed as she slammed the door shut. I was still laughing as I pushed the truck back out into the traffic and headed towards my office a few blocks away. I let the city air fill the truck. It was definitely a different air than the ocean air I had been breathing in. It felt alive but hurried, like there was always some reason not to stop and breathe deep. I had always craved city life when I was little and made it my life to goal to live in a big city. I achieved that goal and now, I wanted nothing more than to go back to my cottage and the slow pace of living it offered me.

Pulling into the parking garage of my office building I had a strange feeling wash over me, I couldn't place exactly what it was. It had me feeling uneasy, but safe at the same time. I had to take a deep breath to shake out the feeling.

I parked old blue in the parking spot that had my last name on a metal sign. "F. Owen Lead Investigative Journalist." I grinned at the sign, debating whether or not I would steal it when we left the city, or leave it for my unknown return date.

I locked up old blue and was tempted to go in to the building. I did want to talk to my boss about what my options were and see a few of my coworkers, but at the same time I didn't. I walked past the main entrance, grateful that the door told me that the office hours were done for the day and I would have to return in the morning.

I walked back down the street I had just come from, heading back to Amy's apartment. It had been only twenty minutes when my phone beeped, Amy's text telling me she did indeed decide to claim everything damage and call it a day. She wanted to eat more than she wanted to sit around, cataloging destroyed property. I chuckled and sent her a text telling her I was on my way.

Tucking my phone back into my jean pocket I walked down the same streets I had walked a million times. Every step I took that brought me closer to Amy's apartment, the heavy strange feeling came creeping back. It was a feeling I couldn't place no matter how hard I focused on it. Only knowing it made me feel warm and made my heart beat a little faster with every step.

I turned the corner to the block of my destination. The city was starting to come to life with evening activity. People were slowly coming out of buildings, migrating to dinner or drinks. As I stood at a red-light, eavesdropping on the conversation of the couple behind me. They were bickering about which restaurant to have a late lunch at. The woman wanted to do a three star and the man was adamant on doing a four star restaurant. I shook my head as it reminded me of the same small fights Christopher and I would have on the nights we went out for dinner, which was usually every night. When the light turned, the couple pushed past me still bickering. I sighed, and kept walking. I passed more couples chatting about their evening plans, bringing back more memories of Christopher and our evenings. I clutched my bag tighter, trying to focus on anything other than old memories that I thought would be happy ones. Now they were memories that made me feel stupid for not seeing the truth behind the glitz and charm of a handsome man.

Another red-light stopped me. I stared ahead and tried to tune out another couple's conversation when the warm feeling I had overwhelmed me. This time clearly giving me a sensation of warmth, comfort and it pulled at my heart in a way that I hadn't felt in a long time. My heart began to beat faster as I felt tingles in the air around me. So much so, that I had to close my eyes and steady myself. A slow wind came from nowhere and pushed my hair free from the ponytail I had. Forcing me to run my hand over my hair, I looked to my right.

What I saw made my heart leap into my throat. Across the street on the opposite block stood a tall brunette. Her head was down, buried in a magazine as she stood at the redlining waiting for her turn to cross. I stared at her, a sense of familiarity coursing through my body as I willed her from afar to look up. My heart knew it was her, I just need to see her so my mind would agree. After a moment, the brunette looked up and I couldn't hold the gasp that fell from my mouth.

Carey was standing on the corner. She was watching the traffic pass, a small smile on her face as she shifted the bag on her shoulder. She was dressed down, wearing jeans and a light shirt with a hood, her hair was down and draped over her shoulders. Carey literally glowed as I stared at her, it was as if the city lights knew I was looking for her and provided me a spotlight. My eyes were transfixed and I couldn't move. I was watching her, trying to convince every inch of my being to believe she was real and she was standing a block away from me. I swallowed hard and begged my body to compose itself and prepare for the run I was about to make the moment that light turned green. I started whispering at the light, "Come on, come on, come on." When Carey turned my way.

Her eyes locked onto mine, even though we were a fair distance away and there was plenty of people in our path, she looked through everything as if she had x-ray vision and locked onto my eyes. I watched as her eyes widened in a slight panic, then a slow sense of recognition settled in. Her lips curled up into a huge smile, forcing mine to follow suit. I raised my hand a little in a childish wave, making Carey smile and look down at her shoes. My heart pounded as it was pulled in the direction of where she was standing. She was the reason behind the sensation I had been feeling, something was pulling me to her.

I looked at the red light, about to step off and ignore it when it finally turned green. I began to half walk and run towards Carey. Glancing up at her to keep track of her as she also moved towards me. The crowd seemed to thicken around me with every step I took towards her. I had to push through clusters of couples, hurried businessmen on their exhausted way home, growing anxious with excitement with every step. Carey was doing the same as she tried to make her way to me.

My heart pounded hard, so hard it added a loud tempo that matched my steps. I came across another red-light. I had to stop as the city traffic bellowed out like horses out of the gate. I looked up and saw her. She was across the street from me, watching the traffic in between quick looks at me. I wanted to run to her, take my chances with the rushing cars. My heart couldn't handle it. It was beating so hard at every little glance I threw her way.

When the last red-light turned green, I went to step off and run when I felt a hand on my elbow. A firm hand stopped me in my tracks, followed by my name being spoken from behind my ear. "Francesca? Is that you?"

I turned to the deep voice, yanking my arm free I went to curse them. Instead, I was swallowed up in the strong arms that I had once loved to be held in, Christopher hugged me as he spoke. "I thought that was you, you look do different." He spun us around and I caught Carey across the street. Standing in the same spot she had been. Her face was void of any smile, the sparkle in her eyes when she first saw me was now gone and replaced by a sudden sadness. She looked down and nodded to herself.

I struggled against his strong arms, "Let me go, Christopher. Please." I pushed and pulled at his arms but, I couldn't escape. I watched as Carey turned to the left and started walking away. Christopher held me at arm's length as he ended the hug, his bright white smile shining across his face. "Francesca, I want to apologize for the letter. It was a little harsh of me."

I shook my head, "No, no. Don't do this." My eyes were on Carey as she began to get swallowed up in the crowd. I looked at Christopher, "Let me go." The tone in my voice was one that he had never heard and I could see it hit him by surprise. He dropped his hands from my arms, "I know you are upset."

I pushed past him and ran. I ran across the street just as the light turned red and I had, but a second to spare before a yellow taxi cab clipped me. I pushed past people, trying to hold onto the small glimpse I had of the brunette ponytail further ahead of me than I would like. I shoved, elbowed and pushed through a thick wall of people. I finally found my voice and shouted. "Carey, wait!"

I startled a few around me, but the brunette ponytail kept moving. I shouted again and kept pushing. My determination mixing with the adrenaline coursing through my body. She was so close and there was nothing going to stop me.

I was stopped. The thickening crowd fought back and I couldn't push through. I had to navigate slowly and when I finally broke free I found myself standing on a corner. Carey was nowhere in sight, I searched the crowd across from me, next to me and even behind me. She was gone, disappeared into thin air like a daydream.

I felt my tears rise at the frustration I felt. I was so close to her. I felt like throwing up as the warm sensation slowly drifted away from my body. The pull in my heart losing a clear direction and dimming to a dull ache of loss. I shook my head and walked down the alley next to me. I leaned against the wall and started to cry, my heart begged for some sort of release, anything to let out everything I was feeling. She was real, I know that now. She stood a few feet in front of me, so close to being in my arms. Exactly where I wanted her, and when I looked in her eyes, I knew she felt the same.

I slid down the wall and sat on the cool concrete of the alley, holding my head in my hands, as I sobbed. Cursing Christopher for pulling me off course, again. I cried for what she saw, knowing what it might look like to her. That a second chance of finding me and it was lost to her, that I was lost to someone else. I wiped my eyes, whispering to no one, "Carey, I promise you. You are the only someone I want." I looked up into the sky, bordered by the large buildings on each side of me, only giving me a sliver of the night and the stars. "I'm sorry, but I promise I will find you."

I sat in the alley, my head against the brick wall behind me staring at the stars. I sat there until Amy called me and I told her where I was. I didn't have the strength or the desire to stand up and walk the city streets. I wanted to go home, I wanted to go home to the cottage and write her a letter. Tell her what happened today and to forgive me, wait for me.

Amy found me fifteen minutes later when she pulled up in old blue. She said nothing as she parked on the curb and helped me up. She loaded me into the truck and said nothing other than, "We're going home. This stupid city has cursed you enough."

I looked over at my best friend as she roared through the traffic. "She was so close."

Amy nodded, "I know. I also know that Christopher found you. He called me when you ran off. I told him that he needed to die in a fire and leave you alone. That he has ruined more in your life than he could ever imagine."

I smiled at my best friend and let the tears fall. Amy reached over and grabbed my hand, "We will find her. You know now she is real, that is all you needed. Now, let's make this happen." She squeezed my fingers, "She is real and what you two have is real." Amy looked at me with her bright blue eyes. "We write her when we get home, and fix this."

I shook my head, "I don't think I can. It already happened. Only the past and the future. That's how this works."

Amy began to rattle on about the things we could do. I tuned her out, my heart hurt far too much to listen. I closed my eyes and leaned against the cool glass of the truck window. The only thing I thought about was the first moment our eyes met and how in that moment I knew I was in love with her.

Chapter 9

The drive home was long, longer than the drive to the city. The drive into the city was full excited chatter, laughing and the eagerness of two best friends looking forward to what the city at night had in store. Now, I stared out the window, my head against the back window of the old truck. The darkness of the world around us seemingly comforting me when I finally stopped crying just as the sun fully set and we hit the edge of the city.

I was so close to her, a few feet away from standing in front of her. Staring into the golden brown eyes and finally being able to know if they sparkled like I imagined they would. To finally hear her voice, whisper my name and be able to whisper her name back. To touch her, whether it was a silly handshake, a quick hug or a kiss. It was all so close. I squeezed my eyes shut, fighting the tears back as the flashes of Christopher holding me back and the look on Carey's face tugged at my heart. I made Amy drive around the few blocks where I thought Carey may have run off to, searching for any glimpse of brunette hair, but we found nothing more than couples making their way to the evening plans set before them. I gave in after a few city blocks, quietly asking to be taken back to the cottage.

"Frankie, you okay?"

It was at least the thousandth time she had asked me in the last few hours. I couldn't get mad at Amy, as her voice was full of genuine concern each time she asked. "You don't have to ask every half hour." It came out a half raspy whisper; I didn't bother to look at Amy. I knew if I did the tears would make their escape. I tugged my jacket closer to my body, shifting in my spot and sitting up. "How much further do we have?"

"About an hour, I can push old blue and make it in less than forty-five minutes. Up to you Frankie." Amy glanced at me just as an approaching car's headlights filled the truck cabin. I could see how tired she was. She had driven endlessly since she found me in the alley.

"Pull over at this gas station up here, let's get some coffee and I will drive the rest of the way." I immediately felt bad. I had been so caught up in my misery that I hadn't bothered to do my share of the driving.

We pulled into the bright neon beacon of gas, snacks, and all the caffeine one would need at such a late hour. I filled up old blue while Amy ran for the coffee. I leaned against the truck, watching the digital numbers on the gas pump tick by. I rubbed at my eyes, sighing. Why was this so hard? I had never in my life had a problem getting what I wanted or making it all happen. College, my fancy newspaper job, Christopher. All things I wanted and got because I made it happen, but now, what I wanted kept slipping through my fingertips like sand from the beach.

I just wanted one chance to stand in front of the woman who swept my heart away with her words. But, fate seemed to have different ideas for me. How long until I would have the chance again? I groaned and kicked the back tire out of frustration, startling the big burly truck driver standing at the pump across from me. I waved and threw him a gentle smile, turning my eyes back to the pump. When the truck was full, I went to go inside and chase down Amy.

Walking across the oil stained concrete, I folded my arms and tried to shake out the thoughts crowding my head. A gentle breeze came from nowhere, throwing a chill into my bones. I grumbled and picked up the pace when I felt a warm sensation in my chest around my grandmother's necklace. A sensation warmer than the one I felt when I first saw Carey, one that forced my hand to reach for the necklace and pause in my steps. My fingers wrapped around the worn charm and it began to pulsate against them. I glanced down at it confused when a soft whisper came from the right, coming from the darkened tree line that cradled the gas station as if it was a welcomed disturbance to the world. I stared out into the heavy blackness, squinting at nothing. I shook my head, playing it off to be a result of being over tired and over emotional. I took another step when the necklace pulsated harder against my palm and the soft whisper came again, clearer this time.

"Francesca."

I turned quickly at the sound of my name, but again, saw nothing. I was frozen in my place until I felt a strong pull to move towards the woods. A safe, comforting feeling came over me. It was as if the trees were gently beckoning me to them. I felt my heart beat harder as I began to move towards the trees, my mind telling me one thing while my heart was pulling me deeper in. After a few steps, I was completely away from the overcasting neon light of the gas station, leaving it to only highlight my back. My eyes were able to focus in the darkness, picking up the tree details and the small clearing with a large stone set in the middle.

I kept walking towards the stone, the necklace and my heart driving me towards it. When I was a foot away from the stone, I saw a glimmer of something mixed with the breeze that had made its reappearance. Another whisper, one louder, swarmed around me. "Francesca, it's in your hands."

I began to breathe harder, adrenaline mixing in with the small amount of fear in my veins. I tried to speak clearly but, my fear betrayed me, only allowing a harsh whisper, "Who are you?"

The glimmer around the rock shifted with the breeze, growing brighter, the edges of the shape becoming crisp. I gasped as soon as I recognized her. "Grandma?" My body began to tremble as I moved closer to the glimmer that looked exactly like my grandmother, exactly like the last time I saw her. I was looking at my grandmother and I didn't care that it was a ghost or a late night hallucination from lack of sleep. She was here, in front of me and my heart ached at the sight.

The glimmer smiled and winked in the exact same way she did when she saw me for the first time every summer. She held my eyes with hers. "Little Francesca, it's in your hands. I have given it to you because it is all the power you will need to find her. Don't give up. She hasn't, yet and won't until you are together." The glimmer moved closer to me, illuminating the both of us in a soft, grey white glow. The tears rolled down my face as my grandmother reached out with a shimmery, translucent hand to the necklace. Her fingers pressed against the old Claddagh, sending even more warmth into my body, easing away the fears and hesitations I had felt the entire time. I immediately felt safe and loved.

"I gave this to you because it will always pull you in the direction of where she is. To the purest and truest love you will have ever known, my girl. I knew it the moment she walked into the cottage that she was special." Her hand moved away from the necklace and up to my cheek, sending warm sensations through the skin. "You have the power, she is waiting. Don't waste any more time." My grandmother smiled and dropped her hand, stepping back away from me.

"No, no wait! Please wait! I have so much to ask, so much to tell you." I went to reach for her as she began to fade, I was panicking. I had so much in my heart in that moment to give to her, "Wait! Please! I need you to help me find Carey!"

My grandmother smiled, "It's in your hands, Little Francesca. Fight for it, fight for her." And with that, she disappeared into the night, the breeze following suit.

"NO!" I looked around me, as my eyes readjusted to the night. I rubbed at my eyes, hoping to conjure anything up. Nothing, there was nothing, but the darkness and the trees. Even the warm feeling began to dissipate. I pounded on my thigh with a tight fist out of anger and frustration. Anger at not telling her I was sorry, that I loved her. I shook my head and wiped away the tears, turning to go back to the gas station. My mind wanted to cancel out my heart, telling me I was dreaming, hallucinating or just plain crazy. But, my heart told me otherwise, that was my grandmother. My grandmother appearing out of thin air to tell me more cryptic messages. The necklace still pulsated, but slowed down with every quick step I took back to the truck.

I met Amy as she exited the gas station, arms full of snacks, coffee and energy drinks. She grinned at me, holding up a bag, "They had BBQ ranch pork rinds! WOOT!" she shook the bag and when I didn't respond, she frowned. "Uh oh. Why the angry face?"

I shook my head, yanking the driver's side door open, "I think I'm straight up losing my mind." I slammed the door behind me.

Amy ran and hopped in, dumping her snacks on the seat between us, "um, okay." She handed me the large coffee while I started up old blue. "What happened? I saw you creep over to the woods. You see that beardy trucker peeing in the woods? Or doing other creepy trucker things?" She raised her eyebrows at me.

I shook my head, throwing the truck into gear, "No creepy peeing trucker. I just saw the ghost or spirit of my grandmother. Came out of nowhere to tell me some weird cryptic message about her necklace and Carey." I shook my head harder, "I'm losing my mind."

I could feel Amy staring at me, boring holes in me until she finally asked. "What did grams the ghost tell you?"

I gripped tightly to the steering wheel, pushing the truck back onto the two lane road, "She told me that I have all the power. She then reached for the necklace and told me that it will always pull me in the direction of wherever Carey is. And that Carey is my one true love and I need to fight for her." The words spilled out quickly with a tinge of anger and frustration. I sighed hard, "I'm losing it. Plain and simple."

Amy shuffled a few snack bags around. "You're not losing it. You just aren't listening. Listening to me, listening to ghost grams, listening to that heart of yours that you ignore every day."

I shot a look at her, "What?"

Amy sighed, pulling open her pork rind bag, "For someone with a college degree and the ability to read people like you do." I could see her shaking her head at me, disappointed. Amy dropped a few pieces of pork rinds in her mouth. "Frankie, you know what you have to do. I told you the other day, you have the power. I don't believe in ghosts or aliens, but I believe that ghost grams had to come out of the heavens to basically kick you in the ass and tell you the same thing I have been. Can I ask you a question?"

I shrugged. "Yea, fine." I snapped out the words, tired and irritated of all this friendly advice that made no sense to me.

"Oh, don't you put on the sassy pants with me." Amy slapped my shoulder, "Are you in love with this Carey?"

I paused, my heart started beating faster at the simple mention of her name. My body came alive in so many ways when I thought about her, looked at her picture and imagined the possibilities of being with her. Something I never felt before, something so strong that it canceled out any of my other so called loves. I had never felt so strongly for anyone in my entire life, or craved to find them like I did her. My body, my heart and even my mind agreed, I was falling in love or already hopelessly in love with a complete brunette stranger.

I took a slow breath in, "I am, Amy. I can't talk myself out of it or find anything to explain what I feel for her. When I looked in her eyes that slow moment when we saw each other. My heart swelled, my body came alive, and I only saw her." I stopped, clenching my jaw and blinking away the tears. "I pushed and shoved to get to her. Then, he stopped me."

I swallowed hard, whispering into the dark truck cab, "She's all I think about."

"Then what is holding you back? Fight for her. Fight time and this crazy future vs. the past time warp thing. Get her, and let no one and no man stop you." Amy poked my arm as she spoke, "You. Have. The. Power." She dropped the bag on the seat, "The power of love is the greatest power of all. Great enough to bring your grams down here to push you and follow all the little clues she has left you. I never met the lady but, I can tell in the things she left you, that she loved you more than anything and more than anything she wants you to find happiness and love."

I kept my eyes on the road, listening to the strange wisdom of my best friend. It was slowly starting to sink in. There were clues from the moment I went to the cottage. The package, the chest, the gentle guidance of my grandmother showing me the way to happiness. Through her own special magic, she was giving me all the pieces to put my heart back together and find the one thing I had always wanted even as a little girl. The one thing all of my favorite books had in them. A true and wholly pure love.

I let a thick silence fill the truck. It was all slowly coming together. In those stories, I read with my grandmother, the love never came without a fight. It never came to the one searching it out, never handed to them. It was always an uphill battle, a slaying of dragons or journeying over expanse lands to find the true love. I had waited for Carey to come find me, to be one to figure out the best way and show up at my door. When it was, I had to slay the dragons in my way and travel through the restrictions time set upon us all. I had to fight for Carey.

I smiled, pounding my palm on the steering wheel. I finally understood what my grandmother had tried to tell me in the woods. All of the intentions behind her well placed packages and letters. I startled Amy when I reached over, grabbing her into a side hug, "I have the power."

Amy mumbled a duh and continued digging her in food. I pushed the accelerator down to the floor, roaring old blue to life. I needed to get home fast.

Pulling into the drive path of the cottage I was tired but determined. Amy was half asleep and the morning sun was cresting over the roof of the cottage. I left Amy in the truck and ran into the house, up the stairs and pushed the spare bedroom door open. I smiled sheepishly when I saw the floorboard was pushed up, waiting for me. I almost ripped the floorboard completely out of place, my hand finding the thick letter without looking.

I looked at the front of the envelope, "*The heart will always be a mystery.*"

The pages fell out of the envelope as soon as I tore it open.

"*Frankie!*

It worked! I can't tell you how much this means to me that you were able to watch me as I wrote on the wall. I took a chance on my theory and your grandmother's suggestion and it worked! Of course there is no scientific explanation other than we are linked by this cottage and whatever strange other worldly force is allowing this to happen. I racked my brain over the why's and how's but gave up the moment I read your letter telling me it worked. All I care is that it worked and I have some way to share things with you as if you were standing with me.

When I wrote that poem on the wall, I imagined you standing next to me as I read the words aloud to you. The sun pushing through the window and highlighting your beautiful brown hair, your eyes capturing the light in just the right way so they would light up and sparkle. That's why I chose two o'clock. That is when this room fills up with light from the afternoon sun and the reflections from the ocean. What I wouldn't give to stand with you in that room at that time and see first-hand0 how beautiful you are and tell you, Frankie. What I hate most about this strange distance between us is that my heart gently aches for you in the time I wait for your letters. I wish I could figure out how to meet you, but I am in the past and you are in the future."

I set the letter down in my lap, Amy had walked into the kitchen from the truck. I could hear her groaning in her search for coffee. I stood up and walked to my bedroom, sitting on the floor so I could lean against the wall with the poem. When I did, it felt like Carey was there with me as I continued reading.

"I read your other letter, Frankie. I will do what you ask of me. I will leave your past to be your future. I just thought that what I saw was real, genuine and something I didn't feel I should let go if I could do something about it. You take my breath away every time I think about you, Frankie. That night, I can't stop thinking about it and how close you were. I wonder if I had just taken that extra step and introduced myself, we could be friends now. Know where to find each other. You give me so much hope and have given me back my heart and the want to find what made it beat when I was in love.

Which leads me to your investigative reporter question. The one who had my heart and broke it, she doesn't matter anymore. Especially when I have found the one who has put it back together word by word."

I covered my mouth with my hand, trying to hide the massive smile that was creeping across my face. My eyes were glassy and my heart dipped for a moment, why hadn't I pushed hard through the crowd and out of his arms to reach her.

"You do love these postscripts. Is that part of your journalistic nature? Anyway, no mermaid costumes for me. Yes, to singing Elton John in the shower and empty rooms. Please don't tell anyone that, I do have a shy, quiet, moody reputation to uphold.

The books I will return to you, if I can figure out a way to get them to you in the future I will. If I can't, I promise I will leave them as I have the others on the shelf before I move from this amazing cottage. I want you to keep the book I left you, call it a small promise. You can give it back to me when we meet. Your grandmother had told me stories about when she used to read to you. That she was always trying to explain to you how the love stories worked, that it was never an easy task for the hero to find his princess. That there was always something to overcome. She said she wanted to teach you a lesson but many times you were too stubborn to listen and that one day she would do something to make you finally understand it. The rest of the visit went like all the others, we talked about me and where I was going to move. We talked about Natty and her latest crazy adventure of getting stuck in the mud next to the old lighthouse and Sid had to dig her out. Other than that, we sat and I helped her work on a small wooden chest she was trying to carve. She called it her magic jewelry box.

To answer your final postscript. Your grandmother gave me the necklace last week our time. It's a Claddagh, exactly like the one she wears but newer of course. I was embarrassed and tried to politely refuse it, but your grandmother is a hard one to ignore. She gave it to me as a thank you for helping her. Then, told me that I must wear it at all times so that my heart would always know where I was. I wasn't sure what she meant, but it is beautiful and gives me a strange calming feeling."

I closed my eyes, "Grandma, you crafty old woman. Thank you." I leaned against the wall, my head back and looking at the upside down scrawls of the poem, "Her heart would always know where she is." I smiled and shook my head. Whatever magic was at play I would no longer question it, just let it guide me.

"It's getting late. I feel like I have written a small novel to you. Please write me back as soon as you can. I find myself missing you terribly in the moments in between our tattered letters.

I know I told you I have chosen New York City in the book I left. I have and I will wait for you there as long as it takes. I promise. Until we meet and we are standing face to face, I will wait in the city. I will wait because I have fallen for you Frankie and I don't want to look anywhere but towards you.

Let the wind eavesdrop on my whispers and carry them to you.

Carey."

Setting the letter down, I looked out the window and out onto the ocean. I had never read anything more beautiful in my life. I stood up and grabbed my stationary, running my fingers over the poem on the wall as I pulled the chair over to the window. I sat and began to write. I knew what I had to do and this would be the letter that would make it all happen. But, first I had to fix what happened in the city, tell her why I couldn't reach her.

"Carey,

I have so much to say, so much in my heart that I will pour out on these pages. But I have to tell you something. Yesterday, we saw each other. I want you to write down the date and remember it as best as you can, so that when the day comes for you, you will know why I couldn't reach you.

We were both in Toronto. I had gone with Amy, my best friend, to help her with a flood in her apartment. As I walked to her apartment, you were there. Standing on the opposite block. Our eyes met and we both did our best to find each other in the sea of people. When you were across the street, I was stopped. I want you to know and to remember that what you saw was not what you will think it is. I'm not with him, nor will I ever be again. He grabbed me that day, holding me back from you. I fought his grip as best I could, but I couldn't break free in time. I lost you Carey, you disappeared into the alleyways and the side streets. Please, remember this day and remember that it wasn't the right time. That I tried so hard to reach you, but it wasn't meant to be. Now, I know what I have to do. My grandmother told me last night.

So, this is what I want you to do. Two months from the date of this letter, meet me in Toronto. In front of the restaurant where you first saw me. I will be wearing the same dress and waiting for you. Meet me there at six o'clock and I will take you to dinner, drinks and anything else I can think of to spend as much time as possible with you. I want to sit and talk to you until the sun sets and rises again. I want to be with you, because I have also fallen for you. Your words, your unconditional love for my grandmother and the way you make me feel like I'm the only girl in the world and I don't even know you.

I want to give you something but I don't know how I can do that, until I meet you. This frustrates me as much as it frustrates you, Carey. I can't write on walls and have you see it, I can't leave something on a shelf and have it wait for you. So, I have to make this day happen. We have to meet so I can give you everything you have given me but more."

I was frustrated that I couldn't leave her anything or create beautiful poems on a wall for her to see. I chewed on my pen, trying to figure out anything I could to connect with her in the present. All I had were these letter and the ability to set a date in the future.

"The necklace my grandmother gave you is important. Your heart will need it to find you. She wasn't being a silly romantic, she was telling you the same thing I needed to listen to. So, never take it off. My grandmother is trying to teach us both a lesson. We both need to listen to her as if she was writing law.

I love hearing the days you spend with her, I know I have said it a million times. But, I miss her and miss the moments we would have. Sitting in the barn and puttering with her little projects, listening to stories of what the town was like when she first moved there after the war.

If I had one wish, I would wish to go back in time to spend more time with her and to meet you. What I wouldn't give to meet you on the beach, show you my favorite spot out on the edge. Sit with you and my grandmother and share stories. The books can wait until we meet, I know you will take care of them and will be safe in your hands."

I stopped, I had so much to tell Carey but I didn't want to keep writing it in letters. My gut wanted me to save it all until I could be with her. I ached to be with her, and it was driving me mad that all we had were these letters and time.

"Carey. I can't stop thinking about you. Every day I wake up and wonder what it would be like to look over at you. Sitting in the chair by the window, reading the paper or a book waiting for me to wake up so we can start the day together. It's like I have writer's block when it comes to pen and paper. I can't seem to form the same elegant sentences you do. All I can scribble is that I miss you just as much when I have to wait for your reply and every breath I take is filled with a thought of you.

You make my heart sigh at the simple thoughts of you.

We need to hurry time up and meet. Remember, two months from the date of this letter. Meet me in front of the restaurant in Toronto. I will be waiting in a black dress, looking for the most amazing woman to walk into my arms.

Hurry to me.

Frankie."

I stood up, leaning my forehead against the wall, my fingers tracing her handwriting, *"Please wait for me."* I took a deep breath and walked to the bedroom. Performing the same ritual for every letter I had written to Carey, I replaced the floorboard and went downstairs to find Amy.

Not even two hours later when the both of us trudged back upstairs to our respective beds to collapse into mini comas. The floorboard was up.

Amy reached in and handed me a thin envelope with *"It's a date I will remember forever."*

I tore open the envelope with a huge smile on my face.

"Frankie,

It is a date. Two months from now I will be in Toronto. I will make sure nothing and no one stops me. I will also not take off the necklace until my heart, you, finds me.

I will be waiting.

Carey."

I handed the letter over to Amy to read, she had bounced in her spot patiently until I was done. She snatched the letter from my hands. Amy scooped me up in a hug, bouncing the both of us around the room, "Finally! You finally asked her out! Good job!"

I laughed with her, "It's time. I can't sit and wait for her to come to me. She is someone I want and I have to go for it." I squeezed my best friend, I had started the slaying of dragons and long journeys. There was no looking back and I never wanted to. I set Amy down and took the letter into my bedroom. Propping it up next to the picture of Carey on the bookshelf so I could look at it every day. I picked up the book Carey had left me, flipping through the pages and reading some of her favorite poems. When I did it made me feel that much closer to her.

As I read over the small notes Carey left in the margins of the pages, the necklace began to grow warm as if to tell me that I finally started the fight I was supposed to a while ago. I smiled liked a fool, placing my hand over the necklace. "Thank you, grandma."

After that day, time seemed to move quicker. Carey and I wrote each other every day. Sharing our lives and all the silly details one would only share with a love. I told her endless stories of Amy and me, she told me about her schoolwork and the science experiments she was working on. We talked about nothing and everything, she was the link between my grandmother and me. It was healing because I was able to spend the time I had missed out on with her through letters. Tell her about my life after I left for the city and everything I had accomplished and never bothered to share. Every so often Carey would leave me a book or a flower pressed into one of the books on the shelves.

We even shared another day like the day she wrote the poem on the wall. Carey had written on the floor this time. The spot I had pulled the chair to. She wrote as I watched.

"Imagine me here every day, sitting in the chair waiting for you to wake up. Because I am. I sit in this chair every morning and wait. Wait until the day I can share a morning with you. I love you, Frankie."

It was the first time either of us finally said it, but when she did. It felt right and I wasted no time in sending her a simple piece of paper through the floorboard.

"I love you too, Carey."

It was the first time in my life I said it to anyone and knew without a doubt, I meant it with my whole heart and whole being.

The days went by fast and I kept track of the time on a small calendar. Counting down the days until I would climb back into old blue and drive to the city.

Then came the week before the date. I sent Amy back off to the city to return to her apartment and crazy life. It was hard for both of us, we had spent so much time together that we had strengthened our bond of friendship into one of sisters and family. I hugged her tightly on the edge of the walk path, as her cab waited to take her to the small airport down the road.

"Amy, I'm going to miss you terribly. You can always come back whenever you want." I was trying to hold back the tears.

Amy sniffled. "Oh Frankie, Frankie, it's not like I'm moving across the world. You still technically have a job back in the city. And you will be up next week for the big date!" She leaned back in my arms, smiling at me as she wiped away my tears, "This has been the best vacation ever. I have never seen you so happy and so at peace. I hope when you meet her that she is everything and more. I at least owe her a drink for bringing my best friend back to life."

I let out a sigh, "I'll call you after I meet her. I want you to meet her just as much." I chewed my lip and shoved her lightly. "Now get out of here before I kidnap you and lock you up in the cottage."

Amy popped up and kissed me quickly on the cheek, skipping away with her bags, "Wouldn't want that until you get cable television up here. Goodbye my love! I will see you in a week." Amy jumped into the cab and waved frantically as her eyes welled up with tears. I watched until the cab was swallowed up by the giant trees at the end of the road. I folded my arms and took a deep breath of the ocean air, I felt alive and brand new. Next week my life would start over, hopefully start over with a beautiful brunette stranger that I wanted nothing more than to kiss the first chance I got. I smiled as I felt a breeze push around me, as my necklace warmed up. "I know grandma, you are just as excited as I am."

Two days before I was about to leave for the city I sat down and wrote a quick letter to Carey. I wanted to leave her something before I left the cottage and had no contact with her until we met.

"*Carey,*

This is hopefully the last letter I write to you. I know that sounds daunting and final, but I'm hoping it is the last one I write to you because in two days you will be sitting with me at a fancy restaurant sharing a first date drink.

I guess I wanted to leave you something if you find me hideous or horrible. I have cherished these letters and the last few months with you. I know I will never find a love like you in my life and never want to because you are it, you are my one. I have never done the things or shared the things I have with you. You have given my heart back and you have given me the precious time back I missed with my grandmother.

I love you, Carey. More than I have ever loved anyone. You are my heart, my soul and my everything.

Until I see you in a few days.

I love you.

Frankie."

I sealed the letter after dropping one of the rings my grandmother had left me. It was a last-minute thought, one I scrutinized myself for not thinking of doing sooner. It was the smaller ring that I thought was my grandmother's engagement ring. I wrote on the back of the envelope, "Inside is something I want you to have. It's my promise to you."

I smiled as I thought Carey would think it was my marriage proposal. I scribbled underneath, "It isn't a proposal. It's a promise, I mean I can't hardly ask a stranger to marry me."

Dropping the letter into the floorboard I pushed it down for what I hoped to be the last time and returned to my room. I wanted to finish packing so I could leave early the next day. Amy and I had made plans to meet up and try to shake away the rising nerves I felt every day. The what if's that were creeping around in the back of my mind.

I went to bed that night full of hope, full of excitement and full of love.

The loud vibrations of my phone rattling around on the bedside table pulled me from a wonderful dream about

Carey. I snatched up the phone, squinting in the late morning light. It was Amy.

"I will be leaving this afternoon, can't you let a girl get some beauty sleep?"

"This is an emergency! You need to get your ass to the city ASAP!"

I rolled over to look out the window, "What? What are you talking about?"

Amy was talking in her usual hyper fast way, "Oh my god Frankie, I met her. I met your lady. I have no idea how it happened or what the hell freaky powers are at play but I met her and you need to get your ass here. Like leave now, leave in your pajamas or whatever. You need to get here now."

I shot up, leaning against the headboard, "Explain. Now."

"I was walking past your office building on my way to an interview at the bar next door. Oh, shit. Frankie, you aren't going to like this." Amy paused.

"Amy! Tell me what the hell is going on!"

I heard her take a deep breath, "I don't know if this is freaky juju, or ghosty grams magic voodoo. But I stopped at the coffee shop across the street to get go juice for this interview. I was standing in line reading the free paper when I looked outside. There stood your lady. I recognized her immediately with all the times you stared at her picture and told me about her. I knew it was her. I smiled and wanted to text you to let you know the eagle was for sure in town. Then, he walked up to her and stopped her, they talked for a minute."

I cut her off, "Who! Who is he?"

"Christopher. It was Christopher talking to her. They talked for a minute and I could tell it wasn't a happy discussion. Her face changed and she looked like he had just kicked her dog square in the balls. She turned and started to walk away. That's when I ran out after her. The d-bag tried to stop me and ask about you and I told him to fuck off and play in traffic. I caught up to Carey, she was walking fast and I had to grab her."

My heart began to pound, I wanted to throw up as my panic rose. "Don't stop Amy."

"Anyways, after explaining who I was and avoiding a face full of angry brunette fist. Carey told me that Christopher stopped her, telling her that you and he had gotten back together. That you two were set to be married by the end of the year. Somehow he knew who Carey was and tracked her down in the city. Carey was rambling that she knew that she should have let you be with him that day she saw you scooped up into his arms the last time she was here. That day you cried your pretty face off because she ran away. She told me that she had believed your letters, but still worried because of the things she saw. I told her that he was a big dumbass jealous asshole that wanted nothing more than to hurt you as much as possible." Amy paused, "I tried so hard to get her to stay. But, she looked at me with these cold steel eyes and said, "I'm not going to wait anymore." and took off. Frankie you gotta get your ass here. I followed her to the hotel she is staying at and I paid one of the creepy bar backs to watch her until she leaves. You need to leave now."

I threw the phone onto the bed and started yanking on clothes, "I'm leaving now Amy, call me if she leaves. Do everything you can until I get there." I was yelling as I ran around the room. My heart pounding to the point it wanted to explode. I scooped up my bag and grabbed my phone, "Promise me Amy, you stop her until I get there." I hung up the phone and ran out of the house, my mind racing. How in the hell did Christopher know who Carey was, he had only seen her twice in person, and even then, he wouldn't know who she was, and her importance to me. He had nothing to go on other than what she looked like. I cursed, running to the barn I looked at old blue. I had intended to take the truck to the city but now time was precious. I picked up the corner of the canvas tarp, ripping it off my sleek black sports car.

I started the car, throwing my bags in the back seat. I had little time and knew the sports car would get me to the city in half the time the truck would. I would break speed laws and all the laws I could manage to get to Carey. I wasn't about to let this chance pass me by, I would not let fate or coincidence hold me back.

I backed the car up and when it reached the street. The necklace began to pulsate harder than ever before, stopping me and forcing me to look back at the truck. I had a second guess feeling that I should be taking the truck. I shook my head. "Grandma I can't waste time. I have to get to her." the necklace pulsated more, to the point I had to take it off and drop it in the cup holder. I threw the car into gear and spun the tires, squealing off towards the distance.

I raced on the highway, driving like a maniac. Fast and passing the few cars on the road. I was making good time and with every mile I threw behind me, my heart pounded harder. I checked my phone every other second, waiting for Amy to tell me anything. An hour into the drive she called me, "She just left the hotel. Climbed into a silver car and started off. The kid told me she had all her bags and looked like she was in a hurry. He is following her and I will keep you updated. He said it looks like she is heading east. Where are you?"

"I'm just about to the border, I should be there in the city in two hours. She might head back to New York City. She told me that was where she had taken the job in her last letter. If anything, I will just drive there."

I hung up with Amy and focused on driving. I pushed the sports car to its limit and prayed there were no cops on the road to pull me over for excessive speeding. I had to get to her. There was nothing that would stop me.

An hour later I had crossed the border and was once again racing through the highways. The traffic thickened the closer to the city I got, making it harder to pass and navigate. Amplifying my fears that I would not make it.

I gripped the steering wheel when I came up on to a few semi-trucks in my lane, I prepped to pass them when my phone rang. I snatched it up, "Amy." I looked to my left and began to enter the oncoming lane to pass the trucks, pushing the accelerator to the floor.

"Frankie! Stop and go back! The kid has followed her and she is almost to the border, go back!" Amy was practically yelling on the phone.

I looked down at the phone. "Why would I go back if she is heading to New York City!"

"No, no that border..."

Before Amy finished, I was blinded by the bright lights of an oncoming car. I had taken my eyes off the road for a second too long. I looked up and dropped the phone on the floor, Amy's voice calling after me. I tried to swerve out of the way and lost control of the speeding car. I slid off on to the median and the car spun like a tilt a whirl. I hit a guard rail hard, making me slam my head against the driver's side window. I heard horns and squealing tires as the car took its own erratic path. Slamming into guard rails and jolting me around as things went fuzzy and black. I hit my head a few more times before the car seemed to settle on its side. I passed out as my seatbelt allowed me to dangle as if I was a puppet on strings.

When I opened my eyes again I felt nothing but strong hands pulling me from the car, a soft strong voice telling me I would be alright.

My eyes flicked open again when I heard the sirens, and the crunch of metal and glass. I opened my eyes and everything was blurry, just bright blue and red lights adding to the gentle haze I was in. I half listened to the paramedics yelling my injuries to one another. I had fractured bones, and a laceration to my head. I was limp and lifeless when I was placed on a stretcher, male voices surrounding me. I rolled my head and looked at a young faced cop, asking the paramedic, "Where is the one who pulled her out of the car? I need to find that witness and talk to them. They saved her life."

The paramedic pointed off to my right, the cop nodded, then looked at me. "If the driver of that car hadn't stopped and pulled you out. You wouldn't be alive right now lady. It was by the good luck of whatever you believe in they were a doctor."

I tried to say something, but the paramedic pushed painkillers into my IV right before he loaded me up into the ambulance. Pushing me back into a hazy blur of black. Sending me into a deep sleep.

The only thought I had was, I lost her, and I lost her like I did that day in the city. I hadn't moved fast enough then and now I had moved too fast and not listened to my heart when it begged me to take old blue. This was my fate and I had sealed it. She would not know where I was now and think I had given up on her and that Christopher was right.

I had lost her and my heart in a split second.

Chapter 10

Natty sat in the chair across from my bed, holding my discharge papers. The doctor went over the care of the stitches on my forehead and how to take showers with the cast on my right hand. I had fractured my right wrist on the steering wheel and my head had been bounced around like a super ball in the hands of an over excited child. My entire body was sore, but nothing hurt more than my heart. I nodded silently and waited until he was done before thanking him quietly and sliding off the bed. I wanted to go home and sleep in my own bed, darken the windows and heal in isolation.

Natty helped me up and with getting my jacket on. She said very little but I could tell in her eyes she was disappointed with me and scared. It had been told to me more than a hundred times how lucky I was that I survived the crash that if it wasn't for the good Samaritans that stopped and pulled me from my twisted piece of metal that once was a sports car. Lucky there had been a doctor on scene, or I would have died.

I honestly wished I had at times. The times that I would think about how close I was again and how stupid I had been to drive like that. To ignore the massives sign my grandmother was trying to send my way when I pulled off in a mad dash. Ignoring the necklace pulsating and taking old blue. I reached up involuntarily to where the necklace sat and cringed that it was missing. It had been lost in the car wreck. Another piece of my grandmother and my heart I lost out of stupidity.

I leaned against Natty as we walked down the hallway, she held on to my elbow and said nothing until we were outside and she was loading me into the passenger seat of her beat up Volvo station wagon.

"Little Frankie. Your grandmother would have had a heart attack over this. What in your damn foolish mind were you thinking?" Her voice was dripping with held back anger and frustration towards me throwing my car into traffic like I had.

I grimaced, shifting in the seat. I was sore and bruised everywhere. "Natty if I knew I would tell you. I just want to go home and rest."

Natty shook her head, "Everything is set up at the cottage. Old Sid and I will be on call until Amy makes it down to be your personal nurse ratchet." She turned to look at me, "You are lucky to be alive, you know that right?"

I sighed, "I have only been told a million times. So, yes I know." I closed my eyes and shift again. Trying not to put weight on the sorest side of my body. "Did the police ever find the person or the doctor who helped me?"

Natty shook her head as she exited the parking lot of the hospital, "I haven't heard anything. There is a handful of us that would like to thank the nameless superhero. The police promised they would tell us if and when they found them."

I nodded, reaching for my prescription bag. Digging out the bottle of pain killers the doctor issued me. The old car's suspension was killing me when it literally searched out every crack and bump in the road, rattling my damaged body. I swallowed two pills dry and drifted off listening to Natty lecture me some more.

Back at the cottage, Natty and I were met by Sid sitting on the back of his old truck. He smiled when he saw me, running to open my door and steady me while I struggled to get my bearings. I saw the same look in his eyes that I saw in Natty's when she first saw me; fear and relief. I realized in that moment that this small town and its kooky inhabitants had become family. All because of my grandmother and what she meant to everyone.

Sid smiled at me, walking me to the front door, "Hey kiddo. Glad to have you home. If you need anything, don't hesitate to call. Natty and I will be over in shifts to check on you and feed you, as well as my wife too." He spoke softly as he opened the front door. The cottage felt different to me the moment I stepped inside but I couldn't place it.

I squeezed Sid's hand."Thank you Sid. I just want to go to bed and sleep." I tried to smile for him, but knew it was half-hearted. Sid helped me up the stairs and set me on the giant bed. Natty was close to follow, setting down a bottle of water and some fruit on the bedside table. She went to open the giant curtains to let in the light.

I stopped her. "Leave them. I had enough bright lights in the hospital, and I have a headache." I mumbled while I pushed my shoes off. I didn't want to see the poem on the wall or the words Carey had left for me in the room. It would shatter my heart even more than, I had shattered my body.

Natty folded her arms, "Righto. Well, Sid and I will be off." she pointed to the small brown box on the table by the water, "That's a new phone. Amy sent it down yesterday already pre-programmed with our numbers, since yours was lost." Natty drifted off, taking a deep breath. "Anyways, come on Sid. Let's let the kid get some sleep." Sid smiled tightly and walked out the room. Natty stared at me for a moment before saying, "Call if you need anything at all, Frankie." she smiled genuinely and walked out the door. I could feel how much they wanted to comfort me about the car accident and it also felt like they knew what I had lost. That I lost my heart and desire to function like a normal human. I knew my face telegraphed my emotions and I didn't care.

I waited until I heard the front door shut before I slowly stripped my clothes off and fell into some pajamas. I was more broken than I thought, but I didn't want to bother anyone. I had done this to myself and I would suffer for it. I crawled into bed, took two more pain pills with the glass of water and buried my body deep into the blankets, crying myself to sleep.

The next few days I kept myself in a haze. Taking the pain pills exactly on the dot when I could take them and passing out. Sleeping away the day, the night and the visits from Sid and Natty. I vaguely remembered snippets of their visits. They tried diligently to get me up, to eat, to walk around and Natty always tried to open the curtains and I would tell her to keep them closed. The only time I would actually get up was to check my bandages and take a shower. I did open the box with the cell phone and turn it on, replying to the four hundred texts from Amy. She informed me a hundred times she would be at the cottage by the end of the week and I knew I would have to prepare for another round of lecturing from her.

I didn't care though, there was very little I did care about. I only made an effort to keep Natty and Sid from worrying too much, but after they left I would crawl back into bed and cry. My heart was broken beyond belief and every time I closed my eyes I would think of her. When I did I would take two more pills and fall into a listless sleep.

On the fifth day, I woke up to the sound of Sid dragging boxes up to my room. Tom was behind him carrying his own share of large brown boxes. I blinked turning on the light, only half illuminating the room and startling the two older men. Sid smiled at me as Tom made another trip downstairs, "Morning kiddo! How are you feeling?"

I swallowed the cotton mouth down a few times before sitting up. I was still groggy from my hazy, deep sleep, "What are those?"

Sid looked behind his shoulder, "Oh, those came into the post office this morning. I offered to help Tom bring them up to the cottage. I also dropped off some food for you. Fresh beef stew my wife made. You will like it, kiddo." he smiled in a way that told me he was worried that I hadn't been eating. I smiled lightly and tried to look at the boxes. I couldn't make out the writing on the boxes.

"Sid, can you open the curtains? There isn't enough light in here."

Sid nodded and pulled open the curtains, filling the room with the early morning light that I once loved and now ignored. I couldn't keep my eyes from going straight to the poem on the wall and her handwriting. I had to swallow my heart down and fight the tears back. I stood up from the bed, Sid rushing to my side to steady me. I held on to his arm until I found my balance, then walked to the boxes.

"Do you know what's in these?" I looked at Sid. He shook his head but pulled out his box cutter. Kneeling down to open the first box for me. He flipped open the lid and that's when I saw the handwritten address on the front.

My heart stopped and my feet pulled me closer to the boxes. It was her handwriting.

"It looks like it's a bunch of old books, little Frankie." Sid stood up and looked at the address, "All the way from New York City too!"

I covered my mouth with my hand, I didn't want to cry in front of Sid, but I couldn't hold back the heartbreak. I stared at the scrawls and swirls I had memorized and would often see in my dreams. She had sent the books back to me, she wanted to forget me and this was the proof. I had broken her heart by never showing up, never stopping her and letting my past speak in my place. I choked out a sob, scaring Sid a bit. He looked at me, suddenly feeling awkward I was crying in front of him, "I will tell Tom to leave the rest downstairs for you." He helped me back to bed and covered me up. I reached for the last two pain pills I had and downed them. Curling up in the middle of the bed as sobs carried through my body. I didn't hear anything as Sid mumbled something and walked to the door, he paused before leaving, "Oh! Natty said they found the doctor who saved you. She will be by tomorrow to tell you their name and how to find them." I heard him let out a sad sigh, "I know you'll be okay, kiddo. You're a tough one."

I hoped he was right as I let my sobs carry me into sleep.

The bright light that filled every inch of the room also poked at my eyelids. Playfully dancing across them to get me to wake up and enjoy what it had to offer. I groaned and cursed the empty room. I had forgotten to close the curtains yesterday and now my pounding headache made me regret it even more. I rolled over to the bedside table, finding another giant glass of water and a banana sitting next to my phone. I greedily gulped down the water and ignored the banana. I picked up my phone, it was eight o'clock in the morning and I once again had missed phone calls from Amy and texts. I also had an unknown number in the missed call logs. I sent a quick I'm alive text to Amy to reply to the one telling me she would be down this weekend and that I had better be alive so she could kick my ass.

I took a deep breath, stretching out tired muscles and sore bones. I was physically feeling better but that was as far as it went. I picked up the pain pill bottle and found it to be empty with no refills authorized. I used the edge of the bed to push up and walk to the curtains. I tried avoiding the walls and the boxes sitting in the corner. I wanted to darken the room and push the boxes into the other room without looking at them. It was a constant reminder of her and what I had messed up. I took a few steps when something caught my eye, pulling me to look up at the bookshelf.

The bookshelf was almost full. The books were lined up in a strange perfect order and were completely dust free. I stared at the books. I didn't remember anyone coming in last night after Sid left, but again I was in a deep sleep. I was confused as I stepped to them, the boxes were gone and there was only a small stack of the last few on the floor next to the chair. That drew my attention to the chair. It was clear someone had sat in the chair and recently. There was an empty coffee cup set on the floor next to the chair leg, my discharge and after care papers were out and neatly stacked on the seat of the chair. I was even more confused, Natty or Sid would not disturb my privacy to that length. Amy would, but she was still in the city and nothing about her was neat.

I stood staring at the whole scene in front of me, trying to place together what was going on when my stomach roared to life. I was hungry, starving and my body was definitely telling me. I shuffled to the banana and ate it in two bites, feeling better I decided that it was time to try and work through my heartbreak. Or at least try and get enough strength to figure out who was in my house snooping around. I walked out of the room and shuffled past the spare bedroom, I glanced at the floorboard out of habit and found that it was pushed up. The sheer sight of it sent my heart into overdrive. I did my best to kneel to the floor, my stiff body was not as bendy as I wanted, yet. It was hard to be steady with one good hand and one broken wrist. Pushing the floorboard away I reached my good hand in, my fingertips finding the edge of an envelope. I hesitated for a second before closing my fingers around it and pulling it free from the floor.

I took a deep breath and looked around the room. I was afraid to look at the letter, fearful of the words she had written in response to my last profession of love and excitement of meeting her. I would have to tell her what happened and pray that I could figure some way out of the mess I had made just a few days ago. I thought for a second if it was really worth it, no matter how hard I tried and how many dragons I slayed, another one would show itself. I chewed on my lip and let my eyes roam around the room. I began to slowly notice that it was neater than it had been when Amy left and there were two large black suitcases tucked into the open closet. As if the owner just arrived a few hours ago and hadn't yet unpacked. I stood up slowly, walking to the luggage, looking for any tag to tell me who they belonged to. My mind was racing and for a moment I wondered if Christopher managed to make his way out here, the luggage looked exactly like the fancy kind he always preferred. I found nothing to clue me in who the owner was. I started to get angry with the confusion I felt. Someone had definitely been in the cottage unwelcomed. I hobbled back to my room to call Natty and find out who had been in the cottage. I went to set the letter down on the table when I noticed that it was a clean, brand new white envelope. I held the envelope up and turned it over to the front.

There was nothing on the front, no handwriting or anything. I hesitated before sliding my finger under the flap and tore it open. There was only a small piece of paper folded in half.

When I opened it, there was one sentence.

"*Frankie.*

Go outside to the beach."

I blinked a few times, and began taking quick breaths. I set the paper down on the bed, grabbed my sweater and pulled on shoes. I did my best to walk down the stairs and out the back door. The cool ocean wind hit me, forcing me to take a deep breath of the fresh clean air. Filling my lungs and chasing out the last of the haze and headache I felt. I walked as best as I could. I had been in bed far too long and it showed with every stiff step I took.

I huddled my arms closer to myself when the wind found the tiny holes in my sweater. When I came to the end of the walk path that opened the beach up to me I spotted Natty in the low tide area of the beach. She was wearing her usual hip boots and huge fisherman sweater. She was elbow deep in the mud digging up clams. I walked towards her as she turned to see me actually out of the house. Natty threw me a cheeky smile, and began to move my way. Leaving her bucket and tiny shovel in the mud she waved at me. Meeting me at the edge of the mud, "Good to see you up and out of the house." Her smile was wide and I saw the edges of relief in her eyes that I was up and about.

I smiled, nodding, "I guess it's time." I looked around the beach, in the distance was another clam digger. Wearing a bright yellow raincoat with the hood up, knee-deep in the mud and digging as Natty had. I took a deep breath, my heart begging for me to ask about the things I had seen in the house. "Um, Natty, have I had any visitors today?"

Natty smiled, "I came over earlier, but you were dead to the world. I wanted to tell you about a phone call I got last night, about the doctor that pulled you from the car wreck and saved you." Natty reached into her jean pocket and pulled something out. She grabbed my hand and pressed something cool into my palm. "They also found this."

I opened my hand. In the middle of my palm sat my grandmother's necklace. I felt my hand tremble at the sight. "How did they find it?"

"The doctor found it in the car. After you were pulled out." Natty kept smiling at me. I kept my eyes on the necklace in my hand.

"There's luggage in the spare bedroom and the books are unpacked, did you do that Natty?" I looked up at her with glassy eyes.

Natty winked at me, "I didn't." She reached into my palm and picked up the necklace. Moving closer to me, Natty slipped the necklace around my neck. She then turned and pointed to the other clam digger in the near distance, "She did."

As soon as the charm of the necklace set against my chest, it began to pulsate and pull me towards the direction of where the yellow raincoat was standing. I had to reach for Natty's arm to keep myself from stumbling. Natty pulled me closer to her, linking my arm with hers as she whistled towards the yellow raincoat. The raincoat straightened up and turned in our direction, throwing a hand up, waving at us.

The yellow raincoat started walking towards us.

With every step closer, the stronger the pull of the necklace became. I bit my lip as I began to shiver, not from the cool wind swimming around us, but from the hope in my heart. It couldn't be. After everything, all the mistakes and almost killing myself. It couldn't be.

The yellow raincoat was a few feet away from us, I couldn't see a face as it was hidden from the giant hood of the raincoat. A gloved hand reached up and pushed the hood back, allowing me a full view of her face.

I gasped, swallowing whatever sound that wanted to come out. She looked at me with those golden brown eyes I dreamt about endlessly. Golden brown eyes I only looked in once before and feared I would never see again. Now, they were moving towards me, smiling and sparkling with the wide smile that carried across her face. Her brunette hair was up in a ponytail, small stray strands blowing around with the wind. She was beautiful, even more so as I watched her walking towards me, her eyes never leaving mine.

She stopped a few steps away from Natty and I. The necklace was warmer than ever and began beating with my heart, both were pounding like an elephant stampede through my body.

My voice was lost, only allowing me to choke out one word, "Carey?" I could feel my tears dampening my cheeks. I didn't care that I was crying like I was. I couldn't and wouldn't tear my eyes away from her. I reached out with my good hand, desperate to touch her and know she was real.

She pulled off her glove and took my hand in hers, they fit perfectly together, her warm fingers wrapping around mine as she whispered, "It's nice to finally meet you little Frankie." The smile on her face widened as she blinked back her own tears.

Chapter 11

I let out a sob entangled with a laugh, pulling her into my arms with all the strength I could muster. I wrapped my arms around her, not caring that the raincoat she wore was damp and muddy. I buried my face into her shoulder as I continued to laugh through the tears, holding her tightly. Sighing as I felt her arms come up around me, holding me just as tight.

I whispered against her ear. "You're real."

Carey laughed and leaned back in my arms, meeting my eyes with hers. Her hand left my back, pushing some hair out of my face before resting against my cheek, "I am." She bit her bottom lip and smiled, "Let's get you back into the house. It's a little too cold out here for you."

I grabbed her hand on my cheek, pressing it against my face as my eyes closed. I wanted to memorize this moment and try to convince myself that I wasn't dreaming. I opened my eyes; she was still standing in front of me. I knew I had a dazed look on my face and was frozen in my place. Carey ran her hand down my arm, finding my hand again. She looked over at Natty, "We will meet you inside for lunch."

Natty had a huge grin on her face, "Take your time, I think you both have a lot to talk about." Natty squeezed Carey's shoulder, "Good to have you back, doctor."

Carey blushed and moved closer to me, wrapping an arm around my waist to help me walk back to the cottage. I couldn't tear my eyes away from her; I was shivering from the cold and all the emotion running through my body. I was so cold I couldn't force my arms away from their folded position across my chest. Carey noticed my shivering and pulled off her raincoat, draping it around my shoulders. I snuggled up into the raincoat and found myself leaning into her, drawn to her body warmth and strong arms that held on to my shoulders. It all still felt surreal, like a fantastic dream I would be horribly ripped from and wake up to a harsh reality.

We said nothing during the walk back. I would just sneak glances at her. Her perfectly angled jaw, her pinked cheeks from the ocean breeze, her brunette hair and the way she seemed to always carry a small smile. Carey kept a tight grip across my shoulders, squeezing here and there to make sure I was still with her. When we walked into the back door, she pulled the raincoat from my shoulders. Hanging it up on the hook she smiled at me, "I will make some hot tea. Go upstairs and climb into bed. We can talk when you're comfortable."

I nodded, but didn't move. I watched as she pulled off her boots, dropping the gloves in the tops of them. "Carey." I loved the simple joy of being able to say her name, to her in my cottage, to say her name while she stood a foot away from me, straightening up the coats on the old pegs by the door. My body was flooded with a cascade of feelings from all across the spectrum of ecstatic joy to deep-rooted fear.

She turned her head to me as soon as the sound of her name hit her ears. "Frankie." she had a half-smile creep up to the corner of her eyes.

I looked at the floor, the intensity of looking in her eyes made my heart skip with my stomach. "How did you...Why are you here?" it was a silly ill phrased question, but I had to know. How did she find me? I thought I was lost to her the day of the accident.

Carey took the three steps to stand in front of me. Her hands rubbing warmth into my still cold arms, "We have a lot to talk about." She nodded in silent agreement with the strange tension hanging between us. We had professed our feelings multiple times, but now, as we stood face to face, nerves were thicker than anything. Carey squeezed my elbow, "Go get comfortable and I will be up in a minute."

I bit my lip and let my eyes drop to her chest. The top few buttons of her soft lavender flannel shirt were undone, giving me a perfect view of her beautiful collarbones. Between them and at the base of a long neck I wanted to run my fingers over, sat the necklace my grandmother had given her. My cast covered hand snaked free from the long droopy sleeves of my sweater. Carey had begun to turn her head to make her way to the cupboards. My fingers grazing over her warm skin stopped her. I picked up the charm between my fingers, running my thumb over the hands and heart. "You never took it off."

"How else was my heart going to find me without it?" Her hand closed around mine, pressing our hands gently together against her chest. She took a deep breath and whispered, "If you had left yours on, you would have felt me coming to you that day."

I looked down at the floor, my hand sliding from underneath hers. I stepped back and tucked my cast back into the sleeves. I turned away from her, I felt embarrassed and stupid when the memories of that day came rushing back. "I'll be upstairs."

Climbing the stairs my heart felt heavy. This was not how I wanted our first meeting to go. I wanted to meet Carey like I had planned. Scoop her up in my arms and hold her. Now things were tentative and there was so much I felt I had to explain. I climbed the stairs slowly and the second I saw the bed, exhaustion crept in. I kicked off my shoes and crawled into the bed. I was so tired but I had to stay awake to tell Carey everything and hope that her feelings were still there for me.

I pulled the thick blankets up, leaning against the headboard I let my gaze drift to the poem on the wall. Getting lost in a happier memory, one that felt so long ago now. Carey came into the room quietly, the soft creaking of the floor following her steps, making me look at her. She stood close to the bed as she handed me a hot mug of tea. I took it and let the heat course through my chilled hands and deep into my arms. Carey walked to the window, looking out on to the ocean. Holding her cup with two hands, she stood straight, appearing nervous to be in the room with me.

"This view is incredible. Your grandmother kept her bed against the opposite wall so she could fall asleep and wake up to this view. She said, it made her feel like she lived in a different world. One where the simple sight of waves, were all that one needed to know how beautiful life can be."

Carey's voice filled my ears and my body, settling around my heart in a way that made me crave to pull her into bed and hold her. I had often thought about the time I could hear her voice whenever I wanted, listen to her talk, and tell me random things. But, as I listened to her I could hear something in her voice that frightened me. There was a hint of hesitation in her words, like she was nervous trying to cover any other emotions that she was holding in. I had to change the subject and start the conversation I knew we needed to have.

I cleared my throat, growing even more fearful to ask for answers and forgiveness. "I forgot to ask Natty. She told me that the police found the doctor who saved me." I reached for my phone to call Natty.

"I was not even a mile away when I saw the smoke. I thought nothing of it until the necklace began to pull me towards the smoke. Pulled, more like pushed me in such a way that I couldn't ignore it. I was on a mission to get to you, hoping to stop you at the cottage before you came for me in the city." Carey kept her eyes on the ocean, her voice softer. Each word was chosen carefully and delivered carefully. It was now clear she was struggling with her emotions. It made my heart hurt to realize it.

Carey moved her head slightly to look at me but, her eyes drew down to the floor, "I tried to ignore it. The strange sensation when I heard your grandmother's voice in the back of my head, urging me to follow the pull." she took a breath, "You had just crashed when I finally arrived at the scene. People were running towards the car and calling for help. I knew it was you in the instant I ran towards the car, my necklace told me so."

Carey turned to look at me, "I had to climb on to the side of the car and with strength I never knew I had, I got you out of the car. Then, carried you away from the twisted, smoking wreckage. When the paramedics arrived I helped them get you on to the stretcher and before I could do anything, go with you. The police pushed me away. Determined to get your name and find out how intoxicated you were." Carey walked to the bed, sitting on the edge. Her hand came to the side of my neck, her finger dipping below the collar of the sweater and finding the chain of my necklace. I could feel how nervous she was in her delicate and purposeful movements. She lifted the necklace free from my sweater, "I was drawn back to the car, and some otherworldly push came with a gentle breeze. Pushing me to go back." she let the necklace lay against her palm, "I found this hanging on the gear shifter. Dangling and glinting like a bright light of peace in a scene of havoc." She let the necklace fall from her hand, "When it was in my hand it throbbed, more so the further I was away from you." When the charm settled back against me, it began to pulse ever so slightly. It had been the entire time Carey was around me, I just didn't notice it until she broke the connection.

I felt my eyes turn glassy, "I took it off when I left to come to you that day. It tried to tell me something, my grandmother tried to tell me something and I ignored it." I took a shaky breath, "I was in a hurry to get to you. After what Amy told me...that you, he..." I swallowed, "You told Amy you were tired of waiting."

Carey nodded, "I was. That's why I left the city to come back here. To the cottage, because I knew this was where you were." She stood up and moved to the wall, looking up at her poem on the wall, faded but still readable. "I still don't understand the science behind this."

Carey ran her hand over the wall, obviously fascinated at the aged markings. I watched her brow furrow ever so slightly in thought. She was avoiding something, something that she wanted to tell me but for some reason the odd tension we now carried wouldn't allow her.

The words fell out quick, "Every time you saw him, with me or in front of the coffee shop. It was all lies that came out of his mouth. This last time, I was afraid. Afraid that you had given up, especially with what Amy told me. That's why I raced to get to you, to do what I should have the last time I saw you." I felt my voice tremble in the words I spoke. I was afraid now, that the next thing Carey would say would be the end of this. I went to say the words I wanted to, needed to, but before I could she spoke.

"Christopher and I have known each other through the years. Not by my choice." Carey sat in the chair, leaning forward she kept her eyes on the cup in her hands. "That first night, the night I came across you in the street and you had no clue who I was. He chased me down at the next street corner. At first, he was charming, introducing himself and politely asking a few questions. I answered them, he is definitely a charming man. But, I could see in his eyes the gentle suspicion all men have when the beautiful woman on their arm is suddenly distracted by someone else. The second time, that day we stood on opposite street corners and I watched him swoop you up in his arms. I remembered what you told me, and I walked away." Carey half smiled in a painful way that made me want to cry.

She nervously ran a hand over her hair, pushing loose strands behind her ears, "My heart hurt, but I knew that it wasn't the right time. He found me in the city later that night and basically told me to leave you alone. That you were his and there was nothing I could do about it. Because of the letter you sent me, telling me that you tried to get to me, find me but I had disappeared on you. I ignored him; my heart was tied to your words and to you." Carey glanced up at me, her gaze turned sad, "Christopher had followed me back to the hotel that night and while I stepped out to grab a late night coffee, he swindled his way into my room. Found your letters in my bag. Read all of them and started to alter his own future, to try to bring you back into his life."

Carey smiled tightly. "A jealous man becomes a determined man." She set her empty mug on the floor carefully, "That last day."

She paused, I watched her jaw clench, "I will never know how he knew I would be in the city that day, but a man of wealth and determination can make almost anything happen. He magically found me outside the coffee shop. Where he proceeded to feed me a story that you and him had found your way back to each other. That you took him back and it was best that I forget you and return to New York City."

She leaned back in the chair, meeting my eyes. Carey was fidgeting again, the struggle of whatever she was holding back clear on her face. She would stare in my eyes for what felt like an eternity and then break it roughly; it was as if she was afraid to look at me for too long. She looked over her shoulder, back out the window.

I watched as she lost herself in the waves for a moment before her voice broke, trembling with held back tears, "You have to understand Frankie. I hadn't heard from you in almost two years since that last letter. Dated almost two years to the date the day before we were to meet. I had lived on the faith and the promise you had written." I heard her inhale sharply, "You are my heart, my soul, and my everything. I would go to sleep every night you were gone, imagining you whispering those words to me. It was what made me hold on during the entire time I had to wait."

My eyes never left her as her words hit me, my words spoken back to me through her. One thing I dreamt about, but now it was painful to hear mixed with the revelation that time moved differently for her and I didn't think much of the time between us when I sent that last letter. All I knew, all I cared about was that I would be meeting her in a matter of hours, where for her it was a matter of years. Years of waiting for me to follow through on a promise. "Carey, I..." My own quiet voice shook, barely carrying across the room and to her.

She smiled softly and shook her head, "It's not your fault, and mostly mine for letting a jealous man get into my head like he did. Amy caught up to me, and explained everything as fast as possible. I was angry, hurt, and frustrated. I immediately thought the time between us, the silence between us had allowed things to change. Feelings to change, that I waited for you like a war bride and you found something, someone else. A promise you couldn't keep."

She gasped slightly, as if she was holding back from crying in front of me. She clenched her jaw again, her brow furrowing in thought. I knew Carey was a strong woman, but I was watching her crumble slowly in front of me. I wanted to interrupt her and shout at her that I had waited for her, that I kept my promise, that I was hopelessly in love with her and that I just didn't understand how her end of our connection work. My heart ached in knowing she had waited for me for as long as she did then, having Christopher confront her. I understood her struggle. Her hesitation and the fear that was now radiating around her. But, something in the back of my head told me to let her finish, let her empty her heart and mind of all the things she held in for far too long.

Carey cleared her throat, "Then, Amy blurted at me you were still at the cottage, intending to make your trip in the afternoon. That's when I told her I didn't want to wait anymore. I had to come to you and ask you, look in your eyes and know if you still loved me like I loved you and have every day for the last almost two years. I didn't want to wait when you were closer than ever. I left the city to come to you." Her eyes locked on to mine, her soft golden browns were glassy and littered with hidden emotions.

Silence suddenly filled the room, neither one of us broke the stare between us. I didn't know what to say, I was still absorbing the fact I had left her for as long as I had. That she had to fight harder than I did to wait for me. My fight was the dragons in my life, Christopher and my own doubts. Hers was the lengthy journey over the expanse of time, and it never occurred to me her struggle would be equally as great or greater.

Carey stood up quickly, snagging the empty cup with her finger, she took a breath to say something and paused. Running a hand through her hair she smiled, in a way that made it seem as if she was defeated, "I haven't stopped thinking about you since that first night. The midnight black dress you wore, and the way your hazel eyes lit up when you looked in mine and the few times after when we crossed paths for a split second. That was the moment I fell in love with you, and haven't stopped every minute of every day since. Because, Frankie, you are my heart, my soul and my everything, still." Her eyes were now filled with tears, desperate to fall, "I should let you get some sleep. I will come wake you up when lunch is ready." She drew her gaze down to the floor again.

Carey moved closer to the bed, her hand reaching for my half empty cup. My good hand acted on its own, grabbing her hand. Startling her enough that she met my eyes, one lone tear slipped out. Carey wiped it away before it found any further path.

"Carey." I gently squeezed her hand, pulling her closer to me. Silently asking, begging her to sit on the bed with me. She was resisting and stayed standing. I took a deep breath, becoming more nervous about what was happening in this room. "Everything I said to you in the letters was the truth. To be honest, I have never been that truthful to anyone in my life. But, again I have never been more in love with anyone than I am with you. You are my one, Carey." I felt her hand twitch under mine. I turned it over so our fingers could link with each other. I ran my thumb over her slender fingers, "I should have known, paid attention to the science of how this magic, our magic worked. If I had, I promise you I would have found you sooner and never left you without a letter every day until you were in my arms."

I began to feel my necklace grow warm, urging me to keep going, to keep the fight going, "I would talk to you in my sleep, Carey. Then, in my dreams I would beg for the slightest touch from you. The times I was so close to you and you slipped away, hurt but made me determined. That's why that day I raced to you, that I would change my fate and go to you. Stop waiting on time and distance and foolish men." I paused and looked up at Carey. She was staring at our hands, clenching her jaw to hold back even more tears.

I bit my lip, then it came to me. I dropped her hand and rolled out of bed. Holding on to the bedside table to gather my bearings, I dug in the small drawer and pulled out the black marker I had kept in there from when I sent Amy a care package. I clutched the marker in my hands and shuffled over to the chair. I dragged it awkwardly with my good hand and then, pushed it against the wall. I climbed up on to the chair and popped the marker cap off. I wobbled from lack of balance and had to push my broken hand on to the wall, making me yelp a little at the sudden sharp pain.

"Frankie, your hand is broken, what are you doing...." Carey's voice was barely above a whisper.

I ignored her and began to scrawl in the blank space on the wall next to her poem. I wrote fast and large.

"Will you sit and watch the waves with me until they are gone? Will you end my sleepless nights with your arms wrapped around me? Paint our love with the breaths we share? These are all wishes I want to make with you, because now, the time that was the space between us, I banish it now and forever.

I will always and forever only love you Carey Murphy. Time no longer exists with you by my side."

I turned to look at her, wobbling again and pressing through the pain of my broken hand I dropped the marker. Her eyes were focused on the poor attempt at a love poem. I held my hand out to her, "Carey, I love you. I have never loved anyone like I love you. Give me your heart and I will always give you mine."

Carey smiled weakly and walked towards me, "You're hurting your wrist." Her hand slid into mine, warm and strong as she went to help me off the chair. I yanked her closer to me, throwing her off-balance that she had to let go and grab my hips to stop herself from falling into me. I took advantage of it. My good hand slid across her neck and up to the back of her head, guiding her towards me fast enough that she couldn't move away. The moment our lips connected into a deep kiss, we both let out small moans and whimpers. Her lips were as soft as I imagined. I pushed my mouth harder against hers when I felt her hands squeeze hard on to my hips, sending a surge of desire through my body. I let go of the wall and fell forward into her arms. We were chest to chest, her hands leaving my hips to slide up my back and lift me from the chair and hold me as we kissed passionately, urgently and full of pent-up longing. It was the most amazing first kiss I had ever experienced in my life.

The urgency of our kiss slowed into slow and purposeful for a few more seconds until she broke away, as I could hear her heart racing. Her lips still hovering over mine with just enough room that we could both catch our breath. I couldn't hold back the smile as my hand went to her cheek, my thumb running over her lips. When I looked into her eyes I saw that there was no longer fear, hesitation or a struggle behind them. There was relief filled with love, mirroring what I felt. I leaned forward, my lips brushing hers as my nose nuzzled against her soft skin. "Never doubt what I feel for you Carey. I love you."

Carey pulled me closer to her, my head fell into the space in between her shoulder and neck. My arms slid to wrap around her waist, she fit perfectly in my arms. Her body warming mine in a way that I knew I would grow addicted to it and her. She let out a slow breath, "You know I never kiss before a first date or on a first date."

I leaned back in her arms and looked at her, confused. Carey smirked and kissed me quickly and softly, "I guess you're an exception, Frankie." She looked dead in my eyes, "I love you, Francesca. I have for a very long time and will for a very long time after." She bent to kiss me again and I leaned back, smirking, shaking my head.

"Nope, not until our first date." I went to pull my right hand free, when I caught it at a weird angle. A quick burst of pain shot through my hand. I groaned and stepped out of her arms, cradling my sore hand. Carey snapped into doctor mode, gingerly guiding me back to bed. "Back to bed, no excuses. I will get you some aspirin. You need rest."

I didn't fight her, my hand throbbed from the abuse I had put it in over the last few minutes. I crawled into the bed and laid back. Carey left the room and came back just as quickly, water and aspirin in hand. She sat on the edge of the bed, looking at me with a concerned doctor look as I took the pills and drank the water. She took the empty glass from me and stood up, "Take a nap and I will check on you after I get lunch sorted." Carey went to take a step when I grabbed her elbow.

"Lay with me, please?" I bit my lip as the nerves came from nowhere again. This woman made me nervous for all the strangest reasons but, all the right ones. "It's one of the many things I have dreamt about sharing with you for a long time." I wiggled her elbow, "We can talk about where I'm taking you on our first date?"

I watched as she blushed and tried to hold back the grin on her face. Carey set the glass down on the side table, "I will do you one better." She walked out of my gentle grip. Moving to the bookshelf she bent over as she looked over the perfectly placed books. She freed one from the shelf and walked back, "Scoot over."

I smiled and slid to the other side of the bed just enough to give her room to get in but not enough that our bodies wouldn't touch. I couldn't hold back the soft sigh when I felt her arm come around my shoulder and guide me closer. I rolled on to my side, snuggling up into her, my hand finding its way to settle on her stomach as if it always belonged there. I watched as she grinned wider, her hand covering mine on her stomach as she opened the book. Finding the first page she began to read out loud.

It only took a few sentences to recognize what she was reading. My own smile growing wider with every word that she read, her soft smooth voice adding the perfect inflections to the story. I held on to the woman I loved tighter as I drifted off to sleep, listening to her read the Chronicles of Narnia to me.

Chapter 12

The sudden chill in the room woke me up. I shifted in the bed ever so slightly, feeling the pain from my wrist, but also feeling completely rested. I ran my hand over the pillow where it lay, hoping to find a warm shoulder lying across from me.

My hand found nothing but the cool expanse of my bed. I pushed myself up and looked around the bed, I was the only occupant. I sat up in the bed, facing the opposite wall. I began to wonder if everything that happened was a dream. That I had medicated myself into one of the best dreams ever, but that it was only a dream. I sighed, pushing my messy hair back. The room was darker than when I had fallen asleep. The curtains were drawn, darkening the room even more. I turned around in the bed to the only soft light in the room. I pulled at the tangled blankets to free myself from their soft imprisonment. I wanted to shut the light off and go back to sleep. Idly thinking I could will myself back into a dream where I woke up next to her.

When I swung my legs free from the bed, I looked up at the origin of the soft light. My heart finding gentle relief, it wasn't a dream.

Carey was sleeping soundly in the chair I had climbed on earlier in the day. Her chin was tucked against her shoulder, her chest moving up and down slow and evenly. An opened book was pressed against her chest with one hand holding it there. A blanket half covered her legs propped up on a stool. I stared, letting the image burn itself into my memory for when I wake up and doubt if she was real.

I quietly got out of the bed and walked over to Carey. I didn't want to wake her. She looked so peaceful and so beautiful as she slept, I didn't dare to wake her for my own selfish needs to hear her voice again. When I reached for the book, slowly pulling it from her hand, she woke up, murmuring something.

Her eyes opened and met mine. Carey cleared her throat and sat up in the chair quickly, "Frankie, I'm sorry. I think I fell asleep." She reached over and set the book in her hands on the stack next to her, making movements to get up, "You seemed to be in a lot of pain after you fell asleep, I snuck out of the bed and decided to read a little. I didn't want to leave you until you settled into a deeper sleep." She smiled at me, "I will head to the other room." I watched her eyes drift to the clock on the dresser. It was a little past two in the morning, "It's late." Her nervousness was still present but much less than earlier. I wanted to break her from it permanently. There was no reason for her to ever be nervous or afraid for being in my room or close to me.

I leaned forward, my hand settling on her arm gently holding her in the chair. She turned to me, the look on her face questioning if I needed something else. I silenced any words she dared to utter with a kiss, a soft, gentle kiss. One that went no further than our lips touching in an innocent way. I sighed, leaning my forehead against hers. "Be warned, I will be doing that any chance I get." I took a deep breath, enjoying the soft smell of her shampoo and the warmth she seemed to always radiate. "Stay with me, Carey." It came out as a whisper, one tinged with nerves and hope.

Carey's hand came up, her fingers tracing my cheek before stopping against it, "As you wish." She held my eyes with her for a few moments. A small smile drifting across her face.

Carey dropped her hand, leaving me with a small shiver at the loss of contact. She stood up, stretching, "I will be right back. I'm desperate to get out of these muddy jeans."

As she walked past me, she placed her hand on my back. Letting it trail down as she stepped around the stack of books, and exiting the room. I had a momentary thought of offering to help her. I chastised myself for thinking such an inappropriate thought when we were just starting. But, her touches, her looks and that smile sent so much want and cravings in me. It would be hard to keep with simple kisses and not move faster than my heart wanted, but my body desired.

I missed her instantly and quickly busied myself with fixing the bed to make room for her. I had a desire to change the sheets and all the bedding. Knowing that I had slept fitfully for the last few days in a sweaty medicated state. I smoothed out the sheets and fluffed the pillows, wondering what side of the bed she normally slept on. I was caught up in the small details, pulling on edges of blankets and straightening corners that I didn't notice Carey come back into the room.

"Frankie, I can sleep in the other room if it makes you comfortable." Her voice was low but carried through the room.

I turned quickly to the doorway, smiling at the view of Carey in baggy blue flannel pants and wearing a Property of the NYPD t-shirt. I smirked at her shirt, "I thought you were a doctor?" I pointed at the grey shirt with a yellow and blue badge in the middle.

Carey glanced down at the front, smiling sheepishly, "I am. This was a gift from one of my admirers at the hospital. She is a police officer I met once I moved to the city."

A strange shot of jealousy ran through my body, "An admirer?" I tried to keep the jealous tone to a minimum. I knew I had no real right to be jealous. When she told me that it had been years where as it had been days and hours for me, I understood that there could be others, admirers, lovers and even girlfriends in the time I was missing. I knew I should accept it, but it didn't mean I had to. I didn't want to think of anyone touching her before me.

Carey nodded, moving closer to the bed, "An admirer yes." She stood in front of me, she was about to reach for my hand when I shivered. The room had grown colder in the short amount of time I was out of bed.

Carey motioned to the bed, "Which side do you prefer?"

I kept my eyes on Carey, trying to sort out the unfounded jealousy coursing around in my body, settling itself firmly into my mind. "Um, I usually sleep in the middle."

Carey brushed past me, "I usually sleep on the left side." She crawled into the bed and scooted over to the left, then held her hand out to me. "Come, warm up and I will tell you about my admirer. Since I can see the questions all over your face, Frankie."

I let out an embarrassed sigh, taking her hand and letting her guide me into the bed. As I slid in, pulling the blankets up, "I know that time was not on our side and that there might have been one or two people, admirers that could have kept you occupied in the time I was silent." I wanted to scoot next to her, feel her warm body pressed against mine, but it didn't feel right. I just rolled on my side so I could look at her, laying my head in the freshly fluffed pillows.

"There were admirers yes. Many." Carey looked over at me as she sat against the headboard. She dropped her hand down and found mine. Pulling it closer to her. Her fingers lacing into mine, "Frankie, I won't lie to you." Her head tilted, her eyes meeting mine, "I moved to New York shortly after your last letter. I pushed myself into work at the hospital I had chosen on the advice of your grandmother and you. And for you."

I squeezed her hand, "Carey, it is okay. I understand." I suddenly didn't want to talk about Carey with others.

She continued on, determination in her voice, "I had many ask me out on dates, send me flowers, candy and even one mix tape. All of them ranging from fellow doctors, nurses, firefighters and the occasional celebrity that I treated. They seemed relentless in breaking my walls down to figure out why the quiet brunette doctor always went home alone." Carey's thumb ran softly over my fingers as she took a breath, "There was no one that captured my heart like you Frankie. The only one that came close was the police officer, but she soon became my best friend and constant therapist in the days I felt like you were forever away. The few times I saw you, those were the hardest after. I threw myself deeper into my work. It was Annie who kept my mind on task with my heart."

I cringed when the words hit my ears. My thoughts running rampant at the relationship Carey had with this Annie. I looked away from Carey, I knew the jealousy in my eyes was thick. I shifted in the bed. When I did, Carey's grip on my hand tightened. Silently asking for my attention back to her.

Carey let out a slow breath, "She could never compare to you. No one could, and no one will." Her warm brown eyes had a sheen to them. Carey smiled the tears back, "How could I ever love another when you have my whole heart Frankie?"

Her words filled my heart, "Carey." I sat up in the bed, moving closer to her. The jealousy I felt melted into sadness. Sadness in knowing how much Carey had to suffer, "I love you." It came out softer than I intended, but I had no idea what else to say. I just stared into the eyes of the woman who I loved and would defy time to stay by her side as long as I could.

Carey smiled as she leaned forward, whispering, "And I love you." The kiss took me by surprise. It was soft but full of purpose. I felt her hand come up to my cheek, her touch warm, as her hand slid across it and to the back of my head. Pulling me closer to her to allow the kiss to deepen. I let the moan I had stifled out, as well as the desire I was holding in. My hand found its way to her hip. I gripped on to Carey and used her as leverage to pull my body flush against hers. I smiled against the kiss when I heard her gentle moan. Carey's tongue glided against my top lip followed by a light nip, as this was her way of asking me for more. My heart pounded with my body, but it was my mind that was asking me to slow down. I wanted Carey and I knew the moment I gave her tongue permission, I would lose all control I had, the little I had left.

I leaned my head back slowly, breaking the contact of her lips with mine. Allowing the both of us to take much needed breaths. "What happened to the first date rule?" My voice was heavy with lust and frustration of stopping what I very much wanted.

Carey blushed, a wide smile following with the rise of color across her cheeks. "Whenever I'm near you, all rules beg to be broken." She rolled away from me to lay on her back. I instinctively snuggled into her as if her body was a magnet and mine was made of steel. I rested my chin on her shoulder, staring at the angled features of the flushed woman. Carey was truly stunning, even more so close up. The longer I ogled her the more my libido began to rev up again. I cleared my throat, "So, our first date. Where would you like to go? Do?"

Carey's arm snaked under me, her hand resting against my back. The smile still bright on her face as she stared at the ceiling. I could feel her heart pound from across her body, I smiled knowing that she was struggling just as much with a hyperactive libido. "Actually, I'm taking you out." She turned quickly, looking deep into my eyes, "But it's a surprise. A first date I have been planning for years." She winked at me, "We should probably get some sleep, though." She turned back to stare at the ceiling, holding me tightly.

I moved closer to her, laying my body flat against hers. My arm moving across her stomach to allow my hand to settle on the gentle curve between her stomach and the edge of her hip. I had to close my eyes tight when I heard her sigh and tremble when my hand brushed the top of her hip. I mumbled against her neck, "Yes, we need to sleep."

I kept my eyes closed and focused on matching my breaths with hers to chase away the thoughts of what her skin would feel like against mine. Finally falling into a warm and safe sleep in her arms.

The rattle of my phone vibrating against wood next to my head, woke me up. I was in a hazy state, coming out of a deep sleep and reaching blindly for my phone. I mashed it against my ear answering it, "what."

"Frankie! I'm going to kick your ass a million and a half times! I almost had to send in the old people rescue squad if you didn't finally answer me!" Amy's voice was loud, bordering on shrill. I went to sit up when I heard a soft mumble coming from the brunette's head pressed against my chest. I grinned, my hand running over Carey's hair making her snuggle deeper into me. I pressed back into the pillow "Amy. Relax and lower your voice. If you wake up Carey, I will hang up on you."

"Whooooaaaaa, wait! Did you say Carey? The one and only mysterious brunette letter writer?"

I let my hand drift from the soft hair to the strong shoulder, my fingers moving on their own as they traced patterns. "Yes, that Carey. The only Carey I ever talk about." I glanced down at the sleeping woman, the smile growing wider at the simple fact one more wish of mine had come true. I had woken up with her in my arms. "Speak, Amy."

"I think I'm speechless! You finally got your girl! You have to tell me everything! What's she like? You ask her to marry you yet? You guys turn your love story into a NC-17 rating, yet?"

"Speechless, huh? Amy, get to the point. Please."

I could feel the smile on Amy's face, "Ok, ok. I just wanted to tell you I will be down this weekend. Unless you have other important plans."

"Not so far." I looked back at Carey, "I want you to meet her Amy." I drifted away, getting lost in the features in my own private sleeping beauty. I barely heard the rest of what Amy had to say. I mumbled I would see her in a few days and hung up just as Carey began to stir awake.

She stretched, leaning away from my body. I immediately missed the contact.

"Sorry about using you as a pillow all night. I hope I didn't drool on you." Carey sat up, running a hand over my sleep shirt, checking for any drool spots as she smiled.

I sat up with her, setting my phone on to the bedside table. "I wouldn't hold it against you if you did." I slid out of the bed. I had a sudden urge to get out of bed and start the day, the first day with her, "I'm going to shower and then, I will start on making breakfast." I walked to the curtains, throwing them back to let the morning light fill the room up. I smiled as the warmth touched the bare areas of my skin. I turned to look at Carey, grinning at the sheer beauty of the woman. "Today is day one."

Carey smiled and looked at me sideways. "Day one?"

I nodded, walking to the bed and crawling over to her. I hovered in front of her face, my lips brushing hers, "Day one of the rest of our lives together." I kissed her quick and deep, pulling away the second I felt her hands on my upper arms. I knew if I didn't it, we would end up spending day one tangled in sheets. I crawled back out of the bed and to my dresser, picking out clean clothes. "Take your time. I will be downstairs in the kitchen." I glanced back to see a flushed brunette sitting in the middle of the bed, blinking at me as she licked her lips. Carey nodded slowly as I walked out of the room.

The cold shower helped to focus my libido on other things. Like trying to find the pots and pans I needed to make a proper breakfast. I was digging around in the cabinets above the stove, cursing silently. I had been looking for the last five minutes determined not to give up and resort to milk and cereal.

"Did you look in the pantry? That's where I kept the frying pan."

I couldn't hold back the slight sigh that fell from me at the sound of her voice, I shook my head without turning to her. "I forgot there was a pantry. I have been eating only cereal and take out since I have moved here." I went to move from the cabinet, when I came face to face with Carey holding the frying pan I had been looking for.

She was dressed in a grey V-neck t-shirt that fit her perfectly and dark fitted blue jeans. Her hair was down and flowed over her shoulders in a way that made me want to reach out and brush it away.

She continued to hold out the frying pan to me, I was too busy staring at her that I forgot about cooking.

"Um, I can make breakfast if you would like Frankie." I watched her swallow, I was making her nervous with my staring.

I shook my head and grabbed the pan, "I may not be a five-star chef, but I can make eggs." I waved her over to the table, "Sit and tell me about the work you do in the hospital." I turned, breaking my stare to focus on digging in the fridge. "What kind of doctor are you, Dr. Murphy?"

Carey laughed lightly, sitting down at the table with a cup of fresh coffee I had made before my pan search began. "I'm an Oncologist now, still working in fertility research on the side, but it was your grandmother who inspired the change from research medicine to actual treatment of patients. She always told me my bedside manner was one that could heal on itself alone."

I looked up from the bowl of eggs and milk I was attempting to turn into an omelet, I bit my lip to hold back the tears forming from what I was about to say. "Thank you for being there for her. When I couldn't..." I shook my head, squeezing the tears back.

"Frankie. She loved you." Carey stood up and walked over to me. Her hand pulling my chin to look at her. "You know it was her that told me about you. The moment I knocked on her door, the newspaper ad for a room for rent in my hand. She took one look at me, smiled and immediately said, "You should meet my granddaughter. Mrs. Owen sorted out a broken woman, put her back together and pushed her in the direction of her true love...you." Carey let her hand drop from my chin when my eyes locked on to hers, "Every day I sat with her and told her about the letters, she would tell me that she knew I was the one for you."

Carey smiled, "Your grandmother was special. In a way, that I'm not sure I can ever explain other than she was magical." she looked around the cottage, "This place is magical. Natty tried telling me that your grandmother had mystical gifts. I would ignore it because I'm so deeply rooted in the hard evidence of science. But then, you fell into my life, the letters, and the time difference. When I went to ask your grandmother about it, she would only tell me that the best magicians never revealed their secrets. In time, I gave up on finding the science and just believed in the magic of our love. Your grandmother saved me by guiding me back to my heart and helped me find the one purpose of living again. To find love."

Carey took a step back from me, "The day she passed away, I was with her. She was happy, ready and not afraid. She told me to do everything in my power to get to you, that she would find you in your time and give you the old grandma push to keep you on your path. That day she pressed her necklace into my hand, asking me to place it in her old blue jewelry box she hid in the barn. She then told me to tell you." Carey paused, wiping away the tears I had no idea were rolling down my face, "To tell you that she will always love you and that when you are in this cottage, she will be with you. She also told me to tell you when I finally met you that you can stop asking for forgiveness, you have nothing to be forgiven for."

I smiled and let out the soft sob, I wiped at my eyes as the tears were flowing down my face. My heart felt instantly lighter and warmer. I glanced up at the table where Carey's steaming cup of coffee sat.

The shimmery image I had seen in the field by the gas station formed at the empty seat next to the cup, slowly shifting into a clear image of my grandmother. She was smiling at me, placing her hand over her heart. I felt my own heart grow warm, so much so I had to place my hand over it. I kept my eyes on my grandmother. She winked at me and nodded at Carey. I heard her voice in my head, "Live within the love you two have. You will need nothing else, Francesca."

In a blink my grandmother was gone. I only felt Carey's hand on my lower back, her voice filled with concern, "Frankie? Are you okay?" My heart was still warm but now it felt different. It felt healed, free from the last lingering regrets I had about missing out on the last few moments of my grandmother. She had planned everything and she was truly magical in a way that I never wanted an explanation for. She had sorted out my broken heart and brought me to Carey.

I looked at Carey, grinning, "More than anything." I wiped the last of the tears away and nudged Carey with my shoulder, "Go, and sit down. I have breakfast to finish."

Carey looked in my eyes with concern. I nudged her again, "Go! Sit and tell me all about New York City."

I finished making breakfast as Carey told me all about the city, the hospital she worked at and the view from her large apartment in Brooklyn. I let her ramble, enjoying the way her eyes lit up when she talked about her favorite patients. Carey was a passionate woman when she let her guard down.

We sat at the table well past the end of our okay omelets I had made. Carey looked up at the clock, "Oh wow, I have rambled for almost two hours." she stood up, picking up my plate with hers.

I stood up with her, "I like it when you ramble." I followed her into the kitchen, setting the coffee cups into the sink.

Carey blushed, "I tend to do that when I get a chance. I rarely feel comfortable enough with anyone to talk more than just business." She rinsed the plates, "I will finish cleaning up. Go grab your coat and meet me by the barn, Frankie."

I wiped my hands with a towel. "Okay?"

Carey grinned, reaching for the towel. Her golden brown eyes smiling with her, "Our first date starts now." she brushed her arm against mine, her face moving closer to mine as she whispered, "You wouldn't want to be late for it, now would you?"

I took a deep breath, the feelings this woman brought out in me in small touches and whispers. I was beyond addicted. I shook my head slowly, swallowing down the urge to kiss her silly, "Not at all."

"I thought so." Carey turned back to the sink, back to rinsing off the dishes. Smiling to herself, satisfied with the reaction she received from me.

I ran upstairs, grumbling when I couldn't find my favorite coat. Cursing more when I realized it was lost to the accident when the paramedics cut it up to get to my broken wrist. I had to settle for one of my older leather jackets that was slightly too big for me, but fit. I ran back downstairs and past the now empty kitchen. I could see Carey standing outside by the barn, wearing a brown leather jacket, twirling a set of keys around her fingers as she looked out over the glistening ocean.

The day was absolutely perfect the moment I stepped out of the cottage. It was just warm enough to keep the jackets on, the sun was bright and the sky was blue. Emulating the perfect calm feeling I was now carrying.

Carey smiled as she saw me, holding her hand out for me to take. She said nothing as our hands met, only turning to walk towards old blue sitting in front of the barn doors. I looked over my shoulder and saw the shiny silver sports car parked next to it. I went to say something when Carey spoke, "I only bought it because it was fast. I figured if we met and I had to commute, I wanted something to get me to you as fast as possible." She shrugged, "I might sell it now."

Everything she said to me made me love her more, the simple things she did with purpose seemed to be all for me. I had never felt more loved or loved more in my entire life.

I let Carey guide me to the passenger side of old blue. She opened the door for me and helped me take a seat. When she climbed into the driver's seat I couldn't help it, "Where are we going?"

She shook her head, "Patience." She put old blue into gear, pushing the old truck on to the single road.

Carey could feel I was going to ask another question, she smiled and put her hand on my thigh. Squeezing it, "Stop being the investigative journalist and trust me."

I covered her hand with mine, "I have from the moment I met you." I turned her hand over so I could hold it properly.

When her fingers fell into mine, I bit my bottom lip and turned to look out my window, letting myself enjoy the ride.

I started to recognize where we were going as the scenery changed from trees to hills and the air was thick with ocean salt. I knew we were headed to the next town over. Carey pulled the truck into a parking spot along the main road that was filled with shops and restaurants. It was early afternoon and the street was filled with the occasional tourist that the town often attracted. Carey exited the truck and opened my door, taking my hand again as she helped me out.

She stood in front of me, "First, I'm taking you to lunch at my favorite place." she pointed at the small restaurant she had parked in front of. I followed Carey into the small restaurant, excited at the first stop of this first date.

The hostess smiled as she greeted Carey acknowledging the reservations Carey made for us to sit out on the back patio of the restaurant. Giving us an unbroken view of the ocean that made it feel like we were the only two people in the world. I sat across from Carey, looking out on to the ocean. "This is amazing, Carey."

She nodded, "It is. I found this place one day while I was trying to find a place to stay out here before I found the cottage." She looked out on to the ocean, "It was where I picked up the local newspaper with the ad from your grandmother." Her hand came across the table and held mine, "It is also where I read your first letter Frankie."

I looked into her eyes, making her smile more, "So basically, this is where we first met?" I felt the goosebumps as I said it.

Carey laughed. "Cheesy, I know, but yes, this is where we first met."

The waiter broke the moment and the hold Carey had on my hand, taking our drink order and filling us in on the daily specials. As soon as the young man left, Carey leaned forward, "It's your turn, tell me about you, Frankie."

I laughed, "I think you may know far more than I can tell you. I think my grandmother told you all the highlights of my life." I took a sip of water, "That reminds me, the other keeper of my secrets will be down this weekend. Amy. She has booked us all into a family dinner this coming Sunday." I paused, "If that's okay with you?"

"I think that would be perfect. I would like to thank her, for stopping me and giving me that extra push to come to you." Carey picked up her glass of wine the second the waiter set it down, "But, back to the question, where do you live aside from the cottage? Where do you work? Do you like cats? Dogs?"

"I work at Toronto Star as their lead journalist. I cover politics, major news stories and whatever could be a front page seller. I live in a small apartment in the city. One, that I'm sure is heavily neglected since I have not been back to it since before Christopher. I prefer dogs over cats, I'm a non-smoker and my astrological sign is a Libra." I grinned at Carey rolling her eyes, "And I'm completely in love with a gorgeous brunette doctor."

The waiter setting down the food distracted me from watching Carey blush again, something I began to love to do as much as possible. We ate lunch while I told Carey how I got into journalism, that I always felt there was too many stories to tell and since my grandmother always told me I had a bold voice, I figured people would listen to me.

I pushed the empty plate away, "The story that got me the job at the Star was the story of the mugger and my grandmother, the one she had me retell you." I took a breath, "My leave of absence ends in a month. I have to go back to the city then and figure out what comes next with my work, my career."

I looked up at Carey, she had been listening intently the entire time. No one I loved ever listened to me intently outside of my grandmother when I spoke. I felt so at home with this woman, so complete that I suddenly never wanted to leave this moment or the cottage. I ran my hand over the stiff linen tablecloth, "But I have plenty of time to think about that. Where are we headed next?" I would think about real life when the time was right. Now was not that time.

Carey twirled her empty wine glass, "Do you want to go back to work? Toronto?" The question was direct but soft.

I shrugged. "I'm not sure. I think I lost my passion for my work when things fell apart in my life. Toronto, I love the city but it's not where I feel at home." I smiled at her, changing the subject. I didn't want to waste more time in the past when Carey was next to me. All I wanted to think about, was what came next for us. "What's next on this date of ours?"

Carey held my eyes for a moment, I could see her thinking about something before the smile came, "Just follow me."

She stood up and held out her elbow. I wrapped my arm into hers, following her back out to the truck.

We drove out of the small town and towards the cliffs that I had always driven past on my way to and from my grandmother's as a kid, but never stopped. Carey drove on to a side road that carried us up to the top of the cliffs to the small opening where one could park and watch the sun set into the ocean. She helped me out and took my hand. Leading me to the edge of the cliffs, climbing up on to a large boulder that had a flat surface that was a perfect seat for two.

I sat next to her, our legs touching. Our hands still together. The afternoon sun graced the side of her face, picking up the small highlights in her eyes and in her hair. Making Carey even more radiant, as if she was glowing.

She turned to look at me, "This. This is where I wrote the letter where I professed my love for you. On a day exactly like this." She looked down at our hands together, before looking back in my eyes, "Since that moment I dreamt of the moment I could bring you here, sit with you and look into the beautiful hazel eyes that sparkled whenever they looked my way and tell you." Carey's other hand came to rest against my cheek, "I love you, Francesca."

Even though she had said it a handful of times already, in writing and in person. This time, it felt different. It felt real and beyond permanent. The four words filtered through my ears and carried down to my heart, wrapping themselves around it like a protective cage. A cage that would never open for anyone but her. She held the key to my heart and would forever. The air around us grew thick with promises of a future with each other. The sounds of the gentle breeze mixing with the distant waves pushing water against obstacles on the edge of the shore was setting the soundtrack to this memory we were making. One that I knew I would look back on vividly and recount it to my own grandchildren as if they were sitting here with us.

"You know, every time you say that you love me, the gold in your eyes around the iris glows." I reached for the hand on my cheek, tugging it down so I could kiss her palm. "Could you be any more perfect?"

"I'm far from perfect, Frankie." She said it sheepishly. She stood up from the rock, looking down at me. Carey now held both my hands, "Come. One more stop on this date." She pulled me up and I pulled back. Gently forcing her into my arms for a hug. I loved how fit perfectly in each other's arms, as if we were meant to be this way. I kissed her neck before laying my head in the space between her neck and shoulder. "I have a confession to make."

I heard her mumbled an oh really, next to my ear.

I smiled against her shoulder, "I used to look at these cliffs from the back patio of the cottage. Day dreaming as a little girl of the day I could come up here with someone I loved. A prince or a shining knight from one of the stories that were read to me nightly. Even as a teenager I would stare this way, dreaming of the moment when I could stand in this spot, like this. I even went so far as to plan out my own proposal scenario, no longer willing to wait for my knight in shining armor or the prince to climb the castle." I leaned back in Carey's arms so I could look in her eyes, "Ever since that first letter you have made every one of my dreams come true. You are my knight in shining armor."

Carey smirked, "At least you didn't call me a princess." She bent forward and kissed the tip of my nose, "We are turning into our own little fairytale, aren't we?"

I nodded and kissed the edge of her jaw, "We are. One that I think will always be my favorite one." I backed out of her arms, grabbing her hand to lead her back to the truck. "Take me to the last destination on this date of ours. I'm more than ready for the good night kiss."

We drove back to the cottage. Carey parked old blue in front of the barn and told me to meet her on the back patio while she went upstairs. I made a quick stop in the kitchen to grab the last bottle of expensive wine and two glasses. I sat in the chair closest to the edge of the patio and held my glass of wine. I could feel the permanent smile on my face and my heart. For the first time in my life I didn't care about tomorrow or what the future held. I was finally living as my grandmother did, day by day and to the fullest. All because of the quiet, shy brunette that now walked out on to the patio and set a brown package on the table between us.

I handed Carey a glass of wine, my eyes looking at the package, "What is that?"

Carey smiled, pushing it closer to me, "Open it."

I raised an eyebrow at her, setting my wine glass down, I picked up the package. I tore open an edge and as I tore the paper down, my heart raced. I raced through the rest of the paper and stared at the dark red bound book in my hands. My fingers running over the old cover and spine.

"Your grandmother had told me you had lost the copy she had when you were a teenager. That you forgot it on a bus and even though you searched and searched, you could never find it."

"I wasn't paying attention on the trip back from the museum. I was too distracted by some boy I had a crush on. I borrowed it from her for a book report, because it was my favorite." I looked at Carey, "It took me a year to forgive myself for losing it." I turned over the older than time copy of Shakespeare's "Twelfth Night". The one book I coveted more than any other in my grandmother's entire collection. "The story was what inspired me to write. Viola was an inspiration that I could do anything in the world I wanted too."

I stood up, clutching the book to my chest as I moved to the railing, "I was made fun of carrying it with me everywhere that whole week instead of those silly teen magazines every girl read. I even wrote my full name in the back cover under my grandmothers." I sighed, "Then, I lost it. It felt like I had lost a part of her with that book. She told me it was no big deal, a book could never replace our connection."

I looked back at Carey, "What I wouldn't give to have the original now."

Carey stood up, moving towards me. Leaning against the rail she tapped at the top of the book, "Open it up. Read from the back for me."

I furrowed my brow and removed the book from its place against my chest. I shook my head, "I can quote the entire thing to you, as I spent most of my summers here buried in this book before bed." I went to recite the first lines as I slid my hand to the back cover, pushing it open. There in my bubbly teenage handwriting directly underneath my grandmother's elegant handwriting sat. "Francesca A. Owen."

I stared at it, "How..."

"Magic is the best way to explain it." Carey's hand came to the necklace around her neck, "And the gentle guidance of this. I found that book two weeks ago in a vintage book shop near my apartment in New York. I was digging for some old anatomy books for my collection when I felt this incredible force pushing me into the literature section. My fingers moved on their own as I moved across the ancient spines of books when they settled on that book. Sending bolts of lightning through the tips. I always remembered the story she told me about you losing the book and I would always look when I was in a shop but never found the exact book or one close to it."

I listened as my own fingers traced the two names in faded ink.

"There are only two Francesca's I know of in the world."

I closed the book, pressing it back to my chest and looked up at Carey. Her smile faded a little when she saw the look in my eyes, "I just thought that it needed to come home, to you." She was stumbling.

I closed the small gap between us, my free hand going to her cheek as my mouth followed quickly behind. Kissing Carey deeper and harder than I had. I pressed myself flush against her body when I heard the groan followed by her hands tangling in my hair to hold me even closer. I opened my mouth wider, gently coaxing hers to do the same. When our tongues met I felt my desire rise and my control slowly dissipate. When we parted I licked my lips, enjoying the lingering taste of wine and her lip gloss.

I said nothing. My hand left its soft prison in her hair and trailed down her arm. Finding her hand still tangled in my hair, I linked my fingers into hers. I turned and walked back into the cottage, Carey following me up the stairs to my bedroom. Since my hand was locked around hers, she had no choice but to follow me.

Chapter 13

The air grew thick the moment my hand left hers to open the door to my bedroom, both of us knowing what was to come. I knew what I wanted next even though my nerves were beginning to override the desire that had flooded in my body. I swallowed hard, walking to the bookshelf, sliding the book back into the spot it once held.

I then turned to look at Carey standing in the doorway, looking everywhere but at me. "Um, I hope I didn't overstep my bounds. I just know how much you loved her books and, I...I couldn't help it when I found it."

"It's perfect. You are perfect, Carey." I stood up and walked to the middle of the room, holding my hand out to the fidgeting brunette, "Come here." My voice dropped, heavy with want.

Carey kept her head down even as she took my hand, "I might have gotten a little excited, but, it felt like I had found a long lost treasure." She was still trying to explain away the reaction I had when I held the one book that I loved and sought out for years. I had no way of explaining my reaction; I just knew I wanted to show her.

When she was close enough, I let go of her hand. Sliding both of my hands to her flushed cheeks. My body moved on its own and pressed against hers. I looked into her eyes. I could see the same desire in them that I knew was reflected in mine. It had only been a couple of days being in this woman's physical presence and I couldn't wait any longer.

"Carey, stop overthinking. Anything you do is with purpose and filled with love. I could see in the first scribbled words of your first letter." I paused, swallowing hard trying to keep my libido in check as I could feel and hear her heartrate pick up. The smells of her perfume and shampoo mixing with her body heat was beginning to drive me wild. "I may be a journalist, but I could never put down into words how you make me feel every minute you are around me and that every little thing you do makes me love you more." I took a deep breath, leaning forward, inches away from the soft lips I already cherished, "Let me show you."

I didn't hesitate a second longer to give Carey a chance to say anything else. I kissed her, slow at first but then I began to deepen the kiss as my control was slipping through my fingers like sand. I wanted to make love to the woman in my arms all night. Show her how perfect she was to me and how much I craved to touch her.

It took a second for Carey to respond, but then I felt Carey's tongue move against my lips as her hands came around to my waist, pulling me hard into her. We both stumbled at the quick motion of her pulling us closer together. My knees almost gave out as I felt her leg slip between mine on accident to balance the two of us. There was no going back as lightning coursed through my body as her hands gripped my thighs and held onto me tightly against her leg.

I moved my arms to encircle Carey wanting her even closer to me. Even as our bodies were melded together, our breasts pressing into each other. When Carey bit lightly at my bottom lip, all I could think of was the feel of her bare skin against my hands and how that had to happen now.

Kissing her still, my hands wandered slowly from Carey's waist to the edge of her soft t-shirt and slid up and under. The first touch of the skin on her back was hot on my fingertips. I felt her flex as skin brushed against skin, making her push back into my hand out of reaction. Her skin was soft and the muscles underneath toned. I pushed my hands up further when I heard Carey let out a small moan as she felt my hands travel further.

I suddenly felt Carey push herself hard against my hip, making her gasp at the involuntary movement of her body. I let out a small moan against her mouth, knowing that I had such an effect on her. It drove me insane and I couldn't control myself any longer. I moved my hands from her back, across her stomach and up. My fingertips stopped right at the bottom swell of her breasts. I could feel her heart pounding as I hesitated for one second before I took the last few inches to touch skin I had fantasized about for far too long.

I took my time, dragging my fingers over the fabric and finding the edge of her bra that would allow me access to her. I kissed her neck slowly, working my way back up to her lips. I was determined to make this last all night even as my own body began to ache and scream for more.

My middle finger slipped under the fabric and grazed the edge of soft, heated skin. I moaned and moved my hand back, about to push the bra out of my way when Carey mumbled and gripped my upper arms.

"Frankie, wait." Her words came out almost breathless.

I barely heard it, continuing to the corner of her mouth before I kissed her hard again. My hands were still on a mission.

Carey leaned back from my kiss, "Wait. Please." She reached up and grabbed my cheek. Making me stop all movements and focus on the golden brown eyes that were now riddled with emotions. Two of them distinctly being desire and fear.

I immediately withdrew my hands from the warm confines of her shirt and skin, letting them rest on her hips. "Are you okay?" My heart was now pounding, from our kiss and now from what I saw in her eyes.

Carey swallowed hard, her face dropped as she took a step back, "I don't know if I can do this." She moved away from me, folding her arms close to her chest.

It was my turn to panic and ramble, "Is this going too fast? I can slow down." I suddenly felt embarrassed with my empty hands hanging there as if she was still in my grasp. I went to reach for Carey, beginning to feel desperation in having some sort of physical contact with her. "Carey, you are irresistible and I know you have the first date rule and it probably extends to what I had planned when I dragged you up here. But, you have to know how much I love you and how much I want you in every aspect. You drive me crazy like no other and, I don't know. Maybe this is going too fast."

Carey cut me off, "It's not anything like that Frankie." She looked up at the ceiling, smiling painfully as she let out a nervous laugh, "You make me feel the same thing, maybe a thousand times more. If you only knew how many times a night I let myself drift off into thoughts of what it would be like together. Touching your skin, our skin touching, all of it."

I felt tears as she spoke. I moved closer to her, placing my hand on her folded arm. "But, what Carey? What is it?"

She closed her eyes tightly, taking a deep breath trying to summon courage, "I'm afraid, Frankie." She opened her eyes and looked directly in mine. "I'm afraid because even though you are the one who put my heart back together...I haven't been with anyone since the one who destroyed my heart." Carey paused, "It's been two years and I haven't touched anyone or wanted to since I met you. I'm afraid for a multitude of reasons that my logical mind won't allow my passion and desire for you to overcome the fear."

I cringed at her words and the tone in her voice, I could feel how long it had been for her to wait for the intimate touches of another. Whereas, for me it had only been a few months. I had a sudden pang of anger in my body. One for the ever present and stupid time difference between us and for the one who had broken Carey as badly as she did.

I shook my head, "Whoever broke your heart, let them go Carey. Or they will keep having some sort of power over you and us." I went to drop my hand to walk back to the window as the afternoon light began to turn into a deep orange color. I needed the waves to calm the waves inside of me.

"I gave up on life, Frankie. That's why I came to this sleepy ocean side town. I was going to lose myself in the endless water and resign to being alone." Carey stood in the spot she seemed to be rooted to; she kept talking to me even as my back was turned. All of the tension in the room had shifted from heightened passions to one of unknowing certainty.

"The one who broke my heart, shattered it. My first real love, well what I thought was a real love. She and I had met in high school and dated throughout high school, college and to the edge of me leaving for MIT. Marriage was on the horizon, children's names were tossed around and plans to move together were made." Carey was speaking slowly, in a way that it was apparent she was recounting painful memories.

I kept my back to her to hide the hurt and jealousy I was beginning to feel as I listened to how someone else had her heart.

"A month before I was ready to leave for MIT, she got a job in Toronto. A good, amazing, high paying job at some lawyer's office that she was beyond excited for. We agreed that we would try a long distance relationship for a few months. I wanted her to be happy when I knew I was going to be knee deep in studies." Carey moved to the bookshelf, sitting on the arm of the chair. "Three weeks before I moved here, and met your grandmother and set into motion the wheels of change. She called me and off handedly revealed to me that she no longer loved me, that she wanted to end it. She had found someone else that made her feel electric, loved in a way she could never imagine and that she no longer saw a future with me."

I stared out at the distant lighthouse, my own emotions swirling around, "I fully understand what you are feeling, Carey. The same thing happened to me." I turned to look at her, "But all of those feelings of hurt and sadness were replaced by you and how much I love you and that I literally cannot see anything past you."

Carey glanced at me, "What hurts more than anything after the fact was when I found out she was sleeping with her boss, the lawyer she worked for." She stood up from the chair so she could face me, "That night when I first saw you I had spent the day in the city meeting up with her to collect some random things I wanted back. Standing in her apartment while she dumped things into a box, I looked around at the way she was living. Not recognizing in any way the woman I had once thought I loved completely. The pictures in her apartment echoed her new life in that city, her and the lawyer and her new friends."

I shrugged, "That was the past, Carey. Let it be the past, let us be the future." I said it softly not wanting to upset Carey. There was something in the back of my mind telling me that this all felt all too familiar, more so than a similar circumstance of a cheating lover.

"Frankie. When I first met your grandmother the second thing she told me after telling me I needed to meet you was that our fates would intertwine. I had no idea what she was talking about until that night when I first met you and you were with Christopher. Do you remember when you told me to let your past become your future? And not to interfere?"

I sighed, "Yes and I don't regret it. My future became you. My future will always be you." I struggled with the emotions that wanted to flow out faster than I wanted. I didn't want to scare Carey any more than she was.

Carey nodded, "I know. I also don't regret it. But, I left out a one small thing that I didn't think was important until just now. Maybe my heart is seeking a way to purge the last horrible things in my life."

I stared at Carey. Things were jumbled in my head at all Carey was telling me. "Just say it." I wanted to know why she was still so hesitant and afraid of this perfect love we both had stumbled upon.

She took a deep breath, "Our fates intertwined the moment I saw Christopher with you that first night our eyes met. I immediately recognized him as the lawyer in the pictures in the apartment. That's why I wrote to you that I wanted to fix what you two had. My past was corrupting your happiness and I panicked because I didn't want you to experience the heart shattering hurt I did. I would have done anything to protect you from it, but then you asked me not to." Carey cringed, swallowing back tears, "I did as you asked and then he kept popping up, telling me you and him were--"

I cut Carey off as the small familiar clues became the strange revelation that hit me suddenly, "Wait. Ashley? Was your girlfriend's name Ashley?"

Carey nodded, staring at the floor. "Yes."

I let out a breath that I had no idea I had been holding. I ran a hand over my hair, things suddenly making so much more sense. Carey's fear, her strange behavior when we talked about the moments where we almost met and Christopher prevented it. He had been meddling in her life in more ways than one. Things were making sense to me now and why she was so afraid of what we had and taking it to that extra step. Our fates had intertwined and in the most painful way of all for her. I had only thought it was because of my ignorance of the time and space between us when it was so much more. My stupid former fiancé had been the catalyst of her heartbreak. I stood blank, letting everything sink in. I was no longer angry and all of the feelings of jealousy disappeared like a quick summer breeze. My heart ached for Carey and I only felt embarrassed for having the slightest anger towards this incredibly strong woman.

I whispered, "The fate of one becomes another's destiny." My hand holding onto the necklace around my neck. I had been closer to Carey for longer than I thought. I fully understood why my grandmother had set her magic into motion; we were destined for each other. Both of our hearts just had to be shattered so that they could be rebuilt on true love.

Carey didn't hear me; she shifted and jammed her hands into her pockets, "I never wanted to tell you Frankie. And god knows I want you more than I needed air, but I can't with my heart holding onto this last bit of fear. I know you and him are nothing, I know that I have your heart and you will always have mine and I know that I love you and will love you for the rest of my life. I just need a little more time before we...." She waved an awkward hand in the space between us.

"Carey, take all the time you need." I walked over to the woman, pulling her hands free from the jean pockets so I could hold them, "I promise as I have before, you are it for me. There is no one else." I looked up into her sad, tired eyes, "I love you. You know that because I will tell you a hundred times a day. I don't care about the past and the assholes we both have in it. When I told you this morning that today was day one, I meant it." I took a slow breath as I smiled, "As much as it will kill me to wait to see you naked, I will wait for it."

Carey half smiled, squeezing my hands in hers, "It kills me just as much, Frankie." She tugged on my hands, wrapping my arms around her waist so she could envelope me in a hug, "Do you know how perfect you are Frankie?"

I smiled against her shoulder, kissing it softly, "I'm hardly perfect."

Carey held me tighter, "I would have waited an eternity to meet you." It came out as a gentle confession, one I knew that freed up even more of the heaviness she had been holding around her heart.

I leaned back in her arms to look in her eyes. I felt mine gloss over as I stared into the eyes of my future, "I made you wait far too long, my love." I pressed my hand against her cheek, my thumb running over her lips. Carey sighed and closed her eyes, pulling me back into the tight embrace she had me in.

I could tell how exhausted she was in the way she slightly sagged in my arms. I ended up giving in and letting her go. Suggesting that she take a nap while I ran into town to pick up more groceries for the weekend.

I had to push her towards the bed, "Go, nap. I will be gone for at least an hour. Amy requires more food than the average teenage boy. Trust me when you meet her you will fully understand."

Carey laughed lightly, her eyes beginning to sparkle as they once did, "I can go with you and help. You still have that broken wrist."

I shook my head, "You need to rest. I will manage or force old Sid to help out." I pushed her again, "One hour and I will be back. Anything you need?" I reached for my jacket when I was satisfied that Carey had actually climbed into the bed.

Carey smiled and shook her head, "The only thing I need is for you to hurry back, Frankie. This bed isn't the same without you in it."

I would have read into her comments more if it wasn't such an innocent statement. I grinned, "Is that doctor's orders?"

Carey nodded, tucking herself under the blankets, "Yes, so I suggest you follow them." She winked at me as I blew her a kiss and ran down the stairs.

I ran to old blue when I had a second thought. I ran back into the cottage and to the front sitting room. I dug around in the old cabinet where I had tucked my grandmother's old wooden jewelry box after I saw the bookshelf had been filled with books. I sat the box on the top of the cabinet and opened it up, taking out the two remaining ring boxes. I opened both of them, double checking that the two rings were still there. My plan was formulating in my head. I would also wait an eternity for Carey but, first, I would ask her to be mine for eternity.

I smiled to myself as I tucked the ring boxes back into the bigger one. I carried the wooden box back up to the bedroom. Smiling even wider when I saw Carey was already passed out and sleeping heavily. I quietly pushed a few books to the side on the shelf and set the box in an inconspicuous spot. I stood up and looked back at the sleeping brunette, knowing that I would spend the rest of my life with her. If she would have me.

Chapter 14

I spent more time in the grocery store than I expected. For some odd reason I no longer felt a sense of urgency to rush through life. She would be there when I got back, she would be there when I woke up. There was no reason to rush for anything. I could take all the time the world had to offer me to continue this slow and incredible love we had found. I smiled to myself as I set the few cloth bags full of groceries into the back of old blue. I looked around the magical little town that was starting to bustle with closing up shops for the night and heading to dinner at the few diners and restaurants around.

I leaned over the edge of the truck, smiling to myself when my eyes caught the flower shop across the street from me pulling in the flowers for the evening. I smirked, pushing off the edge of the rusted metal. I had never bought flowers for anyone in my life. She would be the first, another many firsts I had experienced in the short time Carey had been in my life. I jogged across the street to catch the young man before he draped the closed sign over the wooden door.

"Excuse me. Do you have time for a last-minute customer?" I threw a bright smile on.

The young man turned to me, an easy smile on his face.

"Of course." he held the door open for me, "I took most of them inside already. I can help you pick something out if you would like, what kind of occasion are you having?"

"The love of my life is asleep in bed and I would love her to wake up to some fresh flowers." I scanned over the masses of colored flowers. Trying to decide what kind would be perfect for her.

The young man moved towards the pile of beautiful roses set near the counter. He ran his hand over the bright yellow, red, and white blossoms. "These roses bloomed this morning, fresh as fresh can get."

I shook my head, "Roses pale in comparison to her." I met the young man's eyes as his lit up. There was a silent message passed between us. He looked directly in my eyes, I suddenly felt like he could see Carey in them and the incredible love I felt for her.

"Of course." he walked to the other side of the shop. Bending over to a huge bucket full of lilies in different colors. He took a deep breath of the fragrance they emitted, and began pulling the biggest and brightest flowers out as he spoke. "Lilies are my favorite. They are often regarded as a lesser flower compared to the popular rose, daisy, and sunflower." He moved slowly as his fingers drew over the expanse of petals set before him. I watched him, mesmerized. He knew flowers and it was as if he could speak to the flowers through his fingertips.

He continued picking when he stood up slightly, "All flowers have meaning if you choose to look past the commercial message." he turned to me, holding a large bouquet of yellow, orange, and white lilies. "Roses have always been the stand out for telling one how much you love them. But these, these little gentle elegant creatures, they are the ones that hold the true meaning of how much one can be loved. The dare one to love with all they have in their heart. Innocence, devotion, love and a sense of purity that a true love should have."

I was entranced by the young man's delicate and deliberate words. Watching him as he wrapped up the bouquet in brown paper. He continued speaking while winding twine around the bottom to hold the flowers together, "I often feel that giving the one you love lilies is telling them that they have your love until the end of time and beyond." he looked up from the stunning and perfect bouquet, "I can see in your eyes that the woman you are giving these to deserves more than a tacky rose. You carry the sparkle of a love that many are envious of, one that very few of us will ever experience."

I was silent for a moment, "It really is written all over my face, isn't it?"

The young man grinned, "Only to someone who has also found their own true love." He held out the bouquet to me. "These are on the house. I rarely get to see the workings of true and honest love carried in a person. I sell enough roses to keep me in business for the rest of my days."

I picked up the wrapped package. The bunch of flowers in my clutch was absolutely perfect. Each flower was placed in perfect synchronicity with the one next to it. It perfectly reflected Carey, her beauty and how much I loved the woman. I dug into my pocket for a few bills, "I have to pay you, these are too beautiful and the help you gave me."

The young man reached out, grabbing my arm gently to stop my digging for money. With a giant warm smile, "Just have me provide the flower arrangements for your wedding." He winked at me, handing me his business card.

I blushed and grabbed the card with my free hand. Glancing over it for his name, I nodded, "Of course I will, David." I took a deep breath, thanked him again and left the shop.

The sun was slowly dipping away but, it still invigorated me. I was eager to get back to the cottage and wake Carey up and tell her about the flowers and the experience at the flower shop. As I drove the old truck back to the cottage, the flowers on the seat next to me. I entertained the idea of letting out the last part of the conversation...the part about the wedding.

I set the groceries down in the kitchen, rushing around to get things set in their place before I walked upstairs. When I was done, I dug around and found an old glass vase that held the bunch of lilies as if they were meant to be. I breathed in their gentle scent and smiled.

She was still asleep when I pushed the bedroom door open. The light from the window cascaded through the room and laid delicately across her features. Amplifying the curves and angles of her face in a way that even the greatest painters would be envious to capture. I stared for a moment, holding the vase in my hands. When I didn't think she could be any more beautiful, I would see a picture like this in front of me. My heart would race faster, a larger smile would crawl across my face, and time would stop. Stop to the point that all that existed was her and I and the way she made my heart beat in a way that I would cherish for the rest of my days.

I had no idea how long I stood there, staring. Until she slowly shifted in the bed, rolling around and swiping away the hair that had fallen across her face. Carey half opened one eye, catching me standing in the middle of the room. She smiled sleepily and rolled over on to her side, "Hey you." Her voice was soft and raspy from the long nap she took.

"Hey you back." I walked over to her, setting the glass vase on to the bedside table. The light pushing through the glass and water. Reflecting prisms of golden and rainbow light across the bed and Carey. I sat on the edge of the bed, reaching over and pushing more soft strands of hair away from her face. Smiling more as sprinkles of light caught the accents in her eyes. Making them glow. I sighed uncontrollably at the sight, "I'm sorry for being gone longer than I promised. How did you sleep?"

I watched as her eyes drifted over to the large vase of flowers, "I probably need to sleep more. I passed out the instant my head hit the pillow. I think the last few months of sleepless nights and overworking have caught up to me." Her hand went to the lilies in the vase, her fingertips grazing the orange petal of one. "These are beautiful, Frankie. Did Natty bring these over?"

I smiled, bending forward to kiss her lightly. "I bought them for the beautiful woman I left in my bed." I ran my hand down her neck to her arm, until it was drawn to her hand. I moved closer to her on the bed as she sat up, her face creeping up with an embarrassed smile.

"For me?"

I nodded, "For you, my love. I've never bought flowers for anyone and I couldn't resist." I watched as she bent closer, taking a deep breath of the scent the lilies were beginning to fill the room with. "Carey, you make me want to do things I have never done. Reach deep into my soul to the lost hopeless romantic and do all the beautiful things you deserve."

Carey turned to look at me in the eyes, her hand squeezing mine. She bit her bottom lip as she began to flush, "Frankie, you being here with me is more than I will ever need."

I grinned at her words. I took a deep breath, "I have a little story that goes with the flowers. The young man who helped me pick them--" I smirked, "He wanted to sell me roses until I told him a rose pales in comparison to your beauty. So, he started telling me about these lilies. That they stand for eternal love, purity, innocence, devotion and to dare the one you give them to, to love you for eternity." I pulled her hand closer to my chest. Her eyes never left mine, slowly glossing over. I held our hands against me so she could feel the effect she always had on my heart, "So, I dare you Carey Murphy." I winked at her, "The best part of the story is as I was leaving, and he gave me his card and told me the flowers were on the house. That the only payment I had to give him was that he would be the man to provide the flowers for our wed..."

The front screen door of the cottage slamming cut off my words. Carey and I both looked towards the sound. I thought maybe it was the wind catching it when I heard the most familiar obnoxious but, loved voice of my best friend carry up the stairs.

"FRANKIE! Come down here and pay the cab driver. I still haven't gotten a pay check from the new job."

I let out a small chuckle, looking back to the brunette whose gaze was stuck on the open bedroom door. "And that is Amy, the best moment breaker I have ever met in my life." I stood up from the bed, still holding on to her hand. Amy hollering once again about making sure I give the driver a good tip.

"I will get her settled. Come down when you're ready." I slowly let go of her hand, "Be warned, she will interrogate you." I went to walk out of the room when I felt her tug me to stop.

I turned to Carey, my eyes wide with questioning. She slid out of the bed and said nothing as her hands cradled the sides of my face. She held me still for a split second before bending forward, her lips meeting mine in a soft, delicate way. Carey kissed me slowly at first, then drew out in to a deep, passionate dance of our lips and a gentle introduction of tongues. It was just enough to make me moan and press myself against her, my hands finding their place on her hips to hold her. I could feel the fire only she could stoke, begin to build into a bonfire of desire.

I had forgotten all about Amy, only focusing on being in this woman's arms and kissing her.

Carey broke away when the second loud "Frankie!!!" Ringing through the cottage.

I groaned and frowned, "I'm sorry."

Carey smiled, kissing my cheek, "It's okay." She leaned back in my arms, her hands still gently holding the edge of my jaw. "I just wanted to thank you for the flowers. No one has ever given me flowers with such beauty and thought behind them." She let go of me and glanced back at the vase, "I've only gotten roses, and I hate roses." She slid out of my arms, making me groan and frown harder. I folded my arms across my chest to try and trap the lingering body heat from Carey.

I turned and walked towards the stairs, when I heard Carey call softly out after me, "I accept the dare, Frankie and I will forever."

I couldn't hide the grin that exploded across my face. I didn't turn back around, knowing if I did, Amy would be left to her own devices as I attacked the woman still glowing from the setting sun.

I ran downstairs and was met with the sight of a grumpy cab driver leaning against his yellow cab. Amy appeared out of nowhere to stand behind me, "I will pay you back, I promise."

I shook my head and pushed the screen door open. I paid the cab driver off and gave him a huge tip. I turned back to the cottage and shot my best friend a look as she sat on the porch, eating.

"I thought you were coming Sunday?"

Amy shrugged through bites of a bagel, "I took a long weekend." She munched happily, "You seem irritated, you never get irritated when your bestest friend in the world graces your presence." She suddenly attacked me in a rib crushing hug, "I swear to all that is holy, you try to drive your sports car like an Andretti and wreck it like you did. I will hunt you down and kill you myself. You are my best friend and my family." I heard Amy sniffle slightly, and I felt terrible.

I took a deep breath and looked up at the cottage, my eyes drifting to the one window that lead down the hall to the bedroom where Carey was. "I love you too Amy. I promise, never again." I squeezed her tight. She leaned back in my arms and caught where my eyes were scanning. I was lost in thought of what I did, almost loosing that day when I tried to kill myself out of stupidity.

Amy shot me a look. Then, it hit her, making her stand up straighter quickly, "Oh shit! I forgot! She's here, isn't she?"

Amy turned around and scanned the house, "Where is she? Where is the great mystical brunette doctor of poetry and prose from the past?" She wiped away the few tears that had escaped, her mood suddenly turning to excitement.

Amy kept scanning, backing up to get a better view of the entire cottage. She kept going until she bumped into me. Spinning back around to meet my eyes with bright quizzical blue ones. "Have you guys? Were you guys? Did I interrupt?" she jiggled her eyebrows like a pervy little brother.

I sighed and shook my head, "No and no." I stuck out a hand and gently pushed Amy back a step, "We are taking it slow. Learning each other." I let out a breath, "And we are both ridiculously nervous about everything." I swallowed hard, "This time difference between us. Carey has waited two years, alone for me. I had no idea when I sent her the last letter the few days before I went to her that it would be it for her. Two years of waiting for me in silence." I held back the tears, "I understand her fear and nerves. But, it a makes me nervous. Nervous that this might all fall away in a heartbeat."

Amy threw an arm around my shoulder, "Love like what you two have would make any one nervous. Nervous because it's a rare thing to find. True love that you defy the world for. She waited for you that long and I'm certain she will fight for you as much as you have." She yanked at me, "Come, and introduce me to my future sister-in-law properly."

I glanced at Amy curious. Amy nudged me again, giggling, "Oh Frankie, Frankie, it's written all over your face. She is your forever. You are glowing like a newlywed."

I shook my head, trying to laugh away the nerves.

Carey was in the kitchen when Amy and I came back inside. She smiled when she saw us, "I was thinking about making dinner."

Amy grinned, "And she can cook!" she rushed over to Carey, her hand sticking out. "I know we met a few weeks ago, but hello. I'm Amy. Frankie's best friend in the world, constant devil's advocate and guidance counselor." Carey laughed as she took Amy's hand.

"Amy, it's nice to finally meet you." she looked sheepish for a moment, before whispering, "I owe you a ton of thank yous." There was a tinge of tension floating between the two. I knew what Carey was trying to say, I wanted to interrupt to avoid any of us remembering that day.

Amy shrugged, letting go of Carey's hand, "Naw, you owe me nothing." she paused, "Well, you could always call up some BBQ take out and that would make us even?"

Carey smiled, "I know the perfect place. Booby's BB-Q." she pulled out her phone and hit speed dial and left the room to place an order. Amy grinned at me, "She's perfect. If you won't keep her, I think I will steal her."

I shook my head, laughing and grabbing Amy in a hug, "Never gonna happen."

Dinner was full of Amy talking about her new job and filling me in on the happenings in the city. I would every so often catch Carey stealing glances at me until I finally found her hand under the table and held it. Making her smile and blush, which in turn made Amy smile wider as she looked at the both of us.

When the food was done and the table looked like a barbecue battle gone wrong, Carey stood up to clean the table. Amy giggled, "And she cleans!"

I tossed my napkin in her face, turning to Carey. "Leave it for Amy, Carey. Sit and relax. I will grab some wine and we can go sit outside. It's a nice night."

Carey shook her head, "It's okay. I will tidy up and meet you two out there."

Amy hopped up at the chance and ran to the cabinet. Grabbing three glasses and the last expensive bottle of wine I had stashed. She then grabbed Carey's elbow as she was in mid toss of empty cardboard containers. "Leave it. Come and tell me everything I need to know about you, Carey. The one who saved my best friend in all the right ways."

Carey stumbled and dropped the containers back on to the table. I shook my head and followed them outside. The night was warmer than it had been over the last few days. The long sleeve shirt I wore was plenty, but I took the opportunity to sit next to Carey as close as possible. Taking her hand in mine as we sat in the large wooden chairs facing the ocean.

"So, tell me everything about the woman that has my Frankie all up in a tizzy." Amy handed us our wine glasses.

Carey smiled, suddenly very bashful, "I don't really have much to say. I'm a doctor, I live in New York City, and I work a lot?" Carey shrugged, looking my way for support.

She was at a loss of words being put on the spot like Amy did.

Amy nodded and looked at her in her way, the way that you could tell she was secretly figuring you out. I took a sip of my wine, feeling nervous at what Amy was about to ask next. Even though I had no idea what she was going to ask.

"Well, you must be amazing." Amy leaned back in her chair, "I have never seen Frankie so open to someone. Someone neither of us thought really existed." Amy let her eyes drift off to the dark ocean and the glints of light the tips of the waves caught, "I have known Frankie for a long time. She's my sister of the heart. I know her better than she knows herself and vice versa." Amy turned back to look at Carey, her eyes soft with honesty as she continued, "I have never seen Frankie fight harder for anything in her life, want something or someone as much as she wanted you from the first word you wrote." She paused and leaned forward in her chair, closer to Carey who was fidgeting nervously in my hand. "Frankie told me that you waited for her. That things were lost in the translation of the magic of this silly little cottage."

She then looked Carey dead in the eyes, "I can tell you, there was no one else for her. Just the mysterious, elegant brunette graduate student that has horrible handwriting who became the reason for Frankie to defy all the rules she set for herself and the world sets for us as humans."

Amy grinned, winking at Carey. "I can see it in the way she glows like a lighting bug in June. You have nothing to fear but, being stuck with her for the rest of your days." Amy took a huge swig of wine and giggled, "You two should write a book about this, it's too perfect of a fairy tale."

I sat in awe of what Amy had just said. Never in my days with her as my closest friend had I ever heard her speak with such direct kindness and pure hearted honesty. She had plenty of honesty when things came apart with Christopher, but that honesty was laden with curse words and unique derogatory names for the man.

I glanced at Carey who was fighting back tears and staring at Amy with a remarkable look. Carey cleared her throat after a moment, "Amy, I have never loved anyone like Frankie." The words came out soft but, full of honest determination.

Amy looked at me grinning before directing her smirk back at Carey, doing her part to cut the tension in the air, "I know. You two were meant to be from the moment that toe smashing floorboard popped up." She held up her wine glass, "A toast to the perfect true love I will envy until I find it myself. Here's to hoping I don't have to break any toes to find it."

After our glasses clinked together, Amy lightened the mood by asking Carey how big the rats in the New York City really were. The rest of the evening was spent with Carey telling us about her first few weeks in New York City. I listened, cherishing the moment with the two of them. My heart filling in all the small cracks that my past heart breaks had left me with. It was truly perfect and as I laid with Carey in bed that night, I sat watching her while she slept. Amazed that a stranger in a floorboard could be the one to seal up my heart with so much love.

The weekend flew by with Amy. She actually brought out a goofy side in Carey and I loved it. Carey was slowly letting down her small walls that were held up by the nervousness that echoed in the quiet moments when she and I were alone. The three of us spent nights playing cards or telling stories of how Amy and I met, how Carey and my grandmother used to infuriate Natty by switching out her full clam bucket with an empty one. Telling her the clams had run away when she wasn't looking.

I stood with Carey as Amy tossed her bags into the back of the cab. Rushing back to me for a hug when she was done, "When will you be back in the city?" She mumbled in my ear. It was getting late at night and Amy had delayed her departure for as long as possible until I had to tell her it would be impossible for her to get a cab until morning and that she had to be at work that same morning.

I leaned out of the hug, "I have at least a month left." I glanced at Carey as she paid the cab driver for the return trip. "But she has changed everything. We haven't discussed much, but I only want to be where she is."

Amy rolled her eyes and giggled. "You two. Ugh, so perfect." she punched me in the shoulder lightly. "When you figure it out, make me your first call?" Amy batted her eyelashes at me. I smiled and laughed, hugging her again, "Of course. I love you Amy and thank you for everything."

Carey walked over to us, "The cab is all set."

Amy hopped out of my arms and hopped into a hug with Carey, "Thanks Doc! You are the best." It took Carey a minute to adjust to the tiny crushing hug. Amy stepped back and winked at the both of us, "I will be back next month for a visit. But, you two are more than welcome to come to Toronto and have free drinks at my bar." She blew us both a kiss and rushed to the cab.

Carey moved to stand next to me, wrapping and arm around my waist as we both waved, "Why does it feel like our grown up kid is heading back to college?"

I giggled and laid my head on her shoulder, "Because in many ways, Amy is a big kid going back to the college of life." I looked up at Carey. "She is exhausting, but I adore her."

Carey smirked as the last yellow bit of the cab disappeared into the trees, "A big kid with a big heart."

Carey and I walked back into the cottage, "I'm glad she came, Frankie." I watched her move to the kitchen and start a pot of tea. "It was good for me to hear what you went through while things worked itself out." Carey was slow with her words, "It made sense that even though time was as much as my enemy, your frustration in fighting it and fighting for me was your enemy."

I walked over to Carey, "It doesn't matter anymore, Carey." I slid my arms around her from behind as she sorted through the tea boxes, "We are here, and we are together. Time has nothing on us now." I sighed as I took deep breaths of her shampoo mixed with the warmth she always gave me. I swallowed and propped my chin on her shoulder as her hands covered mine at her waist. I groaned when my cast prevented her hand from fully covering mine. I would have to see if I could get it off as soon as it was possible.

"She did bring up a good point. Where do we go from here?" I hated asking the question but it would hover over me like a dark cloud until I asked it. I knew I would go wherever she led me, but I wanted to give Carey the chance to make her own decision.

I felt her sigh and push back into me, "I have to go back to New York City by the end of next week. I was going to tell you in the morning. I didn't want to ruin the weekend." She turned in my arms, slowly breaking the hold I had on her so she could look at me. "The time I took is just about over and I need to go back and make a decision of where I will go next." She dropped her eyes to the floor, "I will go wherever you are Frankie, and I can find a job anywhere. But I don't want to wait for you, and be away from you like before."

The softness in her voice made my heart ache. It was filled with so much emotion that it was hard to pinpoint one. I held on to her hips, "Carey, I will give it all up to be with you. My job is just a job, my apartment is just an empty box." I moved an inch closer, "But you, you are my heart, my soul and the only place I will call home is where you are." I repeated the words I had said to her in a letter long ago, a phrase that I knew I would utter over and over.

Carey looked up in my eyes. I ran the back of my hand across her cheek, "I love you. We will figure it out, this will be the easiest thing now. Especially after everything we have been through."

Carey nodded in agreement and went to pull me closer when her phone began to ring. She pulled it out of her back pocket, looking at the screen she frowned. "It's the Chief resident at my hospital. I should probably take this."

I nodded and let her glide out of my arms, watching her as she walked out on to the patio and answered the phone. The reality of life was beginning to sink in around me, we did have lives outside of the magic of the cottage and our coming together. I knew that I would leave my job and close up my apartment for her. I wouldn't ask that of her when I had already asked so much of her in the last two years and my painful silence.

I shut the stove off as the tea kettle began to whistle its call of readiness. I suddenly felt sad, the weight of my self-realized reality of having to go back to lives that were put on pause was bearing down. I set the kettle on to a cool burner and decided to head upstairs and get into bed. It wasn't super late, but I suddenly craved to lie down and wait for Carey. Live in the fantasy and fairy tale for as long as possible.

I changed into pajamas and crawled into bed, leaving the one light by the bookshelf on. I cracked open the window to let some fresh air in to help clear out the clouds in my head. I ran my fingers over the still full and lively lilies. They were still filling the air with their clean scent and I couldn't help but smile when it hit my nose. They would forever remind me of the brunette who captured my heart.

I curled up into the bed and placed my hand over her pillow. The small dent she left from the way she had slept the night before. I closed my eyes and thought about the nights we had shared in the bed together. Wrapped in each other's arms and sleeping blissfully. Before I knew it, I had drifted off to sleep to the sounds of the ocean mixed with the happy beat of my heart and the scent of the lilies surrounding me.

I woke up when I felt the bed shift slightly followed by warm lips grazing across my cheeks. I smiled and opened my eyes to look deep into the golden brown eyes of the woman I loved. I whispered, "I was warming the bed up for you."

Carey said nothing, just stared in my eyes and bent to kiss me. She was hovering over me from the side she was kneeling on. The kiss was feathery and soft, like she was tentative to kiss me. I licked my lips when she leaned back.

"Frankie, I love you so much. I'm smitten with you. I crave you. I think about you even when you are standing next to me." She ran fingers across my forehead and down my cheek, "You have given me the breath of life my heart has searched for."

My own breath was caught in my throat as I saw the honesty, love and desire in her eyes. My heart began to race as the air began to fill with tension. I went to speak when she shook her head, bending to my lips again. When I felt her tongue travel across my lips, the response was immediate.

I opened my mouth, allowing the kiss to deepen. Minutes passed while I bathed in the sweetness of the kiss, the softness of her lips against mine and the warm, smooth feel of her tongue as it met mine. Carey broke the kiss, so she could shift into the bed. Her hand slipping around my waist as she pulled me up to sit with her. I gazed into her eyes, not watching her hands as they found the edge of my shirt and pulled it from me. I drew in a slow gasp when I felt the straps of my bra being pulled slowly down, followed by the clasp being slowly unhooked. The bra fell away and I watched as Carey's eyes drew slowly from mine and carry down my body. Settling on my breasts as I began to breathe quickly.

Her hand came up to sit at the bottom of my throat. Flat against me, it made my libido lurch at wanting more. Carey spread her fingers as she slowly drew her hand down my chest, between my breasts. Her pinky and thumb grazing the round edges of both until it found a place to stop under one of them. I almost yelped when the first touch of her thumb drew across my nipple. I had to clutch the pillow that was behind me to prevent myself from grabbing her. I wanted this as much as her, but I wanted it to go slow. She looked in my eyes and a silent permission to continue passed between us. She was giving herself to me.

Carey held on to me, her thumb drawing small circles while she kissed my neck. Her lips pressing against my pulse as it began to pound harder with every touch from this woman. When I was close to losing the thread of control I was holding on to Carey's hand left my breast and found mine, still clutching to the pillow. She wrapped her fingers in mine and pulled them to her. To the edge of her shirt. It didn't take more than a second to figure it out before I pulled her shirt off. I went faster than she did with removing her bra. As she sat before me, I marveled at the beauty she was. The light would always do her just right no matter if it was full sunlight or ambient. I bit my lip as my hands reached for her. Traveling over breasts that were creamy and a perfect fit in my hands. When Carey moaned at the first touch of my fingers, I couldn't hold back. I lowered my head to her chest and covered her with my mouth, enjoying the breathless gasps I pulled from her with every soft movement of my tongue across her nipples.

Carey gently pushed me away, pulling my mouth up to hers to kiss me in a way that sent lightning bolts throughout my body, making me shiver as it hit between my legs. Carey gently pushed back on to the bed, moving her hands to my thin sleep pants. Slowly drawing them off my body and dropping them to the floor, she quickly stripped herself of her own clothes before returning to press her body against mine. Her thigh had found its path to settle with the softest pressure against me. My hips arched on their own at the pressure she was applying. I had to still my body from exploding, my hands going to hold her steady by clutching on to her sides. I begged in a rasp, "Please...Carey."

Carey smiled knowingly. Drawing her lips across mine, she began to rock her thigh against me.

I had never been so turned on, so close to losing all control of my body. But with every slow, tantalizing movement of Carey against me, I could feel my heart skipping. When I was close to letting my body have what it wanted, Carey began to kiss down my neck, over my collarbone and towards my breasts.

I had to bite my lip to prevent more begging demands to pass my lips. The need and want for release was throttling through my body like a jet engine. When I felt Carey's delicate breath across the inside of my thighs and the gentle push of her hands to give her more access, I had to bite harder. The soft breaths floating across my skin, issuing promises of imminent ecstasy was almost too much for me.

I arched almost off the bed and gasped the minute I felt her tongue against me. I had to grab the edge of the bed with my good hand and fight through the dull pain of my broken wrist squeezing through the sheets I had balled in my fist. It only took a millisecond before the orgasm rocked through my body like a freight train. I couldn't control the shaking and moaning as the waves of bliss crashed over me again and again.

Carey moved up to rest against my body, her hand covering my heart as if she was trying to keep it in my chest, it was pounding uncontrollably. She looked concerned, "Are you okay?" She brushed some of the hair that was stuck to my forehead away, worry that she had done something wrong etched all over her face.

I smirked, and said nothing. I moved, grabbing the back of her head and pulling her into a kiss. I wrapped my arm with the cast on it around her to hold her against me as my free hand traveled down her heated skin. I knew that we were in for a long night, but right now I wanted to make this woman in my arms scream my name and tremble under my touch like she just did to me. When my fingers found how ready Carey was for me, she tore her mouth from mine in a strangled moan. I drew my fingers slowly up and down her wetness, enjoying how her body acted on its own. Pushing down on my hand until I slipped a finger into her. Making her pause all of her movements to slow down her own release. I could feel that she was close and took the moment, slowly increasing the tempo of my fingers until Carey was breathing in short gulps and moans. I watched her, enjoying every second I pushed her closer and closer to the edge she so desperately needed to fall from.

When she began to move faster against my hand, I pressed up into her letting my thumb give her the release she had craved for far too long. Carey began to buck against my hand, she fell against my shoulder as she cried out my name. Her own orgasm intense and filling her body with pulsating waves of splendor. I slowly removed my hand as Carey kissed and nipped at my shoulder, still coming down from the ride. I wrapped my arms around her and held her tight against me. Lavishing in the feel of her skin melded against mine. I kissed her shoulder and whispered, "I wanted to take your breath away."

Carey rolled over on to her side, still holding close to me. She smirked with flush cheeks, "You certainly did." She held my eyes, "You always have taken my breath away."

It was my turn to blush. I went to tear my gaze from hers when I felt her hands draw down my hip and across my lower body. Carey leaned and kissed the corner of my mouth as her fingers found me very ready for another round, making me whimper as her slender fingers slid in easily, "And I intend to take your breath away for the rest of the night Frankie."

I woke up as the first few rays of morning light began to dance across the wooden floor. The cool ocean breeze was giving the room a fresh feel with the chill it pushed through the cracked window. Carey was deep asleep, her hand holding on to the edge of my hip. I sighed, we had made love throughout the night before exhaustion claimed us. I felt alive even though I was sore and probably could use another four hours of sleep. I smiled at the memories of the night we shared. It was nothing like I had ever experienced before, making love to some I was hopelessly in love with. I shifted in the bed slowly as not to wake her up. I put on my shirt from the floor and walked over to the bookshelf and grabbed the wooden jewelry box I had set there a few days before. I sat in the chair and opened up the box, taking out the two ring boxes. I opened the one and smiled at the wedding band. I opened the second and stopped, inside was the engagement ring and the small ring I had sent Carey in my last letter.

I picked it up and held it up to the light. I was amazed once again at the magic of the floorboard and how it worked. The amazement slowly drifted into confusion about why it was back in the box. I held the box, getting lost in thought of why and when Carey would give it back.

"I put it back while you were at the store yesterday." Carey's sleepy voice hit me, forcing me to look up at the tousled brunette who was pulling a sheet over her naked body. "I wanted to return it to the place it belonged, as the promise was fulfilled when I finally met you." she paused, "I wore it every day after you sent it to me. An unspoken reminder to wait as long as it took until I knew you were real." She sat up and ran a hand through her hair, "Its home now, just like I am with you."

I grinned at her. Even though she was as exhausted as I was, she still looked perfect. "I wanted, and still want, you to have it Carey." I held the ring in my palm and went to grab the other one, my heart racing at the sudden decision I had made at her words. "It was and still is a promise."

I walked over to the bed after setting the wooden box on the chair I just vacated. I held out my hand for Carey to take so I could pull her to where I sat. "My grandmother hid this for me to find when the time was right. Leaving me a note telling me that the contents would find their place when I was ready."

I began to get nervous in what I was about to spill across my lips. I had never done this before and it was more nerve-wracking than buying a beautiful woman flowers. I was about to change my life in a few simple words.

I looked at Carey, still clutching a sheet across her body. I ran my eyes over the small marks I had left on her body, pulling a smirk from me. I had to close my eyes and shake my head to clear out the inappropriate thoughts that were building faster than I wanted. "I have never done this before, forgive me if I stumble over my thoughts and words."

I took a calming breath as I felt Carey's hand run up and down my back. "Frankie, what is it?" I opened my eyes and saw that gentle smile that I saw on the first day as she walked across the mud to me. My heart leapt and stole more of my courage.

"I, um, I love you." I blew out a slow breath. My palms sweating around the rings clutched in them. "This is harder than I thought. It's just a simple question."

Carey moved closer to me, her hand going to the edge of my jaw. Making me melt at how warm her touch always was against my skin. "Frankie, what is this simple question you are struggling with?" She grinned at me, her thumb running circles around my cheek. "I like my eggs scrambled, if that's what you want to ask me." She was trying to lighten the tension I was building.

I swallowed hard and grabbed her hand from my face, pulling it to sit in my lap as I opened my palm and took the ring I had given her and pressed it in to her palm. "I want you to keep this, it's yours and it is a promise I made to you a long time ago." I took a deep breath and grabbed her left hand, pulling it towards me. Holding her hand flat in mine, "I have told you a million times in the last few days and week we have been together, but I want to say it again. I knew in the moment I read your messy handwriting and all that your heart held, that I would fall in love with you. And I did.

Faster and harder than I ever could imagine I would let myself go with my heart."

I looked up into her eyes, glossing over with questions and emotion. "I love you Carey Murphy. With everything I have and all that I can give you. I know there is no one else I will ever look at the way I look at you. You have filled my heart with hope and magic that comes from being in love with someone." I took another breath, building the last bit of courage to say it. "The simple question is not how you like your eggs, but I will make you scrambled eggs every morning I wake up with you if..." I stumbled for a second as the words were on the edge of my tongue.

I grabbed her hand and slid the antique engagement ring on to her left ring finger, "Will you marry me Carey?" the last syllable came out as the ring met the end of her finger to sit as if it always belonged there. I stared at it listening to Carey take a deep breath, I didn't want to look at her as I felt her hand begin to tremble in mine. My heart dropped as she pulled her hand from mine. Fears raced through my body, maybe I jumped the gun. I drew my eyes to the lilies and waited for the fears to become a reality.

Chapter 15

The silence was painful. I didn't expect an immediate answer, but I did expect something, anything but the heavy silence in the room. I remembered my own proposal from Christopher. It only took me a minute to say yes, and I did not love him nearly as much as I did this woman. My mind began to race, making my legs quiver nervously, so much so I had to stand up. I couldn't bring myself to look at her, knowing the answer to my simple question in the silence that continued to grow.

One simple question that seemed to change everything between us.

I rushed to my dresser, pulling out jeans and a sweater. Balling them up in my arms I mumbled back at Carey, "I have to go outside." I hurried to the door, "I'm sorry about making things awkward."

"Frankie, wait. Look at me." Her voice was riddled with tears and I knew I couldn't look back at her. The tone of her voice let me know that I had made a mistake; I had jumped the gun for sure by proposing to her. I kept walking and ran down the stairs. Throwing my clothes and shoes on before I rushed out the back door, and to the beach, where I knew I could find the solitude to cry.

I kept my head down as I took quick steps away from the cottage and towards the far rock I always sat at when I wanted to be alone. The morning was bright, sunny and cool, another perfect day but I felt far from it. I wiped at the tears as they came. Instead, I felt embarrassed, stupid and silly that I had rushed something like this. I shook my head and laughed at myself, she would probably think I asked because we finally slept together last night. A first time that was amazing, my first time with her was everything I had ever dreamed of. I was a lovesick fool, tangled in the romantic thoughts of my head. Drunk on how she made me feel. Maybe I was rushing too hard to bottle up this feeling and have her forever. Maybe I ruined everything with a shotgun proposal high on the afterglow of making love to an incredible woman.

When I reached the rock, I fell into the sand and sat against the ragged grey edges. The sound I made as I landed in the sand scattered the handful of seagulls puttering about, digging for their breakfast. I leaned hard against the rock, finding strange comfort as the edges pressed into my back. Staring out into the ocean, I cried. Letting out the emotions of the last few days, the good ones and the bad ones. I had to pull my necklace out from underneath my sweater as it began to throb against my chest. Trying to tell me something, something I didn't want to listen to. I huddled up against the large rock that seemed to hover over me as I shrank up into myself, digging my feet into the sand before me. I let my thoughts drift to the reality that was Carey and I. We barely knew each other and had only been in physical proximity of each other for a handful of days, barely a week or two at the most.

I sat in the sand for minutes, thinking. Deep down wanting to bury my head in the sand until the tide came in and washed me away with my embarrassment. I started thinking of what I would say to Carey when I finally grew the balls to go back to the cottage. I closed my eyes as I began to craft the apology and diatribe I would need to issue to Carey, and hope that I hadn't screwed things up more by letting my emotions get the best of me.

I chewed on my lip when I heard something plop into the sand next to me. Whatever it was hit the sand hard enough to make a firm sound. I turned my head to see if a bird had landed to share the beach with me or a seagull had thrown a crab at me out of disgust for intruding on their morning.

There was no crab or bird. Just a small royal blue box canted into the sand where it landed. It was rectangular and looked brand new. Instinct took hold and I reached out for it.

"Why are you always in a hurry, Frankie?" Her voice was close to my ear. My hand froze in mid-reach as I turned to see Carey sitting on the other side of the rock. She rolled her head to look in my eyes. Hers were red and slightly puffy, my heart aching at the sight. Knowing she had cried and that I could be once again the reason. I pulled away from her gaze, settling my eyes back on the box in the sand. My heart dropping, wondering if she had given the ring back. I stared at the box harder, taking in every little detail and noting that it was not a box I was familiar with. I heard her take a breath, "You need to learn to slow down and take your time. Especially now when time has no meaning for us."

"Carey..."

"Frankie, I have to go home tonight. One of my patients has taken a turn for the worse and surgery will be first thing tomorrow." Carey shifted closer to me; I could feel the warmth from her body. "I wanted to tell you last night after the phone call from the hospital. But you were so beautiful as you slept and after everything Amy and you told me, I didn't want to wait another minute to be with you." Carey grabbed my casted hand, pulling it close to her. Our hands passing over the box in the sand, "You certainly caught me by surprise this morning." Her fingers settled in with mine, her thumb running over the exposed edge of my knuckles, "You didn't give me a chance to answer."

I closed my eyes again, clenching my jaw. Carey's tone was even and it was hard for my hyperactive mind to read her emotions. "Carey, you don't have to answer. I mean you can if you want or you can take all the time you need. I rushed things, as always." I stopped, not wanting to go any further. She had told me she was leaving and it made my stomach turn at the idea of not being around her for however long it was she had to be away. I wanted to yell at her that she couldn't leave when we just finally found each other. To forget my stupid excited proposal and figure out how we would work out staying with me. I let out a stifled breath, "I didn't mean to rush you, and I was excited. I have been thinking about this for a while now, but I know you might not be as ready as I am." I cringed at my forced words, sounding feeble and defeated.

Carey suddenly let go of my hand, grabbing it and turning it until it was facing palm up. I opened my eyes and looked at her, my brow furrowed in questions. I saw a slow smile come across her face, "Oh Frankie. You know I had a plan of my own. It's been in my head and heart for almost a year now. I had it planned down to the last perfect detail." She reached between us, picking up the blue box and setting it in my palm, letting it sit flat against the plaster cast that covered most of my hand. My eyes darting to the box as it felt heavier than I expected.

That's when I caught the engagement ring still as it was when I placed it on her finger. I took a quick breath, looking into the golden brown eyes that were shining brighter than ever before. "I wanted to do this up on the cliffs later today, but you had to hurry things along." She flipped the box open with her thumb.

In the middle of the box nestled in dark purple material sat a simple band dotted with a square-cut ruby in the center, surrounded by two smaller stones that were a light purple color. I was fixated by the simple beauty of the ring as it sparkled in the bright morning sun.

Carey let go of my hand, picking the ring up and out of the box she held her left hand out for mine. "I will only say yes if you will also do me the honor of being my wife, Little Frankie."

I looked back up at Carey, absolutely speechless. Blinking at her even as my left hand took life of its own and found hers like a magnet. I couldn't look away from her as she slipped the band on my ring finger. She held my hand, her thumb gently holding the ring in its place, "Will you come with me tonight, to New York City? I only have to be there for the surgery then, I can finish the rest of the time I have taken off." Carey was speaking quickly, trying her best to fill up the silence I was letting sift around us as I sat transfixed on the gorgeous ring on my finger.

A smile exploded across my face. My hand went to her neck, my fingers crawling up into her hair as I eliminated the space and silence between us by kissing her hard. When the smile on my face grew far too wide for me to continue kissing her. I moved closer to her ear and whispered, "Yes, Carey. Yes, to everything. Yes, to you, yes to being your wife and yes, to going back with you."

Carey's arms snaked around my waist and pulled me against her, her heart and mine beat in unison as our chests met as one. I could feel her smile against my cheek as she returned the whispers. "My answer is also yes. Just promise me one thing Frankie."

I leaned back so I could look into the eyes that I would always find my home in. "Anything for you."

Carey smiled, holding her left hand against my cheek letting me feel the cool metal of the ring as it sat on my flushed skin, "Stop rushing. We no longer have to race through this life of ours."

I nodded as the tears freed themselves, tracing damp lines down my face. I had nothing left to say, leaning into her arms, laying my head against her. Closing my eyes and breathing in deep the moment, letting a slow half-smile form. I knew I would never rush a single moment with her, but in the back of my head I couldn't wait to tell this story to our kids.

Carey and I sat on the beach in each other's arms until the tide began to threaten us. We then walked back hand in hand to the cottage. I couldn't stop looking at the ring on my finger and then to the ring on hers. It all felt surreal but perfectly surreal. I was engaged once again, but this time I knew it would last.

Carey had noticed my on and off stares and when we were back in the cottage's kitchen and she let go of my hand to start the coffee pot. "If you don't like the ring, we can find you another one. I found that one in an old jewelry shop in the city. It reminded me of you in every way." She set down two cups, "It caught my eye exactly like you did that first night." She stared at me adoringly for a minute; I could see the memory of our first encounter flicker in her eyes.

I shook my head and smiled at her, laying my hand flat on the counter so I could continue to ogle the ring she had given me. "It's perfect, Carey. I can't stop looking at it, that's all." I met her eyes as she set a hot cup of coffee in front of me, "I'm still in awe. I never thought I would be engaged again. That my fiancée would be this stunning brunette doctor who fell into my life like a star falling from space."

I grabbed her hand in mine, loving the way our hands fit so the rings we both now wore seemed to lay in perfect harmony. "New York City is a two-hour drive away, right?"

Carey nodded, sipping from her cup.

"What do you say to leaving early and showing me around?" I held my own warm cup, letting the aroma of the fresh coffee waken my senses even more than the woman whose hand I held.

Carey smirked, "I was going to suggest the same thing." She leaned over the counter and kissed me on the cheek, "Maybe we can find a nice restaurant to go to on our second date."

I raised my eyebrows, "Second date? And what are the rules for the second date?" Poking fun at the no kissing on the first date rule we both shattered last night, over and over.

Carey shrugged, "I think the only answer I have is that dessert must be had in bed." She winked at me as she let go of my hand and brushed past me to head upstairs. "On you."

The last part came out in a deep sensual way that made me shiver. I turned and watched her walk away as I called after her, "Then, can we have dinner as soon as we get there? Or just skip it all together."

She said nothing, only throwing one of her melting smirks my way. I hopped off the chair and ran after her, "Carey, be warned. I believe rules are made to be broken. As many times as possible."

When Carey pulled into the city, I became lost in the massive skyscrapers that came up out of the ground like giant metal trees. Casting abstract shadows on the world they hovered over. I had not been to New York City in years, not since my last year in college and a group of us went for a weekend.

I pressed my forehead against the clear glass of the silver sports car. Excited to start this new adventure and learn even more about the brunette who had held my hand the entire drive to the bustling metropolis.

I glanced over at Carey, who was steadily navigating the traffic, "I have forgotten how big this city is. Big on every level, the people, the buildings and the way it feels to stand in the middle of it all."

Carey laughed, "It is intimidating. It took me a few weeks to get used to the claustrophobic feel it gave me. It's big but jammed packed with people and life." She let go of my hand to grab the steering wheel, turning the car into an underground garage that was on the SoHo side of the city.

When we parked, she grabbed her suitcases and my single bag I had tossed in the trunk of her sports car. We both wanted to take old blue, but at the last-minute I suggested we keep the truck at the cottage. It was meant to stay there and be our own mobile picture frame of the life we had there. The most important moments we created were in that beat up truck, I didn't want to taint that.

Carey lugged all of our bags to the elevator and hit the forty-four button. As the doors closed she leaned against the back wall of the steel box, "My apartment is yours to roam. It is rather large, you might get lost in the bedroom." She smiled at me.

I moved to stand in front of her, my hands migrating to her hips, "Are you suggesting that I get lost in there first?"

Carey shrugged, wrapping her arms around the middle of my back. "I will leave that for you to decide, I wouldn't mind it if you did." She licked her lips, before our lips met in a kiss that made my knees weak. I felt her tongue glide over my top lip in the way she always did when she wanted more from me. I opened my mouth wider and pressed us both against the back wall of the elevator. I slid my leg between hers, pushing up to let her know that I wanted just as much from her. Carey instinctively pushed down on my leg, sending waves of desire through my body, making me ache and quiver to have her naked underneath me, again. To taste her skin like I had a night before, to take her breath away with purposeful touches. I smirked as my hands moved from her hips to her breasts, my fingers moving to the pesky buttons on her shirt. I was more than willing to take her in this elevator car. I could tell in the moaning whisper of my name, she was also eager to let me.

The elevator dinged to alert us that we had arrived. The doors slid open to reveal a set of big black double door, the only one on the floor. I ignored it, focused on the skin I had freed by unbuttoning the top few buttons of her shirt. Pressing my lips to her warm, flushed skin again. Carey reached up, her hands pushing on my shoulders to still my kisses. She looked at me with hazy eyes, and bit her lip to regain control.

She whispered, "We have to wait for dessert." I frowned, kissing her collarbone one more time, followed by a light nip of my teeth to let her know I wasn't happy, but I would wait. Remembering her words about rushing all the time.

Carey wiggled out of my arms, clearing her throat and wave at the open elevator doors, "This is home." She reached for the suitcases. I swatted her hands away so I could grab them, "Stop being a total gentleman. You drove; I can at least carry these."

Carey shook her head playfully at me, digging around for her keys. When she pushed open the door I muttered, "Holy shit. This place is bigger than my apartment and the cottage."

She held the door open for me. I shuffled in taking in the grandeur of the apartment. I stood in the middle of a foyer that was stunning and perfectly Carey, with wooden floors and white walls that were capped with crown molding.

Carey tossed the keys on the side table that held a neat stack of mail and files. I looked back at her, wide-eyed. She shrugged again, "It was part of my signing bonus with the hospital. This apartment is mine. I actually wanted to refuse until I saw the views." She grabbed my hand, tugging me to follow her. We walked through the foyer and into a large sitting room that then led us to another room that Carey had turned into a library. The floor to ceiling windows illuminated the entire room as if it sat on the sun. I could see the city from the perfect height, making me feel as if I was on the tip tops of the metal trees that had just made me feel like an ant on the ground.

I walked with Carey over to the window staring out into the breathtaking view. She squeezed my hand to gather my attention before pointing off to the south. "Look over there. You see how the city seems to spread apart for the river, fading off into the trees cresting around the ocean?"

I nodded looking in the direction she pointed. The day was perfect; the view was crisp from the lack of clouds and smog.

Carey turned and looked in my eyes, "That is where the cottage is. Less than a hundred miles away from the last point you can see with the human eye. I took the apartment on this view alone and knowing that I could look out these windows and maybe if I squinted hard enough I would see you." The smile that came across her face was the same one that appeared when she would talk about her work or whatever book she was reading, "I had it mapped out. If I stood in this spot and faced south, I was in the direct path of the window that leads into your bedroom."

I blinked at Carey, utterly amazed. Just when I thought she had topped herself with the romance she would surprise me at how much she loved me and how much of her life over the last two years revolved around being as close as she could to me. I bit my lip, staring at her. I swallowed to clear my throat, "So, what you are saying is that you have been peeping in my window all this time?"

Carey's face dropped and went pale, "Oh my god, no Frankie! I didn't mean it like that. It probably sounds like that." she looked up at the ceiling her mind obviously working overdrive, "I guess it does sound like that." She let go of my hand and fidgeted, "I just did everything I could to be as close as I could to you, Frankie. I honestly thought you might have left the cottage over the last two years."

I laughed and tugged at her elbow, "Carey, I'm kidding." I pushed my hand into the crook of her elbow and snuggled into her side, "You amaze me. All the things you have done. You astound me with how big and loving that heart of yours is." I rested my chin on her shoulder, "You are absolutely perfect."

Carey rolled her eyes, "You keep saying that."

I leaned up, kissing her cheek, "That's because you are."

Our eyes met and nothing was said as we stared. Both of us in awe of what we had found in the most extraordinary of circumstances. Silence was something I had not been used to in previous relationships, feeling as if it was a lack of communication or a subtle hint that one of us was less than interested in the other. But, with Carey, silence was golden. Not in the way the catchy phrase dictated, but in a way that we could emit everything we felt and thought in the silent space we seemed to fall into. We could say everything and nothing at all in the way our eyes locked together.

The perfect silence was broken by Carey's phone ringing. She kissed me on the forehead and dragged the phone out of her pocket, glancing at the home screen. "Feel free to settle in and look around. I have to take this call, it's the surgical team."

I nodded letting her walk away from me, her hand not leaving mine until it was physically impossible for her to hold on to it as she walked away. I watched until she disappeared from the room. I took the opportunity to look around the library I stood in the middle of.

There were massive bookshelves lining the walls. Full of medical texts, magazines and antique books that were a lot like the ones my grandmother collected. I smiled, reaching out and running my fingers down the stiff cloth spines of one row of books. That's when I noticed that the shelf near the edge of the room was half empty and bare. The only thing on the shelf was a picture of Carey with my grandmother, both sitting in her bedroom in chairs against the built-in bookshelf. I moved to the frame, picking it up so I could look at it closer.

Carey had her head down in the photograph, buried in a book that was sitting on her lap. My grandmother was sitting in the chair that was still in the room. She had her head turned to the window; it was obvious she was looking out to the ocean. A book open in her lap, her hand flat in the middle to hold her place. I smiled, feeling my necklace grow warm. I turned over the clear frame and saw my grandmother's handwriting on the back.

"Carey,

You have made an old woman happier than you could imagine in her last few moments in this world. I will always remember the moments we spent reading or talking about books. I hope that you find your heart in this cottage as I know you will, with her. Love my granddaughter like I can already tell you do.

Till we meet again and we will.

Francesca."

I pressed the picture against my chest. I walked back to the window and looked in the direction of the cottage. The necklace growing warmer than ever before. I closed my eyes as everything had come full circle.

I smoothed out the black dress I had brought, checking over the last details in the bathroom mirror. It wasn't the exact one from the past; it was new and better than the last. Carey called out for me from the foyer, asking if I was ready.

I ran a hand over my hair and triple checked my makeup and the small touches I wanted Carey to see. I took a deep breath and walked out of the bathroom and to the foyer.

Carey's face lit up like the sun the moment she saw me. I knew mine did the same the second my eyes took her in. She was stunning in her own grey calf length dress that hugged her curves in a way that made me envious. Her hair was down and cascaded over her shoulders in golden waves. Carey held out her hand to me, whispering a wow the moment our fingers connected.

"Frankie, you. You look amazing."

I shivered as her eyes drew down me. Even though my libido was shouting for dessert to be first, I shoved the thoughts down. I wanted to enjoy this second date before the dress was torn off and thrown to the floor. I took a small step back and took my own slow visual journey of Carey, "I can say the same about you. You clean up nice doctor."

Carey blushed, pulling me closer so my arm could link into hers. "We should get to dinner before I break another rule and have dessert first."

I burst out laughing at the comment. Carey looking at me with a smile, silently asking what was so funny.

I kissed her shoulder, "Great minds think alike."

I stood outside the restaurant waiting for Carey to park the car. The place she had picked was fancy and busy. It made me feel giddy to have a fancy dinner with my lovely fiancée. I secretly wanted to show her off to anyone who would look our way, hold on to her in a way that all eyes that passed over us knew she was mine and I was hers. I giggled to myself at the thoughts, pulling my wrap tighter around my shoulders when the slight night breeze ushered around me. I took a deep breath and looked up into the sky. The stars were poking their head out around the steel buildings as if to wink at me, letting me know they were sharing this night with me.

I looked around me, holding on to my small purse while I watched the city come to the exuberant life it led at this time of night. I was happy and taking note of how happy I was.

"Frankie? Is that you?" A deep, smooth familiar voice came from my left. I turned and my smile faded slightly as Christopher was walking towards me with a half-smile, one you get when you recognize someone in the middle of a crowd. He was walking towards me, his hand holding on to the hand of the brunette I once called my friend. Ashley.

"Christopher." I felt my body tighten up at the mere sight of these two.

His smile fell into the bright white grin he was infamous for. The one that once captured me, but now irritated me. Christopher reached out, his hand settling on my forearm, "Wow, it is you. I thought it was you." I noticed that he dropped Ashley's hand like it was a hot rock.

I took the moment to look at Ashley. I had known her for the entire time I was with Christopher. I never paid her much attention until I caught them. Now I looked over the woman who broke Carey's heart, "Ashley." It came out of my mouth with little emotion. I could be mean, venomous and spiteful. But why? The two who stood before me were the reason why I had found my way to Carey. To the love of my life and a reason to live as much as possible. I smirked and thought for a second I should thank them.

Ashley smiled as best as she could, "Hi Frankie."

Christopher broke in, "What are you doing here in New York? Your little friend told me you had moved to the ocean in that shanty your grandmother left you." He flashed his grin again, "How are you? It is really good to see you."

I could feel in his tone what he was trying to do. Win me over like he once did, make me swoon at the bright smile and his bright blue eyes. I glanced at Ashley as she reached for his arm to try to stake a claim on him.

I smiled, "I'm waiting for my date." I waved at the restaurant behind me, "We are having dinner here tonight." I turned to look at Christopher, when I felt my necklace begin to throb, telling me Carey was close by.

I heard her voice call for me from behind, just like it did that night so long ago. A similar night like this one. A clear, crisp night. The stars bright, my heart full of love but, this time it was different. I reached behind me with my hand, smiling wider as I felt hers slide into it as she spoke my full name again, "Francesca, I'm sorry that took longer than expected."

I didn't look back at her as I watched the faces of Christopher and Ashley shift from cheeky to shock, from jealousy to confusion. I turned to look at Carey; she had not yet noticed the two standing in front of me as she only had eyes for me. I leaned over, kissing the corner of her mouth before I turned to Christopher.

His brow creased as he tried to hide all of the emotions that I knew were racing through his head, making me smile even more. I looked him dead in the eye, "Christopher, I would like to introduce you to my fiancée, whom I believe you have met a few times already."

Carey pulled her eyes from me the moment she heard his name pass my lips. The look on her face stayed the same as she looked at the two people responsible for so much in our lives. I held her closer, "I would love to stay and get caught up, but I have a date with the love of my life. I don't want to make her wait any longer than she already has."

Christopher stammered, "Carey? This woman is your fiancée? But..." he was utterly confused at the sight of Carey and I. I watched as his eyes drew down to the ring on my finger.

I looked up at Ashley, she had tears in her eyes and a smile on her face. It was a look of relief carrying through her face. One that I could only imagine was that of being free in her own way. Free to love the man boy she had chosen over the brunette doctor on my arm, and free of the burden of knowing she had broken Carey's heart in a way that it may never be whole again. She pulled at Christopher, looking at the both of us, "We should go before we miss our own reservations."

Christopher shook his head in disbelief and resisted for a moment until Ashley pulled harder. He mumbled, "I can't believe it. Another woman Frankie?" He took a step back, "But, it's only been a few months since...we were..."

I stood my ground and as he turned to walk away and I looked up at Carey, "Our table is waiting." Carey nodded and kissed me softly before turning to Ashley and Christopher walking away. She called after Ashley, who stopped and glanced back.

Carey squeezed my hand as she looked in the eyes of the woman who broke her heart to pieces, "Thank you."

Ashley smiled, dropping her head down to look at the concrete, nodding in understanding of everything that just happened.

Four lives that had tangled together in a strange mess, had straightened out to form their own complete circles. One that was magical and full of a love that had tested time and fate, and one that was a hard life lesson for another that you can't always win at manipulating life.

I sighed as I felt Carey's hand move to the small of my back to guide me into the restaurant. As expected, all eyes fell upon us the moment we stepped in the room. I beamed when I kissed the woman I was set to marry, claiming her as mine in front of a packed restaurant.

Chapter 16

I laid in bed, looking around the bedroom. Carey had left for surgery two hours ago, sneaking out of the bed while I slept dreaming about the date and the dessert that followed our first dinner together. I woke up as the sun began to warm up the edge of the bed and my feet under the thick, soft blankets I had rolled myself into. I pushed hair away from my face and ran my hand over the empty side of the bed. Looking at the clock I knew it would be a lonely, quiet day waiting for her. She had told me surgery would take her well into the evening. I sighed and rolled over to squish her pillow underneath me, soaking in the smells that lingered. Allowing my sensory memory to place Carey in the room with me even if she wasn't. I smiled and looked around the room I was in, that I spent no time looking at last night as Carey and I wasted no time in having the long promised dessert as soon as we walked into the apartment.

Carey's bedroom was huge, twice the size of the one at the cottage. The large windows that were a prominent feature in the main living areas also carried into her bedroom. A line of perfect rectangular glass blocks wrapped around the top of the room. Bathing the room in an angled light that gave just enough light without interfering with the bed or the one sleeping in it. The bed was also large, barely taking up much of the space in the giant room. It was plain, but soft. The grey sheets and the matching comforter told me that Carey spent very little time in bed or in this room, period. There was only one photograph on the wall, one of the ocean taken from the back patio of the cottage. It was black and white and invoked a true feeling of timelessness. There was only a dresser in the room and two bedside tables.

The one on the side Carey slept on was covered in medical journals and random patient files. The table next to my side held a vintage alarm clock and a light identical to the one on her side. I thought about Carey sitting in this room night after night for two years, holding on to the fantasy that was our love. She only existed in the rooms where she could be close to it, almost reach out and touch it. The other rooms appeared to be only for function, to survive until the fantasy became a reality.

I got out of bed after a few minutes of visually snooping around her room. I wrapped a blanket around me, moving to the dresses we had tossed to the floor in urgency to touch one another. I smirked at the memories of the night before as I shook out the wrinkles in the fabric. Walking to the closet to hang them up. I took a moment in the closet, running my hands over her clothes. Perfectly placed in the order she choose. Business suits near the front, casual button downs and slacks after that, then her jeans and sweaters. The shelves were perfectly organized with her t-shirts and scrubs. I laughed lightly as I saw that she was partial to color coding, a far cry from my toss it in the closet if it's clean and walk away manner of organization.

I dug around until I found one of her MIT sweatshirts. Pulling it on as I dropped the blanket, I inhaled deeply as it instantly reminded me of the woman who had infected my soul and my heart. I walked past her dresser to my bag, foraging for a baggy pair of jeans. I dressed and stood up, fixing my hair in the mirror over the dresser. Catching the engagement ring on my finger in my reflection I could not help the grin that spilled over my face. I ran my fingers over the ring as I walked out to the kitchen to make some coffee, picking up my phone on the way.

Smiling over the handful of texts Carey sent before she went into surgery, I missed her already but her simple I love you would hold me over for the next ten hours until she was done. I took my coffee and went out in to the room with the bookshelves. Sitting in one of the most comfortable chairs I had ever sat in, I watched the city below. Cars moving like little bugs and the people looking like specks that filled in the cracks between the buildings and cars. It was a little after one in the afternoon and I started to think about lunch and what I could do for Carey when she got home. If I could make her dinner, a bath or order take out. I leaned back in the chair, enjoying the feeling of emptiness my heart held. A good emptiness, the only kind that came with being so happy and so full of love there was no room for the worry and heartbreak that one often carried in a day. My life was bordering on complete and it made me actually stop caring about time and rushing through it, exactly as Carey told me to do; stop and enjoy it all.

I began flipping through a book that was on the small coffee table in front of me, a newer copy of the popular fantasy novel series the entire world had been raving about. It made me smile, I would have to ask Carey about it later, maybe poke fun at her for being a little bit of a nerd. But, in a matter of moments and a few pages, I found that I had been sucked into the world of a far off world. One similar to the ones that had intrigued my heart and mind as a child in the pages of "King Arthur" and "Aesop's Fables."

I curled my legs up and began to devour the book when I heard the front door open and a voice follow the slamming of a door.

"Murphy! Sean told me he saw you this morning, and that you were back in the city. I brought those sandwiches you like from that weird organic vegan spot next to Sean's coffee house." The voice was female and had a tinge of New York Native in it.

I set the book down and stood up as the owner of the voice appeared around the corner, mid-sentence, "You have to tell me everything that went down with the magical girl in the floor. You've been gone three weeks and all I get is a text or two. You had me worried Murphy, I almost put out an APB." The woman paused as her emerald green eyes locked onto mine.

The only thing that didn't make me yell or grab a bookend as a weapon was the fact that the tall redhead who stood before me, carrying a large brown take out box, was wearing a NYPD uniform. The woman was beautiful, reminding me of a movie star from the golden age of film. I took a quick glance at her name badge, A. Calhoun.

I smiled gently and broke the strange silence that fell into the massive room. "You must be Annie."

"And you must be the girl in the floor, Frankie." Her jaw twitched for a second, I could tell she was sizing me up for a moment. Like all cops do when they are trying to get a read on a person.

I nodded. "I am."

Another pause and more silence filled in between us. Annie dropped her eyes to the box in her hands, "I will go put this in the kitchen, and I thought Murphy was home." She turned to walk out of the room, "In case you are wondering, I have a key."

I followed the police officer out to the kitchen. "Carey is at the hospital, in surgery. We came back home...to her apartment last night." I was careful with my words. The look in Annie's eyes told me that she was not the biggest fan of me. After two years and hearing about me and the moments of heartbreak I threw Carey's way, I could understand.

Annie nodded as she tucked the sandwiches into the partially empty refrigerator. "These are her favorite, some weird pesto chicken with sprouts. The other is an Italian salami one, with extra provolone." Annie shut the fridge and yanked at her vest under her uniform, "You can eat the Italian one. I have to head back to work." I could feel the awkwardness and the urge for her to leave the apartment quickly.

"Annie. Ask me what it is you want." I watched as she paused, her jaw twitching again. "I know you are Carey's best friend. She told me about you and how you were there for her over the last two years. So, ask me questions, say what you need to, what you want to."

Annie took a firm breath, looking sideways at me. Only her radio and the soft crackle of police traffic was the only sound in the room. She suddenly smirked, turning to face me as she leaned against the back counter next to the steel doors of the fridge, "You know I asked her out five times. Five different times in five different ways that had always worked for me in the past. Her answer was always the same, in that soft Carey way of letting you down she has about her." Annie looked me in the eyes, "She said, Annie I appreciate the flattery and the gifts, but there is someone else. Someone else who has my heart in a way that it will never make sense to me other than its too perfect to let go of."

I bit my lip, folding my hands in front of me in a way that I wanted to hide the engagement ring from the observant woman.

Annie pushed off the counter and grabbed two glasses, opening the fridge again she grabbed the sole bottle of vodka tucked in the freezer door. I gave her a look when she filled two glasses. "I got off shift a half hour ago. I lied about going back to work." She pushed a glass towards me, "I wanted a quick exit from this awkward moment, but now that you are in front of me. Yea, I do have a ton of questions and things to ask."

I spun the glass around in my hand, "I have the time, Carey won't be home until late and she has the car." I smiled to ease the slight tension between us.

Annie chuckled, "Fair enough." she took a sip from the cold, clear liquid, "Carey caught my attention the moment I saw her at the nurse's station, signing off on charts. I was drawn to her and her quiet ways. She was always polite and kind, even to the biggest shit bag patient that came her way. After I gave up asking her out, we became close friends. I really liked her, I mean who wouldn't be taken with an attractive brunette doctor like her. But, I saw in her eyes that I really had no chance, no matter how many flowers and other gifts I sent her way."

Annie reached down and turned off her radio and fidgeted with her belt until she took it off, setting the black belt with all the tools a cop needed on the island between us. She began unbuttoning her patrol shirt and set it on top of the belt, followed by her vest that she dropped to the floor. She let out a huge sigh, rolling her shoulders in the white t-shirt she now stood in, "I've been wearing that for the last ten hours." She leaned on her elbows, "I'm not sure if I broke her resolve, but after a while she began talking about you. I knew she trusted me when she told me the crazy story of the magical floorboard and how the future and the past became one in a tiny old cottage up by the ocean. But, the more she talked about you, the more I could tell that her heart was long gone to anyone, but you." She waved her hand in the air, "Long gone to a pile of letters in a dusty floor."

Annie stared at me, "I can't say I liked you too much for a long time, Frankie. Especially when I had to sit with Carey after her one trip to Toronto. Crying her eyes out about you and some greasy man that had been poking around in her life for the last two years. I sat with her for a couple days talking her out of the crazy ideas she had in her head." she took another slow sip of the vodka, "Talk her out of giving up on you. I could see how much Carey loved you and after hearing the story a thousand times, it made me feel like you two had the fairytale we all searched for. I started to root for you two, push her every day to hold onto the strands of hope she had left."

She reached over to me and tapped on my left hand, "That ring. I went with her to pick it out. That was a year ago, I thought she was getting lost in a romantic idea of you at the time. Considering she had not heard from you in years at that point, only holding onto the written promise of a possible ghost. It's nice to finally see it on your finger and that you are a real girl."

I took a sip from my glass, "I didn't understand our connection. It was just mere days for me when it was..."

"Forever for her." Annie cut me off, "Look Frankie, I'm going to lay it out plain and simple. I love Carey, she is my best friend and there is not a damned thing I wouldn't do for her. So this will go one of two ways, I will end up standing up in the not too far off nuptials of you and her. Two if you mess this up and hurt her, well I'm not going to issue the cliché line of how your body will disappear without a trace." Annie winked at me and drained the rest of her glass, reaching for the bottle to refill, "With that said, tell me everything I need to know about you Frankie."

I smiled, "You sound exactly like my best friend." I grabbed the vodka bottle, "But first, thank you for being there for Carey when I couldn't." I grinned as I held up my glass to hers, "I also look forward to you wearing a bright pink bridesmaid dress." Annie smiled and shook her head, "Good, I hate burying bodies by the pier." She winked at me and laughed as I shook my head at the morbid joke.

The rest of the evening Annie and I ate the sandwiches and finished off the vodka. I learned that Annie was a tough but gentle girl. I told her everything about how I came across Carey and the truth behind Christopher and the moments that almost broke Carey. By the time Carey came home, Annie and I had forged our own strange bond fueled by a mutual love of the tired brunette doctor who came home to two half drunk and giggling women in her kitchen.

One year later it was Annie with Amy as the maids of honor of both sides, that helped calmed my racing heart, fix my makeup and pushed me down the aisle to the amazing woman standing at the end, waiting to say I do. Our wedding was in a small church in the heart of the city. A small ceremony with close friends and the smattering of family that could make it. Carey and I made our promises to love and cherish for life surrounded in the rainbow light the ancient stained glass windows pressed upon us. For a split second it felt like the angels and saints from the panes were standing next to us, celebrating our love in their own colorful way. I had to close my eyes at one point when I felt my necklace grow warm, letting me know that my grandmother was in the room with us. Finally, seeing her granddaughter find the final chapter in the love story she had set in motion the moment I walked into the cottage.

I stood outside the glass door leading into the back room Carey and I had chosen to hold our reception. At the same restaurant we had our first proper date at. The same one that Amy was now the general manager of. I was nervous even though the ceremony was over and I was now married to the woman who silently stepped to my side, her hand falling into mine.

"Frankie, why are you so nervous? The worse is over." Carey looked at me with a sparkle in her eye. Looking equally stunning in her own white dress and flawless makeup and hair. She pulled our linked hands to her lips. Kissing the wedding band that she had placed there just less than an hour ago, promising me for an eternity to stand by my side.

I sighed and leaned closer to her, "I know, I guess it's just happy jitters." I kissed her bare shoulder, "That and I'm afraid of the kind of first dance and hijinks Amy has planned in there."

Carey chuckled, then met my eyes, "Do you even know how beautiful you are right now? And how much I love you, Mrs. Murphy?"

I smiled, loving the way my new last name sounded coming from my wife, "I love you too, Mrs. Murphy."

Carey winked at me and motioned to the door, "Then, let's get the party started so we can get to our honeymoon a little faster."

I saw the look in her eyes, the same one that had always clued me in to what she meant right before our clothes were shed in a hurry. I went to say something when I heard Amy announce the first appearance of "Mrs. Carey Murphy and her blushing bride Mrs. Francesca Murphy." Followed by a thundering applause from the mass of friends and family that sat in the room, smiling and basking in the glow of a newly wedded couple.

After the usual wedding reception formalities and a lovely dinner, Carey and I separated to say hello to the room. Hoping that if we spread out it would take less time. I was over in the corner talking to Amy and her new boyfriend that I knew in a few months' time would be her new fiancé. A handsome, dashing man that she had met while moving into her own apartment. Adam was an architect and was smitten with my crazy best friend from the moment she dropped a box of shoes on him. I saw in his eyes the same magic that Carey and I had. I smiled listening to Amy talk about the cake she had gotten us when I let my eyes roam around the room, searching for my wife. I missed her even though it had only been a handful of minutes since our hands left one another.

My eyes settled on the far corner of the room when I saw Carey standing and talking to a brunette in a black dress. It took a moment for me to realize that the brunette was Ashley. I squinted, not remembering if either of us had sent an invitation to her. I watched for a moment and excused myself from Amy and Adam, curious as to why Ashley had reappeared in our lives after a year.

When I moved closer, sliding my hand into its place on Carey's elbow, I caught the edge of a conversation. Ashley paused when she saw me, a gentle worried smile on her face, "Hi Frankie. I was telling Carey about reading your wedding announcement in the paper." she held up the small gift in her hands, "I know I'm crashing the party but I wanted to give you guys a gift and." She paused when Carey interrupted her.

"Ashley was getting me caught up on things." She looked at me and smiled, "And to apologize for everything."

The look in Carey's eyes told me that I had nothing to worry about, regardless if there was a touch of worry in my heart or mind at the sight of Carey's ex-girlfriend and my ex fiancé's mistress.

I smiled to put Ashley at ease, "All was forgiven a long time ago. If anything I should thank you."

Ashley nodded and shrugged, "I was selfish Frankie. You were my friend and I was selfish." her eyes went to Carey's for a moment, "Sometimes love, or the thing you think is love leads you into a blind trap." She dropped her head to stare at her hands, "I left Christopher that night we all ran into each other. The only reason we got along was that we both were selfish and ignorant to what love is. Breaking hearts is not the way to find true love." she laughed nervously, "Being single for the last year I have had a lot of time to think about my missteps." She looked back up at Carey and me, "Anyways, I wanted to say congratulations and drop off my gift. I wish you two the longest and happiest marriage ever. You two are an example for the rest of us to follow."

Ashley turned to leave when Carey looked at me, both of us having the same idea. I spoke first, "Ashley stay. You are here now and there is plenty of food and drink." I glanced over my shoulder at Annie sitting with the bartender, both watching the baseball game on the TV on the wall, "There is someone we would like you to meet." I turned back to Ashley, "How do you feel about feisty lady cops?"

As I held the card announcing that Annie and Ashley were expecting their second baby boy, I marveled that it had been six years since our wedding and that first meeting of the two. They married a year after we did and lived over on the east side with their first born, Tommy. I set the card down and focused on finishing the last of my packing for the cottage.

I walked around the apartment, double checking doors and windows, grabbing the last few things I needed and Carey had requested. She had gone down to the cottage the day before to start our long weekend. I had to stay back to finish the last few meetings with my publisher before I could head down to meet her.

I shoved the first print of my new book into my briefcase to show Carey. After I moved to New York City permanently with Carey, I quit my job at the Toronto Star and took my turn writing fantasy fairytales. Finally, succeeding after a handful of rejection letters in publishing my first novel which lead to four more and a decent amount of success as a novelist. It freed up my life with Carey tremendously, we had traveled so much in our first year of marriage and I could spend as much time as I wanted writing in the front room or leave it to spend the day listening to Carey tell me about her work or just listen to her read from our massive book collection. I had finally found the slow button of life and hit it permanently, cherishing every moment of my life with her.

My phone vibrated in my pocket, pulling it out I swiped open the text from Carey.

"Are you on your way? I miss you and our other houseguest is getting restless for you. Hurry, my love."

I sent her a quick on my way text. The grin on my face stuck from the simple words my wife sent. Six years later and we were still hopelessly in love with each other and couldn't handle more than a few hours of separation before our necklaces begged for us to be close again.

I walked through the apartment one more time, triple checking before I headed out of the building and to the car. I set my phone in the console, taking a moment to look at the background that had been permanent since the day the picture was taken. It was taken on the day of the reception of Carey and I just as we entered the room. She was looking directly at the camera while I was leaning up to kiss her on the edge of her jaw. The light had hit her brown eyes perfectly and they glowed like two amber stones. It was my favorite wedding photograph from that day and I had many copies of it around the house and on my phone. I smiled and unlocked the phone, smiling wider at the picture that was the wallpaper. A picture of Carey and the other lady in my life I loved. I set the phone to silent and tucked it away so I could focus on the drive to the cottage.

I pulled into the driveway of the cottage, parking the car next to Carey's silver sports car that already had a tarp pulled over it. Old blue had been taken from the barn and ready for the weekend just as much as we were. I shut my blue sports car off and after pulling my bags out, I also covered it with a tarp. Leaving the city behind me for the weekend.

I walked into the cottage and found it to be alive, but empty. I knew Carey would be down at the ocean already. Over the years I had found she was truly addicted to the ocean and always had to be around it to keep her stress in check, it also inspired her romantic side to a point that I would often drag her there just to hear the things that would come out of her mouth or the random gestures she was inspired to do for me.

I walked up to the bedroom, finding it warm and welcoming as always. I set my bags down and set the small gift I had gotten her on her pillow. I also set the brown paper wrapped first print of my new book on the chair next to the bookshelf and the wall that still held the poem she had written for me so long ago. Still making my heart skip whenever I looked at it.

I changed into baggy jeans and a sweater, walking out the back door to find Carey at the edge of the ocean skipping stones with a small sandy brown haired little girl who held onto her hand like a boat holds onto a lighthouse in the middle of a storm.

I grinned and tucked my arms against my chest, walking towards the two girls. Hoping to catch them by surprise when the little girl turned and caught me. My own smile reflecting on her face as she pulled at Carey's hand, making

Carey look up at me and smile. She let go of the little girl who bolted towards me at full speed.

I bent to my knees and held my arms open to catch my five year old daughter in a huge hug. When she slammed into my arms, I lifted her up, spinning her around as she giggled. "Momma! We thought you were going to be late!"

I ran my hands through her mop of hair, "Oh Viola, I raced here as fast as I could. Mommy told me you were getting restless to see me."

The little girl leaned back in my arms, Carey's amber eyes looking back in mine. She squished her face up in a silly hybrid smile of Carey's shy one and my boisterous one, "I wanted you to get here so I could show you how I learned how to skip stones."

I smiled and listened to my daughter tell me how Uncle Sid showed her which stones to pick when Carey and Viola were picking up firewood from the hardware store. Our daughter was a marvel of magic and medicine combined in one. I became pregnant with her a year after Carey and I were married. Carey was able to work with some of her colleagues to figure a way how both of our DNA could be included into one traditional pregnancy. Through the magic of medicine and a lengthy explanation of scientific words, I carried our first child that was a perfect split of Carey and I. Viola Annabelle Murphy was born nine months later, healthy and as I held her, I didn't care about the specifics or the groundbreaking work my wife had done. All I cared was that our daughter had my smile, Carey's eyes and a perfect mix of our personalities. She also showed signs of having Carey's smarts and my charisma, a dangerous combination waiting for us in the years she grew into a teenager.

I listened to Viola tell me about how the grey stones were the best for skipping, when Carey walked up to us. Kissing me on the lips as she whispered a soft hello, trying not to interrupt our daughter's determined speech on stones.

Viola finished and looked at the both of us, before blurting out, "Mommy has a surprise for you. She told me today is your sixth annitersary?" Viola looked confused as she tried to wrap her tongue around the big word. I laughed and kissed her flushed cheek, "Anniversary."

Viola tried again and again, before Carey reached for her rolling her eyes, "I should know that she can't keep secrets." she picked up the giggling little girl looking in her eyes, "Viola and I made you a new notebook to write in for your next book."

Viola giggled when Carey poked her side before setting her to the ground. Viola snatched up both of our hands and dragged us into the cottage, "I wrapped it for you Momma!"

I leaned over the bouncy little girl to kiss Carey on the lips, "I missed you."

Carey blushed as we let our little one guide us back to the house. Stealing looks at me like she did on this same beach six years ago.

Back in the cottage, I opened the new notebook my girls had made for me. Both Carey and Viola wrote little I love you notes in the front page, calling it their own notes of inspiration when they weren't around.

The three of us had dinner and planned out the rest of the weekend. Visits to Uncle Sid and Auntie Natty, playing in the water and at least one quiet night alone while Viola had a sleep over at Natty's. When the sun finally dipped into the ocean for the night, I carried a sleepy Viola into the spare bedroom which was now her room. Tucking her into the quilt and kissing her forehead.

I then moved to the bedroom, finding Carey standing at the large window. Staring out into the deep black of the water and the gentle highlights from the moon and the lighthouse on the tips of the water. I wrapped my arms around her waist from behind, resting my head against her back so I could hear the way her heart always picked up pace when she was close to me.

She held on to my hands at her waist, "Do you remember six years ago? That first morning after the first night we spent together."

I nodded against her, "I do." I closed my eyes, squeezing her tighter against me, "I have something for you." I slid away from her body and moved to the small gift box I had set on her pillow. I picked it up and held it out to her, "Six years and I still love you like I did the moment I saw that messy handwriting of a woman who I'm forever grateful to have found."

Carey took the box, slowly opening it, "Frankie, you don't have to get me anything. You and Viola are all I ever need."

I moved closer to her, my hands settling on her upper arms as she opened the box, "I know, but I wanted to do something for you." I watched as her eyes widened, I pulled the ring out of the box and grabbed her left hand that only had her wedding band on it. "I know you thought you lost it months ago, but I actually stole it with the help of our little one." I held up the new ring. It was the original engagement ring I had set on her finger this same day six years ago, but I had it integrated with the first ring I had sent to her so long ago in my last letter, "This ring was a promise I made to you a long time ago and the first thing I ever gave you besides my heart." I gently slid the ring on to her finger so the new ring sat against her wedding band, "I have Viola and all the things you do for me to remind me of how much you love me, I want you to have this. A symbol of our magic, a symbol of my heart and that it will always be yours long after time has given us our fair share of living in it."

I kissed her finger, "I love you Carey Murphy, six years and counting sixty plus more." I looked into her eyes and saw the immense amount of happiness that was hidden in the tears sitting on the edge.

Carey pulled me into a deep kiss, holding the edges of my jaw as my own drifted to her waist to hold her closer. Six years and I couldn't get enough of this woman, six years of a perfect life that was handed to me by my grandmother and fought for by a shy brunette who overcame the broken heart she carried to find it in my hands one letter at a time.

Carey leaned back in my grasp, our kiss ending far too soon for my liking. She held my face in her hands, "And I love you Francesca Murphy."

I went to kiss her again when I felt the small hand pat at my leg, Carey and I looked down at the sleepy face of our daughter. Clutching to her blanket and the small stuffed monkey animal her Aunt Amy had given her. I bent down, pushing the messy hair from Viola's face, "What's wrong Vi?"

She shrugged, "I can't sleep." she looked at me and then to Carey, "Will you and Mommy read me a story?"

Carey looked at me, leaving it up to me to decide if we would bend to the nightly trick Viola would pull to stay up just a little longer or sneak into our bed. I winked at Carey, "I think I have the perfect story for you." I stood up, "Go climb into our bed while Mommy and I get into our pj's." I watched as the little one ran to the bed and hopped into it, crawling to the middle and smushing herself into the pillows like she did almost every other night. Smiling excitedly at the story to come.

Carey whispered to me as I handed her, her pajamas, "You are such a softie."

I playfully swatted at her, "Can you blame her? I love it just as much when you read to me at night."

I walked back into the room, Carey following behind me. I grabbed the book from the chair, pulling the paper off it as I climbed into bed. Letting Viola lean against me as she spotted the book in my hands.

"Is that a new one, Momma?"

I nodded and kissed the top of her head, "It is." I looked at Carey, "It's the first print of the new book." I held it out to Carey for her to take. She smiled when she read the description on the back page. I snuggled with Viola as I spoke, "My agent thinks it will sell better than the series. That I will find a new fan base with this slight departure from my fantasy series and to fiction romance."

Carey flipped through the first few pages, "What some call fiction, I call my life." She raised an eyebrow at Viola, "Can you read the front cover for us, Vi?"

Viola nodded eagerly, leaning over the book and read in a slow and determined voice, "Letters in the Floor of Love." she squinted at the bottom of the cover, "By Francesca Owen." she suddenly grinned and looked at me, "That's you, Momma!"

I nodded and tickling her lightly, making her giggle until Carey cleared her throat looking at us. Obviously, waiting for us to settle down and listen to the story she was about to start. Viola pressed a tiny finger against my lips and shushed me, "Quiet now. Mommy is gonna read to us."

I smirked against the little fingers, nodding at Carey to begin.

She opened to the first page and slid down closer to Viola and began to read. Her soft, smooth voice making our daughter and I sigh contently.

"Some say if a love is strong enough, it can overcome the physical obstructions placed in its way. It can transcend space and time together. That love, a true love, is the most powerful force a human has to offer the world and themselves. I never thought that to be true, nor did I want to believe it. Until I wanted to meet her so much, I broke all the barriers set before me."

I listened intently to Carey reading the first words of our love story, the one where magic and determination of spirit won in the end. I felt my necklace pulse against my chest, pulling me to look back at the bookshelf. I rolled my head and focused on the chair. A shift of light filled the room and focused onto the empty chair and in the blink of an eye, a glimmering light filled the seat. Quickly forming the image of my grandmother, sitting in the chair, holding a book and smiling at my little family.

I met her eyes and smiled back, she nodded at me. I finally understood that I could continue to share my life with her long after she was gone. I just had to come back to the cottage and bring the family she gave me the chance of having. I clutched the necklace and nodded back at her. She threw me a sly wink and then faded away with another shift of light.

I took a moment before turning back to my wife and daughter, snuggling deeper into the bed as Carey kept reading the magical love story that already had our little one entranced.

My final wish had come true, I was telling my child the story of how I found the most perfect love anyone could ever dream of.

THE END

- A little about the author -

I started this journey writing fanfiction a handful of years and found that I had a lot in my imagination that needed to be shared with the world. The result was my first novel, Redemptio Animae, which I hope you have read and thoroughly enjoyed! That book led to another, Devil's in the Details, which will have a sequel in the near future. I'm currently working on a supernatural series that I think many of you will enjoy. This short story you've just read, was a short dabble into a first person POV tale, and I hope you loved it!!! I have more to come!!! I also thank you for purchasing and supporting an independent author!!!

If you're interested in keeping tabs on me and the future works that will certainly follow this debut novel, head on over to Facebook and find me at Sydney Gibson at Facebook.com/sydney.fivesixthree And then to enjoy some of the nonsensical tweets and updates with future novels and the ongoing fanfiction I still occasionally putter with, find me on Twitter at Syndey563a. There is also an author page on Amazon where you can follow me and be updated when the next book is going to be published.

Thanks to all of you for your support! I couldn't, and wouldn't be doing this if it wasn't for my incredible fans and readers!! Also, if you've enjoyed the cover art, email my friend Ben at benjamincthorne@gmail.com , and he'll make magic happen in whatever your heart desires in the graphic art design world!

Syd!

Printed in Great Britain
by Amazon